SKYSCRAPER

***Also by Faith Baldwin
in Large Print:***

They Who Love
The Moon's Our Home
Hotel Hostess
Marry for Money
Men Are Such Fools!
White Magic
Love is a Surprise!

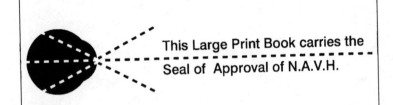

This Large Print Book carries the
Seal of Approval of N.A.V.H.

SKYSCRAPER

FAITH BALDWIN

Thorndike Press • Waterville, Maine

Published in 2002 by arrangement with
Harold Ober Associates, Inc.

Thorndike Press Large Print Candlelight Series.

The tree indicium is a trademark of Thorndike Press.

The text of this Large Print edition is unabridged.
Other aspects of the book may vary from the original edition.

Set in 16 pt. Plantin by Minnie B. Raven.

Printed in the United States on permanent paper.

Library of Congress Cataloging-in-Publication Data

Baldwin, Faith, 1893–
    Skyscraper / by Faith Baldwin.
        p. cm.
    ISBN 0-7862-4086-5 (lg. print : hc : alk. paper)
        1. Women — Employment — Fiction.   2. New York
(N.Y.) — Fiction.   3. Large type books.   I. Title.
PS3505.U97 S55 2002
    813′.52—dc21   2002019934

Author's Dedication

This book is for MAJOR and MRS. PERCIVAL WREN in friendship and gratitude for friendship.

Acknowledgment

To my friends in the trust department of a great bank, to the buyer in a Fifth Avenue store, to the control-room engineer of a radio corporation and to all others who helped me so materially, my acknowledgments and thanks.

— Faith Baldwin

Persons this Love Story is about —

LYNN HARDING, piquant, petite, and 22, is a career girl with a vengeance. A year with the Seacoast Trust Company in Manhattan has started her on a promising future — which only marriage can cloud.

TOM SHEPARD, impulsive, good-natured ex-football player, has his mind on radio — when it isn't on Lynn. Forced to give up Yale and enter banking, Tom would much rather tinker with radio controls. Now if Lynn would only marry him — but she points out that he can't afford a wife.

DAVID DWIGHT, one of the greatest trial lawyers of his time, is exciting and glamorous to Lynn because of his brilliant position. At 48 Dwight is still youthful, ready for new love — his present wife and daughters notwithstanding.

SARAH DENNET, Lynn's boss, is a tall, severely smart woman with gentle eyes. Ten years ago she and David were lovers, but that is all over now, she reminds herself wistfully.

JENNIE LE GRANDE, Lynn's roommate, a Manhattan goddess, Brooklyn style, has the mind of a rather nice animal, asking only to live and let live. Jennie's life as a model doesn't exactly satisfy that breakfast-in-bed feeling with which she was born.

MARA BURT, who supports her bitter husband, doesn't give a whoop *how* she holds her typing job because she knows she wouldn't get anywhere in business without the old S. A. Mara's marital troubles make Lynn even more hesitant about marriage.

BOB RAWLSON, a salesman in the trust department, is a slim, smooth, rather unscrupulous fellow. Lynn distrusts him and deplores the fact that he and Tom are becoming very friendly.

SLIM HOWELL, Tom's lanky roommate, attractive and unsophisticated, thinks Jennie is a combination Venus and Mrs. Socrates, but she won't take him seriously.

FRANK HOUGHTON, married but still playing the field, enjoys taking Mara places. Mara claims it isn't an affair — just a good way to keep her job.

List of Chapters

I. Soaring Steel 11

II. His Kind of Girl. 33

III. Men Are Complications 58

IV. Finished — or Beginning? 76

V. Anything You Wish, David. . . . 92

VI. Harmless as a Serpent. 99

VII. On the Knees of the Gods . . . 127

VIII. After Laughter, Tears 144

IX. On a Note of Heartbreak. . . . 167

X. Two Troubled Girls. 193

XI. Mara's Way Out 219

XII. The Perfect Host 242

XIII. A Secret Betrayed 260

XIV. Dwight Gives His Word. 275

XV. Jennie's Bargain 287

XVI. A Gnawing Suspicion 307

XVII. "Men Make Me Sick!" 322

XVIII. Farewell to Jennie 348

XIX. Sarah Takes Action 371

XX. His Arms, His Kiss 378

XXI. Their Skyscraper. 401

Chapter One:

SOARING STEEL

Midtown in Manhattan, the Seacoast Building rose steadily in a series of sculptured setbacks for more than 800 feet, to challenge the imagination, to utter the most recent, but probably not the last, word in structural engineering.

From the lowest caisson anchored on rock, to the tall tapering of the final soaring tower, incredible tons, impossible masses of steel and stone had been shaped, shrieking their protest, into a pattern of progress, into a concrete expression of man's upward-striving.

Here upon this site, not many months ago, a group of brick buildings, irregular and dingy, had stood. Demolished, they had been, torn apart, vanishing into dust. Then had come an ordered confusion, earth ripped open, earth in a long travail, earth in the preparatory throes of deliverance of a monster. Enamored of the antlike activities of swarming workmen, the crowds had stood still, pausing from their futile, their important, personal affairs to gape dully at the exposed bowels, the torn womb of earth; to watch hour upon hour the heavy open jaws of the steam shovels digging their relentless way through earth to quicksand and running water, through quicksand and running water to the mammoth, the dinosaurian bones of solid rock.

Men. Architects — engineers — contractors — job runners — timekeepers — marble-setters — ironworkers — carpenters — plasterers — masons — painters — glaziers. And back of them, invisible, the forests, the quarries, the mills, and the kilns.

Noise. The discordant hymn attending these gargantuan rites, from the bell signals to the donkey engines, from the clatter of tools to the machine-gun staccato of the riveting-gun. The precise madness of the riveters' gang holds the watching crowd breathless — rivet boys and heater, the magnificently nonchalant catcher, the bucker-up with his dolly bar, the gun man with his pneumatic hammer, are to the audience the star performers of this theatrical spectacle played out against the backdrop of an indifferent and challenged sky.

Two thousand workmen — a dozen languages — tools of all trades — laughter — profanity — and, when the whistle blows, complete and arrogant relaxation over a wedge of pie, a can of coffee; lean backs, broad backs squared against the wooden temporary structures, legs stretched negligently, laughter — *"Some kid! — Hey, baby, what you doing tonight?"*

Silk legs flash by, a chin is lifted in repudiation. The workmen laugh, belly-laughter —

Cement and sand; hoists and derricks; here comes a foreman — *listen* to the foreman if you are not too sensitive —

Skyscraper — not so many months ago.

Now the workmen have vanished. Now the finished building stands; soon the public wonder will concentrate on other miracles. Now the sight-seeing busses make a detour so that the visitors to Manhattan may view the tallest building in town — "On your right, ladies and gentlemen, the Seacoast Building, eight hundred and forty feet high, seventy-two stories, the home of the Seacoast Bank and Trust Company, of the United Broadcasting Company. Hundreds of offices, thousands of workers. Express elevators — and from the towers the finest view of the city obtainable. On your right, ladies and gentlemen."

Statisticians, professional and amateur, contend with one another for space in the instructive press. "If the bricks used in the construction of the Seacoast Building were laid end to end —" "If the steel used in the construction of the Seacoast Building —" "It is estimated that through the bronze portals of the Seacoast Building so-and-so many thousands of people pass, every day —"

A clerk in the minor building opposite turns from his files and thinks of the Seacoast Building in terms of dollars and cents. *"If I had that much money — a tenth — a twentieth —"* he dreams in envy. God, if he had that much money, would he put it into steel and stone? Not he!

An architect, writing for a business magazine, defines the Seacoast Building in terms of the blueprint. He speaks of vertical masses, the absence of cornices and of horizontal accents. "In the Eliel Saarinen tradition," says the architect, for so soon, so swiftly with the passage of inexorable time do the most recent flowerings of the visionary mind become tradition.

A historian, passing by, on foot, looks up. He is dizzy with looking up; is there no end to this building, which to his restricted and tortured vision appears to lean, perilously balanced? He thinks of the lost towers of Babylon, craning his thin neck, while the building slants above him.

From Jersey, a sight-seeing airplane soars over Manhattan and skims like a silver dragonfly high above the tallest tower of the Seacoast Building. The guide murmurs his little lesson: "We are now passing over the Seacoast Building —" The passengers in the plane look down. They see a finger pointing into the sky, they see a pinnacle falling leagues short of its arrogant endeavor. They see a pyramid, built from the blocks of some gigantic child, blocks placed one upon another, setback, step-off. They see something small and aspiring, lifting itself above the striving of other buildings yet never attaining that blue height which their pilot, chewing gum, his hand easy upon the stick, attains. They feel confident and secure. They look down upon this insolence of steel, and it is dwarfed. They are above it.

It is all in the point of view.

A poet is riding in a fractious taxi, at the expense of his broker friend. The poet leans from the window and looks upward; the poet thinks, vaguely, in terms of light and shadow, he sees in the Seacoast

Building an immaculate beauty, with menace at the core. He thinks of the coinage of the country symbolized by the bank on the lower floors. He thinks of people and what money will do for them and what it will not do for them. He thinks of greed and lust, of rescue and rapture. He thinks of the broadcasting station in the towers, topless from a taxi window. He thinks of countries linked by mystery and of the strange dreaming voices of the ether which no man-made filament has yet captured. He wonders if he can get it down on paper. He knows that he cannot — Being a poet he says, "Let's go somewhere and get a drink."

It is all in the point of view.

On Sundays the street is empty. Now and then a car goes by. Now and then a man walks past, talking to his companion. The Seacoast Building stands half in sun and half in shade. The offices of the banks are closed. The other offices are closed also — insurance, wholesale sport clothes, lecture bureau, publishing, investment securities, lawyer, cafeteria, luncheonette, restaurant. Only in the towers are people active, in studios and control rooms, imparting news of the world, secular and church music, sermons, jazz to other

16

people who, slippered, sit at home, the Sunday papers in confusion about them, cartoon and comic, inky sheets, staining the hands which turn them. Who knows when someone will say, "See if you can get UBC, will you? Let's catch a little music —"

This is on Sunday. But Monday releases some spring, animating the routined gestures of men and women. Monday begins the workers' week, and the Seacoast Building opens its doors of green bronze set in black marble and invites them within, to struggle, to attain, to fail, to succeed, to love and to hope, to laugh and to weep, to suffer and rejoice, to envy and wound, to hate and to pity.

In short, to work for their existence.

In the Grand Central district the subway trains jolted to a screaming stop, the doors opened, the people eddied out upon the platform. "Watch your step," intoned the guard. The guard, in the midway car, by pushing a button which manipulated levers, was, for the moment, a demi-deity. Small, dark, a youthful man, in whose veins the South European blood retained memories of laughter and knives, slow, hot sunlight and twisted vines dripping the purple, hazy flesh of grapes, he stood in a swaying car and, as it slid to a stop, reached out a swarthy hand and touched the mechanical contrivance which opens a cage and lets forth an amorphous mass of human beings; a mass which, upon reaching the platform, resolved itself into separately moving, breathing, sometimes thinking, atoms.

"Hey — where the hell do you think you're going?"

"What's your hurry, sister?"

"Out — let me out — let me *out* — !"

A hysterical voice, the last. Some women always became slightly hysterical when their stations were reached. For three minutes prior to the halt they sat tense on the edge of their seats, or, rising, swayed and stumbled, fighting their way toward the doors. — "I'm getting off here — *will* you let me out?"

Men; young men, elderly men, old men. Women; fat and thin, of all ages. Fur coats, too warm, too bulky for this autumnal morning; sleazy, thin coats collared with the protesting pelt of some unfortunate cat, coats too thin for the brisk October winds. Stockings, silk, all grades. Shoes; oxfords, pumps, sandals; repressed but not conquered flesh flowing thickly over straps, bulging from fantastically cut-out leather;

sturdy heels, run-down heels. Powder, paint, lipstick, permanents; perfume, hot, cheap, permeating. Tabloids rustling. Jaws moving in their automatic bovine manner over wads of gum. Worried people; people worried over money, jobs, sickness, sweethearts, women, men, rent, mortgages, life — Crushed together by the doors two lovers, their bodies pressed closely together, his arm in the shabby serge sleeve around her thin shoulder. They were not talking very much. They were smiling, dimly, savoring this intimate moment, a little faint with insufficient breakfasts, with the morning dogtrot to their respective stations, with the fear that they would miss one another, with the beginning of a new working-day.

Other people, as closely allied physically, but strangers. A marriage of strange knees, a welding of limbs, a brief encounter of arms, breasts, shoulders. Breathing each other's breath, sensing each other's personal odors, aware of the texture of each other's skin, the fabric of each other's garments. Revolting, yet impersonal — as a rule.

The floor of the car had become a welter of paper; it looked like the city room in a newspaper office.

In the car there was no knowledge of weather, of rain, snow, sun, shade, warmth, cold. In the car there was nothing to indicate the day. These people were for a little time moles, involuntarily burrowing their way beneath the earth. In the car there lived, also temporarily, huddled together, every type, every kind of human being, one by one and two by two: a modern Noah's ark. In the car there pulsed insanely every sort of human passion, hope and fear —

Forty-Second Street —

The doors opened. "Let 'em off," shouted the guard, knowing that he shouted in vain.

Pushing, elbowing, the small stampede began.

Lynn Harding, arriving by the grace of God and 200 pounds of masculine avoirdupois against her back, upon the platform, shook herself cautiously, as a kitten might, to see if she was all there. She was a small girl, beautifully and firmly made. She settled the trim lines of her coat about her, sank her pointed chin into the fur collar, and fled lightly up the stairs, weaving her way past slower stair-climbers, with something of the fleet intensity of a female halfback, and skirting her way about the intricacies of the upper strata, passing shops and restaurants and the alluring archways to train levels, made her way up and out into the street.

Here there was space, in comparison with what she had left behind her for eight hours or more. Here was air, tainted perhaps with carbon monoxide but by comparison, of a pristine freshness; cold and clear. Here was sunlight, slanting down from tall buildings, but not wholly conquered. Here were hurrying people like herself and under her feet asphalt.

She was on her way to work. She was on her way to the Seacoast Building where, in the trust department of the Seacoast Bank and Trust Company, she was employed to do a job, impressively known as "sales research." She had held the position for a year, starting in the old offices of the company, moving with them two months previously to the new building. She was paid $1900 a year, she lived uptown in a business club for girls, she liked her work, she looked forward to a bigger and better job some day, she was 22 years old and pretty enough to arrest the preoccupied attention of more than one passer-by, hurrying with the insane speed of Monday morning toward his dull or exciting or stop-gap job.

It was early. Lynn was also on her way to

21

breakfast. She had been depressed for months by the cafeteria breakfasts at the club, the girls yawning their way downstairs to the clatter of utensils and thick cups and saucers, serving themselves, selecting cereals with a lackluster eye and balancing their selected calories and vitamins upon tin trays, bearing them to the painted tables, crowded against the painted walls. So, since the bank had moved into the new building, Lynn, arriving earlier than necessary, had breakfasted during her twenty minutes' leisure in the bigger and sunnier cafeteria in the building. She rather liked climbing on the high stool and winding her slim legs about it for support, rather liked the nonchalant, automatically flirtatious attitude of the redheaded young man in the white jacket who always waited on her and was never at a loss for a flung missile of pert conversation between orders. She liked the hurry and confusion, viewed with security from her little perch.

At the club, where she had lived since her arrival more than a year before in New York, she had no intimates. She knew most of the girls, she called them by their given names. She knew their jobs and in some cases their aspirations. She was privy to the love affairs of several. But she had no close friends. And there was something about the slightly institutional atmosphere, hedged about with rules and regulations, something about the pussy-faced, too, too sweet housemother or directress, something about the heavy feminine aura of the place, against which she rebelled. The Marlow Business Club for Girls — heavily endowed by a philanthropic woman who had never lived with 40 other women, who had never obeyed a regulation in her life — accepted for a weekly sum business girls of "good character" and "respectable background," and "employed in remunerative positions" from the ages of 18 to 30. Prior to 18 years of age you did not exist, for the club; nor, it appeared, after 30. Within the narrow brownstone walls the invisible emanations from 40 female personalities clashed and warred and struggled — Frivolous desires, stifling desires, frustrations, disappointments, terrors —

At night Lynn didn't mind. She was usually too tired or too indifferent after a day's work. But to rise refreshed, elastic in her youth and excellent health, looking forward as only youth may, to the unknown astonishments of a new day, and then to come into the crowded dining-room and be smitten full in the face by this intangible atmosphere of caged femininity made her melancholy. Therefore, she elected to breakfast in noise and confusion, surrounded by women, to be sure, but women in whom she was not forced to take a companionable interest and by the healthy loud-voiced argumentative masculinity of, for the most part, freshly shaven and shoe-shined men.

Today she gave her usual order. Orange juice, buttered toast, coffee — but added, because it was Monday and a splendid blue and golden day, a soft-boiled egg. No cereal. The business club was afflicted with cereals — one hot, two cold. And at night, if the hot cereal had not been demolished in the morning, like as not it would appear again in some quaint fried and sweetened guise.

Lynn raised the heavy white coffee cup to her lips.

"Swell day," commented the white jacket flashing back to the enormous steaming containers of coffee.

"Swell," agreed Lynn, contentedly.

Back somewhere in Lynn's Midwestern ancestry there must have been a lithe and laughing Irish girl, a dark-haired, blue-eyed pioneer to new lands, with the soft, breathless voice which such girls possess, a voice with the lilt in it. Such was Lynn's voice, and if the "Western" accent about which her companions at the club occasionally ragged her had been superseded by a hint of New Yorkese the lilt remained; and a young man sitting next to her turned from his own high stool to survey her, jogged, quite by accident, her elbow and changed her for a split second into a startled lady performing sleight of hand with a coffee cup.

"Oh, gosh, I'm sorry," said the young man in contrition, "did — did I spill it?"

He mopped distractedly in her general direction with a paper napkin. Lynn laughed and set down the cup.

"No, it didn't upset; it's quite all right," she told him, her small dark face sparkling from the loosened collar of fur.

"Lord, I'm always doing something clumsy," he bemoaned. He observed her, an open, direct glance, and was in no haste to remove his eyes. He asked, a little hesitantly, "Haven't I seen you before — aren't you in the trust department?"

But, of course! She remembered suddenly who he was. She had met him, about a week ago; Miss Dennet, her chief, had presented him to her one morning when, as she had stood at Miss Dennet's desk, a young man had paused briefly beside it. He was young Shepard — Tom Shepard — wasn't it? the new confidential secretary to Norton, vice-president in charge of the trust department.

"Miss Dennet introduced us," Lynn helped him out, "I'm Lynn Harding. In the sales research."

Tom Shepard grinned at her. He couldn't, he thought, have looked at her very closely that distant morning or he would never have forgotten her, even temporarily. Being a forthright young man, he said so immediately. The white jacket, overhearing, remarked with cheerfulness and envy, "Fast work, brother!" and passed on. Tom Shepard and Lynn looked at one another.

Lynn laughed outright. "Just what I was thinking," she admitted.

"Been with the outfit long?" he wanted to know.

"About a year," she answered.

"Cripes, that's too bad!" he told her sincerely.

His eyes were very blue over the rim of the coffee cup. His hair was of that color which begins as practically flaxen and sobers to a neutral and respectable brown.

That it waved slightly was one of his minor burdens. He had a very square jaw, a crooked nose, a sensitive, finely modeled mouth, close-set ears, and very broad shoulders. He was tall, she remembered. He had also the biggest hands she had ever seen in her life, and she watched them, in fascination, manipulating a fork and knife.

Ugly-good-looking, decided Lynn silently. She liked them — ugly-good-looking.

"You haven't been with us long," she stated rather than inquired. "And what did you mean by 'too bad'?"

He waved a fork perilously. All about them people came in, ordered, rose, paid their checks, departed. All about them was noise and confusion. They sat however on their high stools, heedless of people, of arrivals or departures, and consumed their breakfasts, when they remembered them, and observed each other, and were aware that they were young and that the world was a pretty decent sort of place on a Monday morning in October.

"Oh, I don't know," said Tom, "I'm always sorry when I see a — a girl" — he restrained himself from the qualifying adjective, not sure anyway whether it should be beautiful or charming or merely pretty — "slaving her life away in the toils of a soulless corporation," he ended solemnly.

Lynn laughed again. "I like my slavery," she confessed. "Don't you like yours?"

"Oh, it's all right," he mumbled awkwardly, a little shocked by the talent of all women for the abruptly and purely personal. He added hastily, "Do you always eat in this dump?"

"Breakfasts," she told him, "and generally lunch. I haven't graduated to the luncheonette," she concluded "nor the Gavarin."

The luncheonette was a drug-and-soda, blue-plate, small glass-topped-table affair. The Gavarin was an excellent and moderately expensive restaurant. All three were in the basement of the building.

Shepard nodded. "Me too," he said; and added facetiously, "but I suppose *you'll* be lunching in trust-officer elegance some day."

He referred to the private dining-rooms for the officers of the bank, which occupied the 53rd floor in magnificent privacy and undisputed beauty.

"I hope so," said Lynn sincerely, to his inner amazement. She climbed down from the stool, sliding her modest tip under the saucer. "It's late," she said, and looked at the immense clock ticking inexorably.

Tom absorbed the last dregs of the coffee into his inner man in one large intake of breath, dropped a Croesus-like quarter on the counter to the startled wonder of the white jacket and snatched his check. He reached for Lynn's also. "Here, let me."

But she shook her head. "I'd rather not," she said.

Rebuffed but not cast down, he walked with her to the cashier's desk, unconsciously squaring his shoulders and looking down at her from the physical superiority of his great height. She thought, as they stood at the desk together, *Bet he's played football* —

She asked him.

"Scrub. And in my junior year on the team. Yale," he explained and added, his gay young face momentarily shadowed, "I didn't finish."

They made their way upstairs out of the cafeteria and, wandering in what were literally marble halls, located their right elevator and went sedately to the third floor where the trust department was situated. In the elevator pressed close together he observed her from the corners of his blue eyes. Small, dark, reaching to his heart. Oh, well, perhaps a little more, but let it go at that. Curly dark hair rebelling against the little beret, growing, as he was able to see, in a widow's peak upon her forehead. A smooth and olive skin, faintly flushed, and the lovely accent of gray eyes, the color of a quiet rainy day, rimmed with dark lashes, shining under the thin, fine curve of black brows. Another accent was her mouth, frankly lipsticked into a charming and impossible scarlet. And near one satiny corner there was a tiny, jet-black mole.

He thought, *it's a damned shame that pretty women have to work.*

Now they were walking into the trust department. Here they would separate, she to go to the big room in the corner of which she had her desk, he to enter the more magnificent surroundings of the trust officers' room, and finally his own small anteroom off Norton's private office. He lingered, however. He said, "Look here, you won't think me fresh or anything — How about lunch?"

She was genuinely sorry. She said so. "I have," she said, "an engagement."

"Breakfast then?" asked Tom, with a grin.

She laughed, gestured toward her wrist watch and fled into her room. She was still laughing when she reached there, five minutes late. "What's the joke at this time in the morning?" inquired the blond Miss Marple a little sourly, turning from her files.

The room was flanked with files. It was a strictly utilitarian room. There were no splendid draperies, no massive furniture, no murals, no inches-thick carpet in this room; nor were there any little quiet anterooms where tactful men and women interviewed swathed, draped, and sometimes weeping widows or bewildered orphans. Yet in this room where Lynn worked were filed the futures of widows and orphans; row upon row of green metal files.

In a corner a girl was checking stock quotations with the help of another. Miss Marple, at a file, was looking up something relative to the estate of one Jonathan Smith. Someone else was filing carbons. Lynn, her outdoor things disposed of, sat down at her own desk by the window on the far side of one wall and looked over the work which was set aside for today. In her desk lay, and would lie, the not-so-private lives of many unsuspecting men, neatly docketed upon little blue cards.

Here on a card, one David Whitmore's name, plainly typed. Here, his probable income, his clubs, his family relations, his business connections. Today Lynn would give this card, upon which Mr. Whitmore's financial life and prospects were displayed in cold print, to an eager young salesman. And that salesman would presently call upon Mr. Whitmore and endeavor to interest him in the many and diverse facilities of the trust department, so completely at Mr. Whitmore's disposal and service.

Lynn jotted down a name upon a pad, reached for a copy of Bradstreet and opened the social register. Her day had begun.

Chapter Two:

HIS KIND OF GIRL

A little before noon she made her way into the officers' room and to Miss Dennet's desk. Lynn always entered this room and approached this desk with a sense of subdued excitement. The room was enormous, it was pillared. Heavy velvet carpeting lay upon the floor. The walls were treated with costly and beautiful simplicity. The flat-topped desks, mahogany, were less businesslike in appearance than Lynn's own. There were perhaps twelve of them in the room, amply spaced. Down the middle of the room ran an equally well-spaced aisle of smaller desks, trademarked by typewriters; the desks of the secretaries to the trust officers. The room was subdued. People moved quietly, made little noise. Miss Dennet's secretary, sitting by Miss Dennet's desk, nodded at Lynn, smiled, and slipped away. Miss Dennet reached out a strong white hand and replaced a volume — some one or other on "Bonds" — in its usual position.

Lynn laid a card on the desk.

"We slipped up on this," she reported guiltily.

Sarah Dennet was 48 and looked 36. A well-groomed woman, tall, her hair brushed severely, her face well washed and but slightly powdered, she had large severe features and very gentle eyes behind rimmed spectacles. She wore a miraculously well-cut dress, black, white collar, white cuffs. She smiled at Lynn, and her large mouth had curves of unexpected merriment and amiability.

"That can't be helped," she said. "I expected it." She pushed aside some of Lynn's own blue cards, the salesmen's reports firmly clipped to them, and asked, "Nearly lunch time, isn't it?"

Lynn nodded.

"I'll meet you outside," Sarah told her, "and we'll go to the Gavarin."

Lynn smiled and looked past Miss Dennet's desk, the desk of that trust officer in charge of "new business," to the open door of the anteroom leading into the vice-president's private office. She saw a pair of broad shoulders and the back of a brown head. She hadn't been quite truthful when she had told Tom Shepard that she had not graduated to the Gavarin. She went there, perhaps once a week, with Miss Dennet.

Fifteen minutes later she and her chief were facing each other across the small table in the corner of the rather consciously elegant restaurant. The older woman commented after they had ordered, "Haven't been to see me in weeks, Lynn. Been busy?"

"Not very. A movie now and then. Except — Ken Wilkins — from home, you know. He was in town last week. He gave me a whirl. Theater every night."

"Is that Amy Wilkins's boy?" asked Sarah, interested.

"The same. He wouldn't thank you for calling him a boy. You should see him in New York. He wrote the place!" laughed Lynn.

"Amy was like that," commented Sarah vaguely, over chicken cutlet; but Lynn, who had been brought up next door to the Wilkins family, understood perfectly and lifted amused gray eyes to her friend's.

"What do you hear from your mother?" Sarah asked her. "She hasn't written to me in ages."

"Oh, she's all right; a little rheumatism, now and then, and trouble getting a cleaning woman. She always has that,"

Lynn declared, "for no one she gets ever satisfies father. He howls at the sight of one of them." She was silent, smiling, thinking of her father's untidy, medicinally odorous office on the first floor of their frame house. She remembered when that house had stood in the country, rather than in the town proper. She remembered hearing the wheels of the rig drive out, night after night, on the errands of mercy, of success or failure. She remembered the first car, which had replaced the rig. She remembered the encroaching growth of the small, busy, energetic town.

"Your father works himself to death," Sarah announced, attacking her salad. She hated salad but always ate it, every day, for her health. "He and your mother should get away, for a rest."

"They're talking about going to Florida this winter. Father hates to turn over his practice, though. The new young doctor is clever, he says," Lynn told her, a little resentful of the recent Johns Hopkins graduate and his "cleverness." "But father thinks people depend on *him*. And he's right," she said proudly.

"Of course he's right," agreed Sarah, out of her long loyal friendship with the Hardings. She had been Janet Harding's closest friend, back in that town where both were born. She was Lynn's godmother. And it was she who had poured soothing syrup on the troubled family waters when young Lynn, after less than a year at her state university, had decided she had been enough expense to the family and must therefore come to New York and make her own fortune and seek her own adventure. It was Sarah who had met Lynn at the train, who had found the job for her, and who had urged her to stay with her, at least for the first few months, in the small, charming apartment she shared with another woman, a head of advertising in a large department store.

But Lynn had refused. "There isn't room," she said flatly, "and I'd only be putting you and Miss Frank out. Besides, I couldn't pay my share. And moreover," went on Lynn, small, pointed chin slightly elevated, "you'd think it your bounden duty to look after me — and I don't want to be looked after, Sarah darling! Or rather, I want to look after myself — and live on my own salary — and fight my own battles. You'd make things too easy," she announced.

So Sarah, with many misgivings and several lengthy letters, sent via air mail to the Middle West, had given in, and eventually hearing of the business club, had inspected it with, it must be confessed, a slight sinking of the heart, and had sent Lynn there.

During office hours their relations were pleasant, friendly, and co-operative; but Lynn, determined never to overstep the bounds, out of her deep gratitude to her mother's friend, had acquired a business-like formality toward the older woman which amused and rather touched her. Once a week or so they lunched together, and Lynn came to the apartment for dinner now and then. But she never intruded upon Sarah. She realized that the other had her own interests, her own friends and relaxations, acquired after many years in New York, and it would be impossible for Lynn herself to enter into Sarah Dennet's private life to any great extent. *Lynn,* wrote Sarah to Lynn's mother, *treats me with a curious mixture of attitudes — family friend, sometimes confidante, occasional adviser, and Big Chief.*

"Mother," said Lynn, sighing, "still wants me to come home and teach or something. She's always writing and asking if I haven't had enough of city life!"

"And haven't you had enough?" asked Sarah.

"Well, no. I'm just beginning!"

Sarah thought, looking at the glowing face, the steady, lambent gray eyes, *Of course, you're just beginning.* She thought also, *Here sitting opposite me and crumbling her bread on the table sits possibly my successor.* But she felt no special pang of envy at the other's youth, her prospects, her ambitions, her future. She was in fact imperceptibly grooming Lynn Harding for her own job some day. *If she doesn't go off the deep end and marry some young idiot first and ruin her business future,* thought Sarah, who having survived one disastrous love affair twenty years ago was not given to dwelling with admiration on men, as husbands, as lovers. Yes, Lynn should be groomed for her job, for Miss Dennet had no intention of staying where she was forever.

"By the way," said Lynn, a little too carelessly, "at breakfast this morning in the cafeteria, I sat next to Mr. Shepard — you know, Mr. Norton's new secretary."

"You did? He seems a nice boy," Sarah admitted ungrudgingly, "a little too much all hands and feet, I suppose. I understand that Mr. Norton is satisfied with him so far."

"How on earth did he happen to get the job?" asked Lynn. "He doesn't look the type."

"Must there be a type?" the older woman wanted to know.

"Oh, I suppose not. But nowadays you don't see many men secretaries — at least not ex-football players, all, as you say, hands and feet."

"I believe," said Sarah, not particularly interested, "that he was studying engineering at Yale when his mother, his last surviving relative, died. What money she had was left in trust — Mr. Norton is an old friend of the family's."

"Oh, I see — a direct legacy to the Seacoast Trust Company." Lynn's eyes danced. "But why didn't they let him go on with his engineering?" she demanded.

"I don't know." Sarah signaled the waiter and requested a menu. "Will you have a sweet, Lynn? — Two French pastries then, although I shouldn't, I'm getting fat. I don't know," she repeated, recalling herself to the topic of conversation, "I believe there wasn't enough to put him through, or Mr. Norton thought he had better start in working. There is no surer way for a young man to learn the banking business, generally, than by becoming secretary to a banker. Only so few do. I think that he — young Shepard — took a secretarial course before finally coming in with us."

"But he doesn't take dictation, does he?" asked Lynn, wide-eyed and unable to picture Tom Shepard making pothooks.

"No, Miss Mason does that. His job is to meet people and be tactful, I believe," Sarah told her, "and to keep track of Mr. Norton's appointments and carry confidential messages for him and all that sort of thing."

"General errand boy," murmured Lynn.

The French pastry disposed of, Miss Dennet drank her tea and observed her companion.

"The Wilkins boy pestered you to return home, I imagine," she ventured.

"Oh, about as usual." Lynn flushed a little. "He always thinks when he arrives in town full of the possibilities of the dental-equipment business that I will fall on his neck from sheer admiration — and homesickness. He's a good lad," said Lynn carelessly. "He brought me a box of cake and fudge and cookies and never turned a hair, carrying it under his arm as if it were going to explode all the way up, I suppose. But he never arrives without bringing something from mother."

"Well, I don't know him; but I do know his mother," said Sarah firmly, "and I must say I'd hate to see you go back and be one Mrs. Dental-Equipment Wilkins —"

"Don't worry," Lynn said, and laughed. "Marriage is the last thing that would interest me now, and you know it!"

Presently they went back to work, stopping first on the main banking floor for Sarah to cash a personal check. The main banking floor was stately and beautiful; murals looked down from the walls. Here the conversation, the footsteps, and the ceaseless activities of the bank seemed subdued to a monotone. Lynn spoke to one of the tellers, waiting for her friend to finish her transaction. Then they went into the lobby together and waited for the elevator. The express lifts flashed by, and Lynn watched them, taking on and discharging their human freight. If you waited by the elevators long enough you saw rather exciting people: the artists of the air being transported to the broadcasting studios, seven stories of them, in the tower. You saw Broadway actors and actresses, Metropolitan Opera singers, you saw motion-picture stars and orchestra leaders, crooners and daily dieters, lecturers and saxophonists, people whose following was purely local or people whose names were traditional for their work all over the country.

"There goes Gloria Faye," whispered Lynn, clutching Sarah's arm. "She's on the air tonight. Perhaps she is going up to re-hearse."

Gloria — Radio's Sweetheart — in a summer ermine coat and a little helmet of felt and fur swept with her accompanist into the metal cage. Sighing a very little, Lynn turned back to the local elevator and stepped in.

But when she stepped out again that evening she perceived, lounging by the door, feet planted sturdily upon the floor and entirely unmoved by the surge and press of people about him, one Mr. Thomas Shepard, confidential secretary to the vice-president, waiting, as was evident from his practically shouted greeting, for her.

"Here you are," remarked Tom amiably, and took her by the arm. "Where would you like to eat?"

He had the audacious eyes of self-confidence. He wore assurance lightly, without offense, as if it were a fresh, un-fading flower in the buttonhole of his well-cut unobtrusive blue serge. Lynn was distressed to find herself coloring, stammering even.

"Why — why —"

"Where do we eat?" he inquired again sternly.

"But —"

"But me no buts, why me no whys," he told her, and took her arm with the gesture of a man who knows his own mind. A girl not much older than Lynn, hurrying past on her way home to cook supper for her husband — who was out of a job — glanced at them with cynical understanding and a little envy. She thought, *Poor idiots!* and went on her way, small, alert, redheaded. She forgot the couple by the elevator doors, rushing through those of bronze. She thought, as addled as the White Rabbit, *Oh, dear, oh, dear, I shall be late again!*

Lynn, unaware of that fleeting scrutiny, said, involuntarily keeping pace with Shepard as they moved away from the clicking doors, "You were awfully sure of me, weren't you?"

He denied it, laughing, "No, your error. Awfully sure of myself; of what I want. I couldn't wait till breakfast. Look here" — he stopped dead, heedless of the people who were thronging against him and who bounced back, startled, from the impact with his exceedingly solid flesh and bone, like rubber balls — "look here — you don't *dislike* me or anything, do you? I mean, we were introduced properly and all that —"

"Even if you didn't remember — !"

"Check," he admitted, imperturbably.

"Am I — don't spare my feelings — am I the sort of fellow no nice girl ever goes out to dinner with?" he inquired with a total lack of syntax but complete sincerity.

"Don't be ridiculous!" she said, surrendering.

Now they were hurtling through the doors, now they were out on the street. Tom advanced to the curb and signaled a taxi. Lynn asked thriftily, "Can't we walk — or take a bus?"

"Oh, God, a practical woman!" He helped her into the cab and settled himself beside her. He said, "This is an occasion. After you get to know me better I'll permit you to save me money."

His voice was grave; his eyes danced. She felt suddenly self-conscious. What an idiot he must think her. No, he did not think her an idiot. He thought her, and she knew it, a very pretty girl. He said so, immediately. He said aloud something he had been thinking ever since he had seen her at the cafeteria counter, "It's a shrieking shame that pretty girls have to work."

"What about homely ones?" asked Lynn, delighted.

He liked her. He liked her a lot. His kind of girl, cute as a trick, a regular honey, intelligent as the devil, a sense of humor. He liked her the better for not exclaiming, *Oh, Mr. Shepard, do you really think I'm pretty?* or something equally inane. Not that girls ever said that, exactly, nowadays, but they managed to convey the impression. He grinned cheerfully. He answered, lighting a cigarette and offering her his case.

"Have a cigarette? Homely girls, well, I'm sorry for them, as a matter of course. But, personally, I don't give a hoot whether they work or not!"

Not many men so plainly speak the mind of all men.

"No, thanks. I don't smoke much. After coffee perhaps."

"That's good," he put the case away.

She asked curiously, "You don't mean to say that you object?" She eyed him as if he might prove to be a museum piece.

"Well, no, why should I? Personally, I don't like stained fingers," he admitted. "I meant that girls who have to have their cigarettes in taxis, in theater lobbies, and on top of busses are so expensive! You see, even if they smoke your brand," he confided engagingly, "they always feel it their duty to order another kind!"

"You haven't much use for girls?"

"Not any more. In the plural," said Tom cheerfully.

"Do you know where you're going?" asked the driver suddenly.

They regarded him blankly. His face was appallingly ugly, it was pockmarked. He was so hideous that his photograph, before them, did him complete justice. He looked like a racketeer, a gunman, a thug; or he looked like the general conception of these useful gentlemen. As a matter of fact he was a family man with a strong religious sense and a great reader. Tom remembered vaguely that when, on netting his fares, the driver had mechanically inquired, "Where to?" he had merely waved a vague hand in the downtown direction.

Laughter in the taxi. The driver grinned, sympathetic to youth. He knew how it was. He said over his shoulder, steering deftly in and out of cabs, cars, trucks, and delivery wagons in the usual rush-hour huddle, "I had the missis out in the cab last week and didn't turn down me flag. I got a ticket."

They commiserated with him. Tom said, "I know a little place in the Village." Leaning forward he gave the address.

"Oke," agreed the driver amiably.

Off Fifth Avenue, the little place. Up a flight of brownstone steps. Small tables, dim light, a radio, a fat proprietor in a morning coat. "Haven't seen you for a long

47

time, Mr. Shepard."

"Cocktail? They're very good," promised Tom. "Right off the boat. Fishing smack, Staten Island ferryboat, passage to Welfare Island. Who knows?"

When the small frosted glasses came, Tom raised his and looked at her over the rim. "Here's mud in your eye," he said sentimentally, "and now I'll let Mike there order, it's less trouble. You like veal, don't you? Well, if you don't, you'll learn. Broccoli? I thought so. And some of that fluffy stuff in glasses, with a kick in it. And coffee. Large, I hope." He regarded her anxiously. "Don't say you're a demitasse girl," he implored her. "Be bourgeois like me!"

She confessed to a liking for large coffee with, no less, hot milk and cream. "Swell," said her host in great contentment. "Now that's done. Tell me all about yourself, so I can reciprocate. I promise to curb my impatience while you spin your yarn. Then I'll tell one."

"There isn't much," she told him, laughing, and spoke briefly of home and her people, of her boredom at the university, of her sense that she was wasting time. And of her arrival in New York, Sarah Dennet's protégée.

"Do you live with her?" Tom asked, attacking the *antipasto.*

"No." Lynn pushed a spineless red rim of something about on her plate and eventually ate it, abstractedly. "No, I live in a business club for girls."

"Sounds God-awful," commented Tom. "Hen house or chicken coop?"

"Chicken coop, I fancy. They throw you out when you're thirty."

Tom was silent, visualizing thousands of women of 30 hurtling down the steps of the club, fleeing homeless into the night. "Hard luck," he said, "but you have about fifteen years to go, haven't you?"

She replied primly, "I'm twenty-two."

"I'm twenty-three," said Tom in a superior manner.

They viewed each other across the table. Forty-five years between them. The waiter removed the *antipasto* and brought on the minestrone. "It looks like such a lot!" said Lynn, regarding it with some trepidation.

"Elegant soup," praised Tom. "Times when I'm broke I order me minestrone, and it stays by me all day. Spaghetti is a snare and a delusion. You eat it until it comes out of your ears, but three hours later you could devour the side of a barn. Minestrone sticks. Probably glue in it," he suggested helpfully.

He wanted to know all about the club. She told him — sketchily. Yes, they had meals there, breakfast, cafeteria style, and dinner. Dinner was chicken Sundays and hashed chicken Mondays, and lamb on Tuesdays and lamb hash on Wednesdays.

"Don't tell me any more," begged Tom, "you poor kid!"

But she went on, laughing a little, "We've a radio. And a phonograph. We have to be in at eleven-thirty or do a lot of expert explaining. We've a parlor where we can receive gentlemen visitors." She looked at him, her head a little on one side, gray eyes shining through the black lashes. "The visitors have to meet the directress, and there's an awful rush to see who gets the couch in the corner if more than one girl is entertaining. It's great fun," she added, remembering young Mr. Wilkins and one or two others.

Tom called upon his maker. He said, sighing, "Well, we'll spend our time at the movies then. Do you skate? That's nice of you. We'll skate. Bus ride. Now and then we'll see a good show. Oh," mourned Tom, gustily, "oh, for the good old days when every girl had a back parlor for her personal use, and the family could sit in the kitchen!"

This was skimming over surfaces, and they contemplated each other briefly, confronted so soon by the changing standards and living conditions for young people, who at 22 and 23 like each other very much and do not possess back parlors and complaisant parents.

"Your turn," Lynn reminded him.

"No, not yet. What about this bank business? You don't really *like* it, do you?" he asked her.

"I'm crazy about it!"

He said, a little self-consciously, "I didn't listen, I'm afraid, when your department was first explained to me so I asked old Gunboat about it —"

"Gunboat?"

"Norton. Did you ever look at his shoes? — I asked him today. He was tickled silly. He thought I was beginning to take an interest in the organization. In a way he was right. Do you mean to tell me that you expect to sit at a desk for the next forty years, looking up the annual dues of clubs and things and trying to remember that the Racquet Club is not in Chicago nor yet in Red Hook and that the Junior League isn't a church society?" he demanded.

"Of course, I don't expect to," she told him. "There are other jobs. Better ones.

I'm mad about the work. I'm going to start courses at Columbia, nights, in February; going to learn all I can, I like the whole atmosphere of the place."

"That's more than I do. Oh, well," he shrugged, "what's the use of bleating? I couldn't go on with what I wanted to do, and that's that. Only" — he grinned — "I've been taking night courses too."

Oh, Tom!" she regarded him, delighted. "Banking?"

"No, radio, at the Y. M. C. A."

Radio!"

"It comes natural to me," he confessed, "Gee, I'm nuts about it. I could eat it up! I started to get my M.E. degree at Sheff, you know. Radio! Girl, I've a set I built myself in my rooms that will get anything from here to heaven, and sometimes when the static is bad, a bit of the other place, too. You'll have to come and listen to it," he told her.

She said instantly, "I'd love to." She asked, "I suppose you're always tearing it to pieces? Father has one. It's his only hobby. It never works because he is always doing something to it."

"I know a guy up in the UBC control room," Tom told her. "I sneak up there a lot, and, gosh, it's great stuff." His eyes were suddenly no longer gay; they were wistful. He said, "Well, such is life. It's always the way. Rising young banker longs to be a radio-service man."

She argued with animation, "But — banking? That's constructive, marvelous — necessary. A grand job, I think. Your finger on the very pulse of the world."

"Like a ticker tape?" he demanded. "Not for me! Radio, isn't that constructive too?"

His eyes were blazing with enthusiasm. He ruffled his hair so that, more unruly than ever, it stood up in crests and waves, untidy, attractive. He looked, she thought, about ten years old. She said, dissatisfied, "Somehow I don't see you as an announcer."

"Oh — announcing —" He dismissed it with a wave of his big hand. "I don't want to do that." He grinned. "Me! Imagine trying to pronounce jawbreakers and getting dirty letters: 'Dear sir, last night you said *bin* instead of bean!' Hell's bells, that's the bunk, not but what some of 'em aren't swell guys at that. No, but the control room — the lab — that's where I'd like to be, digging out new ways, short cuts, learning, discovering."

He was off. By the time they had reached the fluffy stuff in a glass she knew more — and less — about radio than she had ever known. Her head whirled. Coils, condensers, high frequency, ground circuits, filaments, oscillation — was there no end to this jargon which contained such mysteries as Nemos and cranking gains? She felt as if she had been transported to a new world and there had heard an entirely alien language.

He said, "You're bored to death!" A mild, but sorrowful accusation.

"No, I'm not, I don't understand half you're saying," she admitted, "but go on, I like it!"

It was perfectly true. She did like it. She liked watching him; liked the grave twisting of his mouth, the changing color of his enthusiastic eyes, the gestures of the big hands which looked so awkward and which must be so deft, so adept with wires and little finicking important things.

Presently over coffee, large, over their companionable cigarettes, he was telling her that he lived in a "dump" not far from where they were sitting, with another man, an engineer with the telephone company. He was telling her of the Long Island town where he had been born, where he had gone to high school. "Used to be all farms, that town; my great-granddad owned most of 'em. Didn't hold on though, more's the pity." Telling her of fishing in Peconic Bay, of swimming, of his first stolen airplane flight with a commercial pilot. "Pancaked right into mother's hen house. No, we weren't hurt, but maybe I didn't get a trimming!"

It was past ten o'clock when he deposited her on the narrow brownstone steps of the club. "Tomorrow night?" he asked. "And I'll see you at breakfast?"

She stood a step above him and looked down; hatless, he returned her regard under the dim light shining from the glass of the hall door. "No," she answered, "I mean, yes, for breakfast, but not tomorrow night; I promised one of the girls I'd go to the movies with her."

"Wednesday then?"

"I'm going to dinner at Miss Dennet's."

"Thursday?" He was grave and stubborn.

She gave in, laughing. "Thursday, then," she agreed, "but no more celebrations. We'll go somewhere very cheap, and fifty-fifty."

"Well, I guess not!"

"Please?" She bent toward him slightly. He could see the clear shining pallor of her skin, the satin texture of her lips, the dark widow's peak pointing the little triangle on her forehead. "Please — if we're to be friends?" She added bluntly, "You can't afford to take me out all the time. This way is better. I won't go unless you say you understand."

"Oh, all right." He was sullen, his male pride wounded. He added eagerly, "But once in a while — every ten days — my party? How about it? Shall we compromise?"

"Maybe. We'll see." Perfectly natural coquetry stirred her to say, of course, "But perhaps in ten days you'll —"

"Don't say it. Not in ten years. Not in ten times ten years!" said Tom.

She fled laughing into the house, disregarding his ardent eyes, his outstretched hand. *Dear Dorothy Dix: When I go out with a young man for the first time, is it proper for me to kiss him? All the boys expect it. Girls who don't kiss don't get dates. Little Eva. Dear Little Eva: Of course not. Decent men don't expect payment for an evening's good time.*

Tom was decent. Tom was — darling.

Lynn whistled her way upstairs. She had a quaint way of whistling. Her generous red mouth was not pursed, the whistle was eerie, emanating from an undisturbed face. She went up two flights and entered her room. Nine by something. Bed, bureau, clothes closet, chair. Chintz, a little worn. On the window sill a pot of flowers the Wilkins boy had sent. They were faded. "Poor things," she said, and poked at the dry soil. She had forgotten to water them.

Mollie Eames stuck her flyaway head in the door.

"You sound happy," said Mollie. "Lend me two bucks, will you? I'm flat broke. Anyone in your frame of mind can afford to be broke. I can't. Had a heavy date?"

Lynn replied seriously. "About a hundred and seventy-five pounds, I imagine."

"Lord, a truck driver! How about the two?"

"Help yourself, there's my purse."

"It's great to be crazy," said Mollie sourly.

Crazy? Perhaps. Happy, certainly. Why? Love at first sight? Such things didn't happen. She'd see him at breakfast tomorrow.

She wouldn't like him as well, perhaps, at breakfast tomorrow. He'd sort of taken her off her feet, that's all. She picked up a book. *Financial Systems*, the gilt lettering read soberly. She opened it. *When bonds have a single maturity date —*

She threw it on the floor and went to bed.

Chapter Three:

MEN ARE COMPLICATIONS

Six weeks later Lynn, just before closing-time, took the express elevator to the 30th floor upon which the Seacoast Company maintained recreation and rest rooms, with a trained nurse in charge for all women workers in the entire building.

She went there in order to return a book from the loan library also installed by the Seacoast Company for the convenience of its women employees. The lavatories and mirrored washstands were crowded with chattering girls and women. Here friendships were made, here enmities were established, and here the gossip of the day filtered through hundreds of pale or lip-sticked mouths, talk of twenty, of forty offices, each with its different activities.

A cleaning woman went by. Lynn stopped her. "How's your little boy, Mary?" she asked.

Mary's dull eyes brightened, she straightened a wisp of straggly hair. "Much better, miss," she said gratefully, "and Miss Raines" — she gestured toward the nurse in the rest room — "has promised to come and see him this evening."

"That's nice." Lynn smiled and went on.

In the lounge several girls were sitting and talking. The radio was on, full blast. In the rest room the nurse was occupied; a girl was lying there on the long couch. Back of the rest room was the small officelike dispensary.

Lynn hesitated a moment and then went in. The nurse, a middle-aged woman with a plain, attractive face and startlingly handsome brown eyes, smiled at her. They had struck up an acquaintance some weeks earlier over a particularly good detective story. "Miss Raines?"

"Yes? What can I do for you?"

"Nothing. But Mary — her youngster's sick," Lynn explained. "She said you were going there tonight." Lynn fumbled in her bag and put a bill into the nurse's hands. "It isn't much, but it might buy them something they need."

"I expect it will. That's good of you. Mary — her husband's no good, you see. Drinks. Hasn't a job, of course. She has all she can do to get along." Miss Raines spoke, tucking the bill into the crisp white uniform pocket.

The girl on the couch stirred and lifted her heavy lids. She was a tall girl, very beautifully formed, with masses of wheat-gold hair, worn in the prevalent and generally unbecoming bob, but not unbecoming to Jennie Le Grande (née Smith) however, who wore hers bunched and curled on the back of her long white neck and looked like a Manhattan goddess.

"She's one of the models from the French wholesale house on the twentieth floor," explained Miss Raines, low. "She came up here, complained of feeling ill, and fainted, literally, on my hands. She's been out of it for some time now. She's all right."

Miss Le Grande swung her elegant legs and slender feet to the floor and smoothed back the damp hair from her low broad forehead. "Musta done a flop," she muttered, disgusted.

She added — long blue eyes sliding toward the nurse — "That was powerful stuff you handed me. Packed a kick like an army mule."

"Spirits of ammonia," said the nurse, smiling. "Feel all right again?"

"A little jittery." Jennie rose and walked toward a mirror on the wall. She sat down abruptly. "Backbone's jelly," she complained.

"You girls don't eat breakfast properly, or lunch," diagnosed the nurse severely.

"We eat all day," Jennie told her indifferently. "The girl brings us breakfast when we get down to work. This morning I was late. Didn't get any. Had some lunch, though it didn't set any too well. Mob of buyers in from the West, had us run ragged, that's what." She added glumly and plainly, "I feel like hell!"

"I'd take you home," Miss Raines said, worried, "only I promised Mary — and I have to get over to Jersey tonight to see my sister —"

Her voice trailed off. Lynn nodded to her imperceptibly and, turning, asked the other girl, "Where do you live?"

"Fifty-eighth, West," replied Jennie, without much enthusiasm, "and I'd better be ankling along."

"That's right on my way! I was going to take a taxi," lied Lynn fluently. "I'll drop you."

"Sure you were going to?" asked Jennie shrewdly, and regarded Lynn for the first time, a full direct glance from sleepy, sulky eyes. She was white, under her rouge, pale beneath the coating of lipstick.

"Sure," said Lynn. "I'll look after you. Come along. Think you can make the elevators?"

Miss Raines said, low, "Thanks a lot," and Lynn nodded, smiling.

The rest room was for everybody, all the women. So you met everybody here. Since the building opened Lynn had spoken to dozens of girls who were not employed in the bank. Some she knew by name. But she had never seen Jennie before. Coming up at closing hour or at the noon hour, Lynn always found the rooms crowded, the radio going. Sometimes girls, bringing sandwiches with them, would make up a bridge table for their luncheon hour. Sometimes they danced. Always they employed their free time for anything but resting, Lynn reflected.

"I don't approve of it," said Sarah Dennet firmly, of the rest room. "It's bound to be a hotbed of gossip! And how do you know whom you'll meet?"

"Don't know. Don't care. I don't gossip anyway," Lynn had laughed in answer. Miss Dennet, in her free moments betook herself to the lounge set aside downstairs for the women officers. But the majority of the women in the building used the building's conveniences. "Hello, Kate," said

Lynn, as she and Jennie went out through the wide door into the hall.

Kate Marple, filing clerk in Lynn's section, raised a plucked eyebrow. Where was Lynn going with the model, she wondered.

"This is certainly white of you," said Jennie faintly, in the crowded elevator. Lynn looked at her anxiously. *Hope she's not going off again,* she thought, and wished, with the shrinking of the healthy lay person from the sick, that Miss Raines had come with them.

"You'll feel better in the air," she suggested, as much to reassure herself as to comfort her companion.

They reached the street and hailed a cab. Jennie sank back against the upholstery gratefully. She said, "You must let me pay my part," and peered into her purse. Then she laughed. "I can't," she said flatly, "but pay day's not far off; I'll meet you up in the rest room then and square myself."

"Please," said Lynn embarrassed. "I was going to taxi anyway."

"Well — if you really were," said Jennie, used to accepting things. She added, "I haven't seen you before. What's your name? Work in the building, don't you?"

Lynn told her name and her position. Jennie gave hers. "Le Grande," she said. "I found it in a book. Pretty nifty?" She laughed suddenly. "Over in Brooklyn," said Jennie, "I'm still Jane Smith!"

When they reached her destination she asked, completely recovered, "Must you go home now? I've got a date but it isn't till seven-thirty. I'd like you to see my place."

Lynn was curious. Moreover, she rather liked this girl, with her graceful height and heavy wheaten hair and Viking coloring. She amused her. She was different from anyone she had ever met. And there was no hurry to get back to the club. It was Tom's night at the Y. She wouldn't be seeing him tonight. Nights bereft of Tom were pretty blank.

She climbed the stairs with Jennie. It was a walk-up apartment house, rather dingy. But the little rooms into which Jennie admitted herself and Lynn with a latchkey were pleasant. A bed- and sitting-room, another bedroom, a tiny kitchen, a tiled bath. Very bright and gay with chintz, and fluffy with far too many pillows, and cluttered with long-legged dolls.

"You live alone?" asked Lynn, looking about. "It's very attractive."

"No, I've a girl friend — She's a model, too, but over in the regular wholesale district — coats and suits," explained Jennie.

"Want a drink? I've got some gin."

"No, thanks," said Lynn instantly, and then added, "If you don't mind —"

"Don't bother to apologize or explain," Jennie said easily. "Lord, my head aches! A little snort wouldn't do me any harm." She walked into the kitchenette and came back with a small measure of straight gin in a bar glass in her hand. "Here's how! And thanks a lot."

She went into the bedroom, calling Lynn to follow. She plucked a note from the mirror and frowned at the purple-inked scrawl it contained. "Here's a swell setup," said Jennie angrily. "Angie — that's the girl friend — has walked off with my heavy date for the evening! That leaves me flat!" she mourned. Then she brightened. "Well, it's all in the day's work; he's a washout anyway. Look here, what are you doing this evening? Stay with me, won't you? We'll send to the restaurant around the corner and get something to eat. My credit's good there. Do say you'll stay," urged Jennie. "I hate to be alone, it gives me the heebie-jeebies!"

Lynn stayed. The club was becoming more and more distasteful to her. It was rather fun fussing about the apartment, helping get supper — no, getting all the supper — from the scraps in the ice-box, supplemented by the restaurant service. Jennie drifted about or lay at full length on the bed divan in the living-room, smoking furiously. By the time Lynn left her, a little after ten, she had learned something of Jennie's background.

Twenty-six years old. Born in Brooklyn. A brief stage career — show girl — "But there's about a million of us out of work now," Jennie explained, "and this modeling business isn't so bad. You draw down your forty per and you get your clothes cheap. When they're taken off the line you buy 'em, those you want. And sometimes you buy the ones that have been made to your measure — the sample gowns, I mean. Our house does evening and afternoon dresses. I get my suits and coats through Angie — the double-crossing little cat!" said Jennie, with no rancor and less energy. She listened while Lynn, after urging, explained her own work.

"It's all too deep for me," Jennie confessed. "I haven't the brains. Or the education. Not that I think brains matter getting along. At least they don't in my line of work. There was a model with us when I first came to Madame Fanchon's — good-looking," Jennie admitted, "but not any better-looking than I am. Now she has a couple of Lincolns for the heavy work and a nice little Olds for tea parties. Two sable coats. I suppose she wears one when it's raining. It wasn't brains got her there," said Jennie.

"Did she get married?" asked Lynn innocently.

"Be yourself," Jennie reproved her, and reached for another cigarette.

Lynn flushed, furious with herself for her momentary display of unsophistication. She knew all there was to know. Several girls at the club, notably those who went in for the "arts" had vanished, to reappear as visitors in better clothes than they could afford, and not on foot. They weren't married, either. But Jennie's recital had been so without whispered eagerness, curiosity, or any of the elements with which the business club had discussed the rise — or fall — of its departed members that Lynn found herself reverting to older and more ignorant days. She said now, firmly, "Well, it doesn't pay — that sort of thing."

"Doesn't it?" Jennie glinted the long blue eyes at her guest. "I'll say it does. Better than forty a week anyway. If you've sense enough to soak it away," she added.

When Lynn left she had a promise from

Jennie to come up to the club for dinner some night. "It's not like anything you ever saw," Lynn explained, laughing. "You'll get a big kick out of it."

Jennie did, a few days later. "I'd just as soon live in a jail!" she said while she was inspecting Lynn's quarters after dinner, during which she had stood the astonished glare of the directress very well indeed.

"It's not so hot," Lynn admitted. "I'm getting pretty fed up with it myself."

She found herself meeting Jennie now and then for luncheon in the cafeteria. And then Jennie and the telephone-company engineer — a lanky, attractive lad named Howell — Lynn and Tom went to a movie together. This was repeated at intervals though Tom protested, laughing, after the first occasion: "Where did you pick her up, Lynn? She isn't your sort."

"What's the matter with her?" Lynn wanted to know, indignant. She liked Jennie. There was something slow and expansive about her, something relaxing. She was almost bovine, in her lazy, effortless movements, in her enjoyment of food, in her tremendous desire never to walk when she could ride, never to stand up when she could sit down, never to sit down when she could lie down. How she kept her amazingly slender figure was more than Lynn could fathom.

Then too, she never posed, except perhaps when on display and then only physically. Jennie was frankly herself. *Take me or leave me,* her attitude said, *and I don't give a damn which you do, personally. I'd rather sleep!*

"Nothing," Tom admitted, "but poor old Slim Howell is crazy about her. He thinks she's Venus and Mrs. Socrates all rolled into one!"

"Oh, Tom, not Mrs. Socrates!"

"Why not? Wasn't she a smart *femme?* Well, he think Jennie is," grinned Tom, "and in my opinion she is a perfect vacuum above the neck." He added, "I like girls with brains."

"Meaning me?"

"You? I don't know if you have any brains or not," said Tom, "and I don't care. I don't like you, anyway — I'm crazy about you. I love you to death!"

This was while bus riding, on a freezing night. Lynn snuggled her pointed chin into her collar. Her hand was warm, the hand which Tom held firmly in his overcoat pocket. It wasn't the first time he had told her that he loved her. It was about the hundred and first. But she wouldn't take him seriously. Or so she told herself, and told him. Without much success, however.

Miss Dennet asked, "Is it getting serious — young Shepard, I mean?" and asked it with anxiety.

"Well, of course not," Lynn answered.

But it was. It was gay and idiotic and enchanting and sweet and — underneath as serious as life and death. She knew it. She tried to pretend that she didn't know it. She told herself, *I like Tom and he likes me. Well, perhaps we are crazy about each other. But it doesn't mean anything. We'll get over it. Why, I can't let it mean anything. I don't want to marry Tom. I don't want to marry anyone,* said Lynn to herself. *It's too much of a risk. And I'm just getting somewhere with my job. Men,* sighed Lynn, *are complications.*

Yet Tom had not asked her to marry him. It was, as Jennie would say in describing something indefinable, something without words, but nevertheless a fact, "just one of those things."

"You're my girl, aren't you?" Tom would tell her, ask her, at unexpected moments and in unexpected places. And before Christmas he had kissed her soundly, delightedly, boyishly, and not under the mistletoe either. There are fewer kissing-bridges for unattached and homeless young people in Manhattan than you would think. By homeless I mean just that. Business clubs and Village bedrooms are not homes to people such as Tom and Lynn. And fastidious young people — such as Tom and Lynn — do not embrace avidly in taxicabs unless the compulsion is so strong that they must, or die of it. Once or twice the compulsion was too strong. But they could hold hands, like any other city lovers, in the darkness of the motion-picture theaters, while their eyes were fastened, not quite seeing, on the lighted screen against which the shadows of life and death, love and hatred, formed their simple two-dimensional patterns.

Lynn thought, sometimes, after Tom had left her, *It can't go on like this — being together a lot, laughing a good deal, talking, kissing, now and then — it can't go on. I mean, we can't get married, can we?*

Her people wanted her to come home Christmas. But the Seacoast Bank was not a boarding-school, it gave no long vacations at holiday seasons. She wrote therefore that she would not be home, and her mother wrote back sorrowfully that she was so disappointed — there would be a tree, and fixin's, and that after Christmas she and Lynn's father were really going South.

Lynn had her Christmas at Sarah Dennet's, pleasant, homelike, but make-shift with the white-tissue-paper parcels tied with red ribbon, stockings, gloves, a string of beads — and a little table tree, dripping synthetic icicles on the damask cloth. Sarah Dennet and her friend Anna Frank had rather outgrown Christmas. To Sarah it meant persuading people to put bonds in children's stockings, to turn Santa Claus into a trust fund; while to Anna it denoted a terrific siege of super-advertising, of concentrating the weary mind upon new ways in which to create public demand, public interest, new sprightly methods of loosening public purse strings. They gave to one another costly but sensible gifts and were relieved when it was all over. "Disorganizing," they said. But Sarah despite an inner reluctance invited Tom for dinner, too, so for a short space there was youth in the quiet, tasteful apartment — and laughter and silly jokes.

Tom had brought them all presents from the five-and-ten. He'd been their guest for dinner before. Lynn had asked sweetly, "Some night, may I bring Tom?" and so he knew his hostesses and their Barbadian maid. He brought them egg beaters and tiny trucks and jointed wooden toys. He brought Lynn innumerable idiocies, a pair of woolen socks to keep her feet warm, a pair of rubbers which would fold up into a handbag, doll's clothespins, and, of all things, because she liked a glass of milk at night, a doll's refrigerator. Lynn who had spent more than she could afford upon the cigarette case and lighter she gave him, was not in the least disappointed. She was enchanted — because he had told her early in the evening, "I've got something for you — very special — but it needn't have publicity."

He gave it to her, going back to the club in a taxi. A ring it was, modest, twinkling, a good small stone. She said, "Tom, you shouldn't."

And he asked, "Don't you like it, darling? I hoped you would like it."

She cried, "I *love* it!" and let him put it on her finger, let him touch with his boy's hard mouth her own parted and surrendering lips, and later asked, breathless, drawing away, "But — what does it *mean?*"

He was sobered, after his moment of blind ecstasy. He repeated stupidly, "Mean?" He said, less stupidly, "Why, *you*, of course — and me — that we belong. We do, don't we?"

They did, of course. Their love affair

had run a natural and normal course with the most prosaic of wavelike temperature charts. There had been small quarrels, and swift yieldings, and differences of opinion and hours of unity; but as yet none of the dangers or complications or obstacles which constitute crises.

She told him, still breathless, "But — we can't bind ourselves to anything now. We — we're too young, Tom. You've your way to make. I've mine. Can't you see?"

He could see. He had to see on the fifty dollars a week the bank was paying him. He said, "I know — I don't mean to bind you, you know that. I thought you'd wear it for now, because we belonged."

She wore it, on her right hand, as a concession.

Jennie commented, looking at the ring, her narrow eyes widening. "That's Tom, of course. When are you going to get hitched?"

"We aren't — that is — not now. We aren't really even engaged."

"I see." Jennie didn't, quite. When girls wore diamonds and weren't going to be married and weren't even really engaged, they wore larger diamonds. Such was her simple lexicon. She added, yawning, "Slim's getting pretty goofy. He's a great kid, but not for me. I'd rather struggle along on the forty per, thank you."

"Has he — ?" began Lynn.

"He has. He wants to make a down payment on a house in Jersey, oh, migod!" said Jennie. "Can you tie that?"

Apparently she could not.

Chapter Four:

FINISHED — OR BEGINNING?

In January Jennie did an unprecedented thing shortly before noon. She wandered into Lynn's room at the bank, walking with the effortless, lazy ease so characteristic of her. Miss Marple eyed her severely. Jennie had been showing models to some of the New York buyers, spring models, and still wore her heavy make-up. She looked like nothing on earth, thought Miss Marple, sliding a pink-tipped finger through the corrugations of her own blond hair.

"Lynn!"

Lynn looked up from a frowning contemplation of a blue card which stated that one Hamilton Yates belonged to the Union Club, had an inherited income of $30,000 a year, had twice been married, begotten three children, paid alimony, and was not, as yet, a client of the Seacoast Company.

"Lord," said Jennie, casually reading all this over Lynn's shoulder, "wouldn't it be a break if you met him some day and said,

'Hello, Ham, old egg, what I know about *you!*' "

"It's one of my nightmares," Lynn told her seriously. "What's the matter, Jennie?"

"Lots. Can you chow with me?"

From 12:00 to 1:00 all the models eat lunch. It is one of the minor mysteries of the trade. At 1:00, they return to work. Why, no one knows, as no buyer is available from 1:00 to 2:00.

"I can in twenty minutes."

"Oke," agreed Jennie, and wandered away again, casting a curious glance at the filing-cabinets, which repelled her slightly, as did the clicking of typewriters, the efficient mechanism of the place. Sales research, any kind of research, afflicted Jennie as did the smooth-running mechanism of the offices. She preferred yawning her way downtown, fighting with the colored dresser over hard rolls as opposed to soft: liked sliding in and out of gowns, made meticulously to her measure, clinging to the smooth skin which just veiled her lovely bones; liked sitting for an hour at a dressing-table smoothing creams over her face, painting her lips with scarlet, stiffening each tiny lash with midnight blue, patting on the liquid powder, dusting on the final coat, creaming her slow lids with faint blue. She liked gossiping with the other girls, liked observing Madame in the throes of creation, liked the unmerciful ragging directed at the willowy salesman with his narrow shoulders and white, tended hands. Best of all, she liked swimming into the show room, on parade before the buyers, men and women who sat back of small tables and observed her as she drifted into their line of vision, with the artificial, somehow enchanting placing of her long, slender feet; liked turning, to all appearances hideously bored, one hand with its crimson nails accenting the suave curve of her hip. She liked it as well or better than rehearsals, back stage, footlight posturings. In a sense, it was less work. And it called for no effort of the mind.

Not that she was mindless. Tom was utterly mistaken in that estimate. She had the mind of an animal, a rather nice animal. Shrewd, intuitive, seeking food, shelter, seeking security and self-protection with, in her case, the minimum of effort. She was capable of unreasoning loyalties, of unreasoning tempers, as an animal is capable of these things. But if she found them consuming too much effort she, as it were, opened her hands laxly, and let them slip through her fingers. So much in life was a trouble, a bore. Slide through life as best you can, exert yourself as little as possible, and you will have an unlined face at 40.

When Lynn joined her at the cafeteria they selected a table for four — there were none for two — and Jennie looked gloomily at the crowds intent on nourishment. "Hope they don't pick out this table," she said, and gave her astonishingly ample order. Lynn, slim and small, had a horror of becoming fat. Her own order was calculated. She might let herself go at breakfast, at dinner, but luncheon was a frugal affair.

"You don't eat enough," Jennie told her, secure in her own incredible slenderness. What she did with her food was a mystery. She didn't burn it up, nor work nor worry it off. But she remained fashionably undernourished in appearance.

"Plenty. I'm not like you. Fat runs in the family. What's on your mind, Jennie?"

"Angie," explained Jennie, "is going to get married. The dumb egg! He's fifty, if he's a day! But he's got money. She's leaving in a week. I can't swing the flat alone. I wondered, would you like to come in with me?" She yawned as Lynn looked up, a little startled, and went on: "We wouldn't get in each other's way; it would be a swell arrangement. You could have your friends to the flat on the nights that I went out."

Lynn considered. She said after a moment, "I think I'd like to. Tell me what it costs to run."

Jennie requested the Deity to have mercy on her. Lynn's mental processes were far too clear-cut for Jennie. She counted on her fingers, guessing where she was not sure. She had never budgeted, nor had Angie. They had paid for things as they went along, inescapable intangibilities such as rent, light, gas. When they bought things for which they could not pay, they paid something on account and trusted that heaven would sufficiently protect the working girl when the final day of reckoning arrived.

Lynn had a little notebook, a pencil. She set down figures, neat and round. So much for rent, so much — very little — for light and gas. What about food? "Food," said Jennie, "puts no gray in your bob, dinner, that is. Not if you know the ropes. Sometimes you snatch a lunch, too."

It was cheaper to eat at home, Lynn told her.

"Not if someone else pays the check when you're out."

Lynn looked at the figures and decided she could do it. It was not, of course, as cheap as the club. But with less put away for savings later to be invested, it could certainly be managed. And she considered that the advantages far outweighed the expenditure. To be free of the club was in itself an enormous lure — to have a place, partly her own, to which she might go at night, in which she would take an interest, to which Tom would come. She decided. "I'll do it, Jennie. When may I come in?"

Any time after Angie's departure, Jennie told her. She was as pleasurably moved as she could be, which wasn't much. She liked Lynn. Lynn was a good scout. No, they would not get in each other's way. Lynn, Jennie judged, would not be interested in Jennie's circle of male acquaintances. She wouldn't, as Angie had done, snatch heavy dates from under Jennie's nose and then marry them — as a crowning insult!

Lynn gave her notice to the club. "I hope it's for your good," said the directress, sniffling, the pink tip of her dampish nose moving like a rabbit's; and hoping, of course, no such thing.

Sarah was frankly disapproving. "My dear child, what will your mother say?"

Sarah had never met Jennie but had heard her discussed. Tom was not well pleased, either. "I don't like it; she travels with a funny gang," he said.

"Well, I don't have to travel with them, do I? And, oh, Tom, I'm so darned sick of the club!"

He wanted her to be happy; if he wanted her to be happy only through his intervention, that was man nature, human nature. But even without his connivance he wanted her to be happy, as long as no other man assisted. He gave in gracefully. He grinned. He said, "Well, it has its good points. Can you cook? I'll be up for dinner three times a week while Jennie goes gadding. Poor old Slim," he added, with apparent irrelevance.

Lynn wondered mutely if she could persuade Jennie to get rid of some of the dolls and pillows. She could, it appeared. Most of them belonged to Angie, anyway, and with her departure all but the shabbiest vanished. Lynn drew out some of her savings and scurried about secondhand stores in her spare time. Mrs. Harding, from Florida, wrote that she was so glad Lynn had settled in her own apartment with a "nice friend." Sarah, it seemed, had held her tongue or, rather, her hand. And when the Hardings returned from the South they would send Lynn some of her own things from home.

Tom painted furniture and carpentered a bookcase. He also built a radio set. On evenings when he was building the set Jennie took herself out. She couldn't, she told her current cavalier, understand a couple of lovers who "acted that way."

"What way?"

"Oh, he sits on the floor all tied up in goofy-looking wires and things, and she sits in a chair and admires him. He's had the thing working, all right, but every night he comes he pulls it apart and starts all over again. He's a nut!" said Jennie sincerely.

Lynn made the living-room into her own. The bed-divan was now hers, and she contributed a cherry-wood chest which, both decorative and utilitarian, served as a bureau; and a small slim wall desk. Jennie had offered her the bedroom, but it was darker, smaller, more airless than the living-room, and besides, Lynn knew that Jennie would be lost without her dressing-table, her pots and bottles and jars of various mysterious cosmetics.

So they settled down for the winter. Jennie was out most of the time. Now and then she threw a party at which Lynn was welcome to go or come. Generally Lynn went out with Tom, or to Sarah's, or up to the club to see the girls, or somewhere, and would stay away as late as possible so that on her return the place would be empty of everyone save Jennie; and Lynn, sleepily emptying ash trays and picking up glasses and plates and opening windows, might prepare for bed.

Yet the flat did not work out. Oh, as far as Jennie was concerned, it did. But when Tom came into it, the flat was proving dangerous. They were in it together and alone far too much. Sarah Dennet said worriedly, still stamped with her generation's conventions despite her madness of twenty years ago, "Does Tom come to the apartment, Lynn?"

And Lynn had replied directly, "Yes, of course, that's one reason why I went in with Jennie. It was too silly ranging the streets together, eating at expensive places. We can neither of us afford it."

"Jennie's there, of course, when he comes?"

"Sometimes," said Lynn.

Yes, but not often; and generally, when she was, Slim was there too, or another man. They were learning backgammon, and, when Jennie's brain reeled with that effort there might be a harmless round of poker; something to eat; something to drink. But these occasions were rare.

It was spring. Spring makes a difference. The poets are right, whatever we may think. The poets are almost always right.

"Tom, please, dear! Jennie will be home any moment."

"Let her come. No, I hope she stays away. Why isn't this our place, Lynn, just yours and mine? Why do I ever have to leave you — at night?"

"Tom —"

"Oh, I won't hold you against your will!" He loosened his arms and watched her gloomily as she walked away from him, and then, her knees relaxing, sat down in the straight-backed desk chair, touching her disheveled dark hair with shaking fingers. Tom's kisses were no longer boyish, delighted. They were adult and melancholy and a little desperate.

He burst out, watching her, the gleam of the gray eyes, the hurt, bruised look of the red mouth, the clear color staining her dark pallor. "Lynn, we've got to get married, I can't stand things this way —"

"Tom, we can't; don't be absurd, darling, you know we can't!"

He crossed the small room in three strides, kicked a silly hassock from his path, came and stood behind her, so that she was forced to turn and look up into his face.

"I'll — I'll cut out all the radio business," he said, a little pale. This was an authentic sacrifice. He was like an explorer giving up sight and feel and sound of strange, enchanting countries. No one knew what radio had brought him. It is a commonplace now. We all afford radios, cash or on the installment plan. We turn a switch and fumble with a dial and listen to music, to human speech, to a drama played by unseen actors. We say, "Rotten!" or we say, "That's a good program," and we listen to the advertisers' sleek reminders with attention or boredom according to our amount of interest in brushes, furs, gasoline, shoes, breakfast foods. That is radio to us. A pleasure when the contrivance works; an annoyance when it does not. To Tom music, lectures, dramas, meant nothing. But the things which brought them to their audiences meant much. There was so much more to be discovered, so much more to learn. But it cost money, not alone the lessons but his own private little experiments, which Lynn found so irritating and yet so boyish and charming.

"I'll give it up, I'll save money; we can manage. I'll hit the old Gunboat for a raise. There's enough in that trust fund to start us — I know I don't get it till I'm twenty-five, but there must be a way, there has to be a way."

She said, after a moment, "With what I make — and what you make — we could manage, I think."

She didn't want to marry; not when she said it over to herself; but with Tom there — and those heart-piercing words still burning in her brain, "Why do I ever have to leave you?" — she surrendered.

She must marry him, or lose him. She took her two small hands and pushed back the hair from her face. The widow's peak was ruffled; it gave her an urchin, elfin look.

"Manage? Do you think," shouted Tom, "that I'd let my wife keep on working?"

He came of a generation of men whose wives had not worked. That is to say, they had kept houses and budgets, borne children, scrubbed and cooked and slaved and fought their way up into a little leisure and comfort. They had been pioneer women some of them, women who carried guns as well as babies, women who could wield an ax.

But they had not worked for money.

Or had they?

They had not, at any rate, worked for wages.

She said, startled, "But, Tom, unless I do go on working, it isn't possible."

"Why not — if you're willing to sacrifice —"

She cried out, wounded, "Oh, I am, you know I am! But look at us — Jennie and me. She gets forty a week, my salary comes to a little less, not counting the Christmas bonus. And *we* barely manage!"

He said sullenly, "I won't always be getting just fifty."

"No. No. Of course, you won't. But," she cried again, "you haven't thought of me at all — of how much I like my work, how anxious I am to get on with it."

"Where to?" he demanded.

She said, gray eyes dark with something near to anger, "There's Sarah's job sometime, if I fit myself for it. She isn't going to stop, either. Tom, I'm only twenty-two — by the time I'm thirty —"

"By the time you're thirty, you'll be an old woman," he said absurdly. Then he went down on his knees beside her, awkward, boyish, touching.

"I do love you so much — and you love me, you know you love me!"

He pulled her down, close, closer, kissed her with longing, with anger, with frustration. After a long moment during which they both forgot all that had led up to this emotional climax, she drew herself away.

"Tom, please — we're insane, both of us, we can't go on like this, you'll have to stop coming here, we'll go out, the way we used to. I wish," she said brokenly, "that I'd never left the club!" What she meant was, *I wish I had not opened this particular door to temptation.*

"Then you won't marry me?"

"Oh, Tom" — suddenly, she was tired, beaten down by fatigue — "oh, Tom, don't be childish! No, I won't marry you and give up my job."

"That's enough, then."

He flung himself out of the door. When Jennie came in half an hour later Lynn was in bed. She was crying. Jennie had her moments of tact. She did not switch on the lights; she walked into her bedroom instead and spoke to Lynn from that distance. "Lousy evening," reported Jennie, with a yawn. "I'm getting fed up with this sort of thing. Give you a two-fifty table d'hôte and think they can get funny with their hands for that price. Boy, even to the buyers my legs are worth forty a week — and hands off!"

Lynn made no answer. She knew Jennie required none. She was grateful to Jennie. She ached all over, she was one vast bruise. It was finished, then? Tom had asked her to marry him, and she had refused. Or had she offered to marry Tom, and had he repudiated her? Both, she fancied, crying very quietly.

She fixed herself some breakfast at home next morning, long before Jennie was out of bed. They did not travel to work together, it was an effort for Jennie to report — for breakfast — before nine-thirty.

"What difference does it make? The buyers don't get in till after ten," said Jennie.

But at closing-time Tom was waiting by the elevators. He said, tucking her limp arm through his own, "I'm sorry, Lynn. I must have been crazy."

It was not finished then. It was, as a matter of fact, just beginning.

They resumed their motion pictures, their bus rides. When Tom came to the apartment, he brought Slim, or made sure Jennie would be there. Jennie was incurious. What Lynn did — or did not do — was Lynn's affair. If Jennie had thoughts on the subject she did not utter them. What's the use? Everyone's funeral is his own.

Then one spring day Lynn, coming into the trust officers' room, hesitated, seeing Sarah occupied. A man sat there by the desk, leaning forward laughing a little. "Come here, Lynn," said Sarah.

Chapter Five:

ANYTHING YOU WISH, DAVID

The man at the desk was David Dwight. He rose as Lynn came up and held out his hand. He said easily, "Miss Dennet and I are old friends; she has told me so much about you."

He was a rather short man, very well groomed. He had heavy gray hair, battered into sleekness. He had tired eyes and a quirked sort of mouth and the face and skin of a great actor, all the features mobile, the skin tended.

He *was* a great actor. He was one of the greatest trial lawyers of the generation. To employ Dwight as your counsel was an almost certain admission that you were guilty and would be adjudged innocent. He had a low voice. It was an instrument of rescue or destruction, according to which side he was on. He had square, long-fingered hands, not always restrained in gesture. He had that thing called magnetism. No man had had it to a greater degree save those historic men who move mountains and make empires.

He was 48 years old — perhaps.

He looked at Lynn and his eyes darkened a very little. He said lightly, "Sarah, I've bored you to death with my business. Why people die and leave their estates in my hands — even partly — is more than I can see. A more improvident and a less trustworthy person never lived." His eyes lingered on Lynn's small face. He thought vaguely of spring, spring outside the great draped windows, spring in the country. His blood, never very stable, quickened. His eyes, never very stable either, were veiled. Then he raised them to Sarah Dennet's plain and pleasant face. He suggested gaily, "Let's celebrate, Sarah. Won't you and Miss Harding lunch with me? Please!"

Sarah looked at Lynn. Lynn smiled a little. A sensational man, David Dwight. She had read about him, heard about him. Why had Sarah never mentioned him? Sarah said, "We'd like to, wouldn't we, Lynn?"

He listened to Sarah, but he watched for Lynn's nod. He rose, satisfied. "I'll go in and talk to Norton," he said, "until you're ready."

He smiled at them both, and together they watched him walking, lightly as a cat, toward the inner office. Lynn could see Tom's shoulders. She could see Tom's head now as he moved entirely into her line of vision. He was much taller than the older man. Yet Dwight did not seem dwarfed. In a courtroom one forgot lack of physical inches. She said to Sarah delightedly, "Isn't that a grand break? I never knew you knew him. He's awfully attractive, isn't he?"

Sarah said yes, absently. Lynn vanished to make the trip to the rest room, to wash her hands, to powder her nose, to draw a lipstick across her mouth with more than usual care. It was exciting, lunching with Sarah and David Dwight. He was an exciting man. A personality. If he argued for criminals, he also argued for lost causes. He knew everybody — people who lived on Park and Fifth, people who lived on side streets, back-stage people, cinema people, people who lived in Paris, London, Rome. Policemen called him by name, gunmen knew him, dowagers knew him; he was the personal, legal representative of motion-picture stars, opera singers, millionaires, inventors, marathon runners, prize fighters, social leaders, murderers, thieves, bishops. His income was enormous and his extravagance a byword. Editorials were written to slay him. He wore an invisible armor. Columnists called him Dave. Judges called him Dave. Taxi men called him Dave. And newsboys.

Lynn went downstairs and joined Sarah and Dwight, who were waiting. Dwight said, "We'll go to a place I know." He laughed. "I lunched with Norton — on this Manning business, Sarah, in one of the private rooms upstairs. Murals and pewter and noiseless waiters and a million-dollar view. And," he added, "good food. But it all smelled of money. How long have you for lunch? An hour? Make it an hour and a half. I know a place with sand on the floor and whitewashed walls, which has stood since the Revolution. It smells of partridges turning on a spit over a charcoal fire. We'll go there. Or would you rather not?"

He spoke to Sarah. His eyes were on Lynn. Sarah said, "Anywhere you wish, David."

She had always said that; anywhere, anything. *Anything you wish, David, all my love, all my youth, all my passion, all myself. Break down the barriers; trample on the inhibitions; anything, David. She had said, in effect. It's over then; it must be right, because you say it's over. Anything you wish, David.*

He couldn't marry her twenty years ago. He was beginning to be known then. She was nobody, a raw Western girl, coming East to make her fortune. He had to marry — well. Marry money. He had done so. Anything you wish, David.

Love had been over long ago; if it was over for David Dwight in 18 months and had lasted ten years for Sarah, that was another matter. It was over now. Her work satisfied her as even he had not; her blood pulsed cool and even in her veins. She had for him an affection, a loyalty, that could not be conquered by months, years, of neglect. Now he came to see her — occasionally. She rested and entertained him. It had been years since he had made any reference to her relations with him twenty years ago. They were friends. She disapproved of him, of his way of living, of his easy separation from his wife, of his utter lack of preoccupation with his children. But she was his friend.

Tom, frowning, saw them go out. This man Dwight — poseur, lecher, bad actor, spendthrift, publicity-seeker — what was he doing with Lynn and Sarah Dennet?

He was doing with Sarah that which he had always done. He was having his own way. *Anything you want, David.* Yet, as she stepped into his car and made room for Lynn and Dwight beside her and the car slid smoothly from the curb, she was not remembering that once she had been this man's lover. She was not remembering that once she had struggled from madness to sanity, from suicidal desperation to a sort of apathy approximating peace. She was remembering nothing. You do not remember the things that are in your blood. You put no names to them. They are. They exist, part of you. You question them no longer.

And so Sarah said, that woman who had been born proud and not humble, but whom love had once made docile and amazed, "It's nice of you to take us out, David," and he answered, "It's sweet of you both to take pity on me, and come," and Lynn asked tritely, "Isn't it the most gorgeous day?" And Dwight knew that it was. He liked falling in love. When he was in love he was young. And when he was young he was unafraid.

Why was Sarah not warned? Why should she be warned? Having said, for so long, "Anything you wish, David," she said it now to an offer of luncheon, unexpected, a harmless pleasure for Lynn. Having once known David Dwight as something less a man than a force of nature, should she not now be on her guard?

But twenty years had passed; and she belonged to the women who make a fetish of possession, of the first man, the first love, which is the last. She had forgotten embraces, save in the subconscious darkness of her nature, which she never contemplated now she had forgotten days and nights; she had forgotten tears and insanity. But she had not forgotten obedience. How should she know that asking her to luncheon, "you and Miss Harding," he was asking her for Lynn?

He knew.

Chapter Six:

HARMLESS AS A SERPENT

Lynn, returning to the office from the ancient tavern to which Dwight had taken her and Sarah, was late. She flew in, and went at the work on her desk with considerable animation.

"Well," commented Miss Marple, shutting a file with emphasis, "You look as if someone had left you a million and you'd started out to spend it!" She glanced carelessly at the clock.

"I had a luncheon engagement," Lynn told her guiltily.

"Tell that to Sarah the Slave Driver!"

"She was part of it," Lynn said triumphantly.

She stayed late at the office that evening, to catch up. When she reached home Jennie was there ahead of her. Opening the door Lynn was greeted by a blast of blue smoke and, rushing into the kitchen, found Jennie indifferently shoving some curious-looking pork chops around on a frying-pan.

"For heaven's sake! You'll have the fire department out."

"I was telephoning," admitted Jennie. "How did I know the blasted things would go up in smoke? Here."

She shoved the frying-pan into Lynn's hand, removed Lynn's hat and bore it off to the living-room closet. Returning, she swung herself up on the little kitchen table, flipped her lighter with a thumb, and drew in a long breath of burning Virginia tobacco. "Thought I'd be domestic for a change and get some dinner," she explained. "I didn't get a break. No one's asked me out for a week."

"You were out last night, silly! Did you set the table?"

"I did. Well, it seems a week ago. What's new with you? You're late."

"Plenty. David Dwight took Sarah and me out to lunch — downtown somewhere, funniest place you ever saw, benches and stalls, sand on the floor and the most divine food."

"What did you eat?" asked Jennie with interest, then she added, "Dwight? You don't mean the lawyer, do you?"

"I do. We had oysters and game pies and —"

"Wait a minute, you're breaking my

heart. Throw the chops out of the window. Dwight?" Jennie rocked on the table, slim hands clasped about slim knees. "He's some boy. Carla Lang — you know, the dancer, she was in that show I glorified. He was her lawyer. First he got her an annulment and a big settlement from the boy's family. Then with her next trial trip he got her a Paris divorce and a hunk of alimony. Then she sued Stuart Whitehead for breach of fountain pen — and what a ready letter writer he was, too! — and dragged down a cool hundred grand. She was crazy about Dwight, too, and she told the world. But he wouldn't give her a tumble. I think he was scared of having to sue himself or something."

"Isn't he married?" asked Lynn.

"Sure, he's married. Don't you ever read the papers? His wife lives in California when she isn't abroad. I saw her picture once — and took my wrist watch to the jeweler's. They've got some kids, I think. Not that that's any gray in his hair."

"Well, he's terribly interesting," Lynn said, the chops disposed of on a platter, the potatoes fried deliciously, if beyond the dietician pale.

He had been. As she and Jennie ate supper she thought over her hour and a half — or was it two hours? — with him. He had told them about some of his spectacular cases, not, however, those involving alimony or settlements. He had talked music to Sarah — who was an inveterate opera-goer, finding in music some unspoken release — and he talked cases, plays, books with Lynn. He had asked questions too. She realized that he knew all there was to know about her — or pretty nearly all. He had an easy way of drawing you out.

She spoke her subsequent thought aloud. "I'd hate to be on a witness stand with him doing a cross-examination," she said.

"Slim?" Jennie who had just concluded a monologue relative to Slim, looked at her in astonishment. "Why, that boy's so darned dumb he couldn't get a rise from a goldfish!" she expostulated.

"David Dwight, I meant."

"Oh! Him!" Jennie speared the last potato and drank deeply of coffee. "He's a good lad to keep away from in court. As far as that goes, I hear he's just about unique in his class, courtroom, drawing-room, barroom, bedroom —"

"Jennie!"

"Well, *don't* you read the papers? Not

that it's all in the papers. Gosh, what a break! He has all kinds of money, his own and other people's, and spends it like a South American. Not that *you'd* take advantage of it," said Jennie, sighing.

"He's an old friend of Sarah's."

"Wonders will never cease," said Jennie. "Tom coming tonight? Bet you anything he won't take kindly to the idea of the new boy friend."

"Don't be an idiot," counseled Lynn. "Mr. Dwight was just nice to me; that's all, because I happened to be with Sarah when he asked her for lunch."

"Not that you're pretty good-looking," said Jennie indifferently, "or that he likes 'em young or that Sarah's neat but not gaudy. If Tom's coming, guess I'll ankle around to the Capitol or somewhere. I told Slim he could lay off, over the phone just before you came in. Maybe he didn't burn up the wires!"

"Oh, Jennie, why? Poor Slim, he's so crazy about you."

"I can't stand men with honorable intentions and small incomes."

"We'll all go to the Capitol," suggested Lynn brilliantly.

"What's the matter? You and Tom cooling off?"

"No, of course not." Lynn rose and started to clear the table. "I haven't seen a good picture for ages."

Tom came. Slim came. "I might have known it!" sighed Jennie, giving him a limp hand.

"Backgammon?" asked Tom, slinging his hat in a corner.

"Lynn and I want to see the Capitol picture," Jennie told him serenely, "if you boys are in funds. We don't want to upholster the chairs until fall if we can help it."

They went to the Capitol. It was crowded; they waited in line in the lobby. Tom, standing behind Lynn, grasped her firmly by the elbows. "Lean back," he ordered, "and take the weight off your feet."

When they finally found seats in couples they were separated by several rows. Tom said, taking Lynn's hand in his own, "I tried to ditch Slim. Gosh, Lynn, I haven't seen you alone for weeks."

She said, "I know —"

"Saw you and Sarah and David Dwight going out together. Waited for you a while tonight, but you didn't show up. How come?"

"I was late. I stayed too long at lunch time," she whispered. "Had to make it up."

"Did you have lunch with Dwight?"

"Yes — Oh, Tom, don't talk; people are glaring at us!"

Tom subsided, none too happily. The picture ran its course. An exodus began with the stage show. "Let's stay," said Lynn, as Tom made a motion to rise.

It was late when they met Slim and Jennie in the lobby. Jennie's color was high and Slim's eyes were sulky. "Let's get a sandwich somewhere," said Jennie, the insatiable.

They went to Fifth Avenue Child's.

Walking home, Tom tucked Lynn's arm closely under his own. "Sore at me?"

"No, why should I be?"

"Because I didn't like your going out with Dwight."

"I didn't know you didn't like it," she answered, not very truthfully.

"Well, I didn't. He's a hot number, besides being twice your age."

"I liked him," Lynn told him stubbornly. "I'll probably never see him again, but I liked him. Besides, he's an old friend of Sarah's."

"Oh," said Tom, a little mollified. He added, "I wish you wouldn't go out with anyone — but me."

"Tom, remember our bargain — no strings!" said Lynn.

"I know — but it's hard," he told her, "to see you dashing off with someone else."

"Well, this is the first time, and doubtless the last," she said, laughing.

They had reached the apartment, were walking up the stairs. Jennie and Slim were well in advance but their voices drifted back. They were quarreling.

"Slim's all shot, poor devil," said Tom. "That girl certainly takes him for a ride. Heartless little —"

"She isn't," Lynn interrupted. "It's her business if she doesn't want to tie herself down, isn't it?"

Tom was silent. They reached the corridor; Jennie and Slim had gone in, leaving the door open. Lynn started to follow them, but Tom pulled her back into the semi-dusk of the hall, took her roughly in his arms and kissed her.

"You feel like that, too!" he accused her. "My God, Lynn, I don't know what to think about you — There's nothing I wouldn't do for you, you know that. I'd go through hell for you, I do most of the time, as it is. You belong to me, you know it, and to keep you mine, to make you mine, I'd lie for you, steal for you —"

"Tom — for heaven's sake —" She

pulled herself away. "Don't talk so wildly. It isn't like you. You know I love you."

She returned to him of her own accord and kissed him very sweetly. He bounded into the apartment a moment or so later singing, "My baby just cares for me," a little off-key but at the top of his lungs. He was perfectly and extravagantly happy again. He had forgotten the fantastic fears, the hot desperation, the sudden smothering sensation of a savage despair, which had briefly seized him a moment before. He had forgotten David Dwight, to whom he had spoken once, in conventional words — "Mr. Norton will see you at once, Mr. Dwight" — and at whose back he had glared incredulously as Dwight walked from the outer room with Sarah and Lynn. He had forgotten that the thought of Dwight had affected his mood, as the hand of the puppet master jerks the puppets from attitudes of serenity into postures of terror and rebellion.

He was very much in love, and 23 years old.

Going home, to sit up the rest of the night, in an endeavor to capture Europe over his home-built short-wave receiver, he tried to console his gloomy companion out of his own superabundance of confidence.

For himself, things would come right, he'd get a raise, he'd make some money somehow. Lynn would give up the damned job, in which she was in danger of meeting undesirable people — which translated read, *attractive men with money* — and they would be happy forever after. As far as David Dwight was concerned, well, Sarah had been with them, and probably Lynn was right, she'd only been included because of Sarah, and anyway she might never see him again. Not that it would matter much if she did, for what could Lynn find really worth her while in a "middle-aged" man?

Forty-eight plus, to twenty-three may seem middle-aged — depending upon your viewpoint and your sex. But Lynn next day pulled a blue card from the files marked *D* and entertained herself with reading what was inscribed thereon. Not that it told her more than she already knew; and the *Who's Who* recountal was little better. She'd probably never see him again.

She saw him the following week. He wandered into the room where she was working, a flower in his buttonhole, a faint smile on his subtle lips. He apologized.

"I suppose this is out of order. I've been talking to Sarah. I've got Scarletti — of the opera, you know, coming to dinner Friday. I thought you and Sarah might like to come too, all very informal and all that."

He added quickly, marking her slight hesitation, "Sarah says it's all right with her."

"I'd love to," Lynn told him sincerely, her heart beating a little faster. She did like him so much, he was so stimulating a personality, and there was about him — the bland actor's face, the rather big head with its shock of gray hair, the lazy, keen eyes — a glamor; the glamor of legend or tradition.

He took out a notebook and a little gold pencil. "I'll send a car," he offered, "say, about seven-thirty. We'll dine at eight. What's your address?"

She gave him the address. He asked, lingering a moment, putting the notebook away, "You're in the telephone book?"

"Yes, but under Le Grande. I live with another girl," she said. "The phone is listed in her name."

He raised an eyebrow. "Le Grande — is it possible?"

Lynn laughed. "Smith, really. She's a model here in the building."

He nodded, smiled again, said, "Friday, then," and departed.

"Holy cat," breathed Miss Marple; suddenly at Lynn's elbow, "who's the grand duke?"

"You're sure stepping out," was Jennie's only comment as Lynn told her over the lunch table. "What'll you wear?"

"There's the black net —"

"Too sophisticated —"

"There's the cherry satin, but that's pretty well worn out!"

"Look here," suggested Jennie, "there's a little dress, it's dusky pink lace, stiffened with wide sleeves and a do-funny of French blue at the waist. It's been taken off the line, it's a fourteen, with a twelve skirt length. I can get it for you. It will set you back $69.50, but it's worth it. It sells for $110, retail."

"Jennie, it sounds marvelous!" Lynn looked at her friend, gray eyes shining. "But — I shouldn't!"

"Sure you should. You've got to dress for the occasion. This Scarletina — or whatever his name is — may be as contagious as he sounds — offer you a castle in Florence and a gondola in Venice. He gets about a thousand a yip, I guess. Hop to it, you're only young once. I'll ask Madame if I can bring the dress home tonight. She's a pretty good fellow. She'll let me do it."

"All right," agreed Lynn. After all she needed another evening dress, she excused her extravagance — and she had not spent her father's Christmas check.

Jennie went upstairs after luncheon and attacked Madame on the subject of the little number 58, size 14, in dusky pink. Madame was agreeable, Madame rather liked Jennie; "lazy, stupid, dependable," was Madame's reaction toward her model, not entirely just.

Madame was very tiny, very dark, with an almost startlingly intelligent little face, and smartly, amusingly dressed. She was as quick as a humming-bird, shrewd, emotional. She designed her own frocks, all of them, bought the materials, oversaw workrooms and showrooms. She was the first of the wholesalers to move over and up into the Times Square district, as a convenience for the out-of-town buyers who entered town via Grand Central. The Seacoast Building welcomed her with open doors, and the Bank and Trust Company had respect for her account. A hard worker, Madame.

Jennie found the frock, boxed it, and put it away until closing time. Business was slow today, but, standing at the dressing-room door behind the drapes, she heard

Sam Pearl, the salesman, Pearline, as he was affectionately called by the models, expostulating with a lone buyer who had wandered in and demanded to see models at, say, $39.50.

"Oh," cried Mr. Pearl, with a short sharp scream, "thirty-nine fifty! Impossible!" He put his hand on his hip and shuddered, large reproachful eyes on the buyer. "Impossible," repeated Mr. Pearl firmly. "Madame *never* expresses herself under sixty-nine fifty!"

Crushed, the buyer oozed through the doors, and Mr. Pearl, with a shrug, flitted to the nearest mirror and ran a little comb through his permanent. Jennie in the doorway giggled once. He turned sharply at the sound, but she had vanished; all was silence save for the voice of Madame rising from the workroom where the rows of machines stitched busily. The draperies before the models' room were hanging limp and motionless. Mr. Pearl moved closer to the mirror and examined a flaw in his schoolgirl complexion which had worried him of late.

I must tell that one to Lynn, thought Jennie.

She did. And Lynn told it, without, however, Jennie's comments and embellishments, to Sarah and Dwight on Friday night. Scarletti was late. The car had called first for Lynn and then for Sarah. There were two square boxes in the car, marked with Lynn's and Sarah's names. Lynn's contained unseasonable gardenias, and Sarah's, orchids. Lynn had never had gardenias in her life. Sarah had had orchids, doubtless. But once she had preferred very red roses, dark, with the dew upon them —

"Look, flowers!" Lynn cried, as Sarah entered the car.

Sarah unwrapped her own. She wore black, severe, well-cut, crystals at her throat and well-shaped ears. She said, "He's very extravagant — and does everything well."

"I never dreamed you knew him. Long?"

"Twenty years, a little more."

"How exciting," said Lynn. "What's he like, really?"

The car purred down Fifth Avenue. Sarah was silent. Presently she aroused herself. "He's a brilliant man," she said. "Erratic, people call him, but a very good friend."

That was what Lynn had thought; she said so. She, too, was silent, thinking it would be pleasant to have a friend, a man friend, an older man upon whose cool, impersonal strength one might lean when things became too difficult for one.

Dwight's apartment was a duplex, the penthouse on top of a lower Fifth Avenue structure. The elevator shot them to the 20th floor, they climbed a winding staircase, stood before the apartment doors and were admitted by a man servant who, following the unexpectedness of most things connected with Dwight, did not look like a man servant. He looked like a man. He had nothing of the stage or Jeeves about him. He looked rather like a prize fighter. He had been one.

That was the last formality, if Wilkins could be called formal. Dwight was standing in front of an Adam fireplace; driftwood was burning in it, for looks, he explained, not because of necessity. It was a lovely spring night, with just the proper amount of chill in the air, as cool and sweet and promising as an adolescent girl. Lynn, during the exchange of greetings, wondered vaguely why all men couldn't learn to wear clothes properly and without effort. She thought absurdly, *I'll bet when he wears a full-dress shirt it stays put!*

He wore, however, dinner clothes, not

too new, not too old. He took them to a bedroom, up a winding stair, a bedroom opening upon a gallery of iron grillwork hung with two beautiful old Spanish shawls. The bedroom was so extremely right that you didn't notice furniture or wall treatment or draperies.

"Hairpins," cried Lynn, delighted, "for the growing bob! And rouge. And powder. And, Sarah, look at the jar of cotton, tied with ribbons, and this atomizer of perfume."

She pressed the plunger like a child, and was immediately enveloped in a frail, faint, bewitching scent which Paris bottles at $20 an ounce.

"Now I've done it!" she said, abashed.

Sarah, regarding herself briefly in the mirror, said, "That's what it's there for." She added, "You look lovely, Lynn."

She did. Dusky pink lace stiffened in little tiers. She looked like a rose-quartz pagoda, or so Dwight told her when he saw her. Black hair, close-waved, a satin cap, the widow's peak pointed a dark arrow on her forehead. Gray eyes, black-lashed, clear color, olive skin, red lips, smooth shoulders rising from the tight bodice. And at her slim waist the waxen ivory of the gardenias thrust through the twist of

French blue ribbon.

They had cocktails in the long many-windowed room. Scarletti arrived breathless, before the second round in a strange Inverness and a broad-brimmed hat. He, too, wore dinner clothes, from which he bulged pathetically. He was a great, dark, fat man just a suspicion greasy, with eyes like a good child's, an enormous appetite — *He and Jennie would certainly get on,* thought Lynn, watching him, fascinated — and a gift of Homeric laughter.

They dined in a room which was glass on three sides, the lemon-silk curtains pulled over the windows with tasseled cords. A perfect dinner, mellow wines, and good talk; talk of travel, of opera, of people, of civilization, of trends and tempos, detective stories and the Russian crown jewels. Then they had coffee in the living-room, and Dwight took Lynn into a smaller room, a little lovely library, and showed her his collection of Japanese prints and of etchings, of old books in fine bindings.

"You like things of this sort?" he asked.

"Yes. I don't know much about them," she confessed.

"Neither do I. But I like lovely things about me." His eyes were on her own, friendly, controlled. He smiled at her and

116

added, "You, for instance. You don't mind my saying that? You've a charming frock — but I'm repeating myself."

She said, "That's the advantage of having a friend who is a model."

Sarah spoke in the doorway, "Can't you persuade Scarletti to sing for us, David?"

"I'll try. I am still complimenting our little friend on her gown."

"Jennie bought it for me," Lynn told Sarah.

Sarah's eyebrows drew down, black and heavy, a smudge across her forehead.

"You don't approve of Jennie?" asked Dwight, laughing at her.

"Not for Lynn. A model," said Sarah.

"Jennie's a dear," said Lynn, flashing into indignation. It wasn't kind of Sarah, she thought, before strangers. David Dwight was a stranger.

Spirit, thought Dwight, *and loyalty.* His interest quickened. He passionately admired loyalty, perhaps because he had encountered so little of it along the road, possessed so little of it himself. He had had it once given him, full measure, pressed down and running over. He had forgotten that gift. He had it still, from the same donor. He could remember this and forget the original bestowal.

117

"Models are all right, Sarah; don't be provincial," he mocked her. "Nice girls. I've known dozens."

"I don't doubt it." Her voice was a little sharp.

"Sarah, don't give me away. What will Miss Harding think?" he murmured reproachfully. "You make me sound like an ogre, a Casanova seeking to devour the lithe ladies of the wholesale garment trade. But really, my dear, your idea of models is outdated. They are no longer forced to entertain the avid buyers from out of town, lest they lose their jobs. As a matter of fact a good model is so rare nowadays that the wholesaler is content with working hours only; and so permits the buyer to seek his own amusements. Let's go back and see what we can do with Scarletti." As they went into the living-room together he said to Lynn, low, "I like the way you champion your friend. Sometime, perhaps, you'll bring her to one of my parties?"

He took it for granted that this was the beginning of a friendship. Lynn's heart had warmed to his defense of Jennie. She smiled at him openly. He nodded imperceptibly, as if a bond had been sealed between them. "Giuseppe, old boy, could you sing for us?"

"Later," rumbled the big Italian, "not now. I am too concerned with the digestion of your excellent meal."

He turned to Sarah and asked a question. They sat down together in the low chairs by the fireplace, and Dwight gestured to Lynn. "I'll send Wilkins upstairs for your wrap," he said, "and we'll go out and look at the view. I'm rather proud of my view. Not that it will mean anything to you — who enjoy the scenic facilities of the Seacoast Building every day."

"I spend most of my time on the third floor," she reminded him.

Wilkins brought the wrap. Dwight put it about her bare shoulders. They went out on the terrace together, and together leaned on the parapet and looked out over the lower city. The terrace was gay with the hardiest of spring flowers, with small, squat trees in green pottery jars, with chairs of decorative metal, swinging couches, tables.

She drew a deep breath of pleasure and astonishment. "How very lovely!" she told him, entranced.

"I like it. Later, we have gay awnings and parasols. All it then lacks is sand and sea," he told her laughing, "but I stay in town — when I'm here at all — until courts close, you know. I've a place on the Island," he went on. "I'd like you to see it. You'd enjoy it, I think."

The mail plane passed overhead. They heard the strong singing of the engine, they saw the steady shining lights —

"It is a wonderful city," he said, so softly, so easily, that he did not disturb her little dream of lights and buildings, of archway and park, of far waters and strange lands beyond. "A city whose symbol is the skyscraper — Have you ever thought much about skyscrapers?" he asked her.

"Why, no —" she answered, startled.

"Of course not. Every day you go to one, are swallowed up by it, every day you work there, never thinking of the life teeming in the building, beating against the walls, unaware of the thousands of people, working, like yourself, passing in and out ceaselessly, through the doors, unaware that many of them spend most of their waking hours under that impossibly high roof. A skyscraper is a little city, it is a little world, it is a strange planet, it is," he went on smoothly, "a phallic symbol. Yet it is also a new pattern against the sky; it is all of ordered beauty and upward growth that many of the workers within it shall ever know. And it must influence them, whether they are aware of it or not."

She listened as he went on talking, weaving a web of significant words; then, abruptly, he was silent. *What had he said,* Lynn wondered. Not much perhaps — perhaps, after all, his words had no significance, or perhaps they were more important than she knew. But his voice had a dark necromancy, his trained, eloquent voice. She stood there in a magic circle, scarcely breathing, thinking yet not thinking.

In the room they had left, Scarletti struck a chord, sitting fatly at the piano, grotesque god of song.

"I've bored you," said David Dwight contritely. "Come, let us go in and listen to our imported songbird."

He stood aside to let her pass before him. But she stopped a moment on the threshold and turned toward the dreaming spires, with the golden squares that were their windows, of downtown New York. She forgot, if indeed she had ever remembered, that the golden squares meant people working, scrubwomen earning their musty daily bread, clerks doing overtime, harried people, housed together in the spring night for the purpose of wage earning.

Little cities — little worlds — strange planets — phallic symbol.

What was that?

She remembered, from her indiscriminate reading; flushed a very little and, turning, went into the living-room. Now Scarletti was singing. He was singing *"Una Furtiva Lacrima"* —

Sarah was listening, her eyes half closed. Lynn sat down in a deep chair. The music throbbed about her, lifted her, high, higher, past the pointed soaring of city buildings which aimed at so far, and so impossible, a goal.

But presently Scarletti ceased to sing, and there was general talk and a rubber or two of bridge. And Lynn did not again go out upon the terrace. She felt, very dimly, wordlessly, that there was danger in terraces above a city, in the anachronistic blooming of spring flowers from soil scattered in cement and set upon steel, danger in dreaming lights, in distant streets, the ugliness veiled and softened, danger in voices speaking precisely patterned words —

"Happy evening?" asked Sarah, as they were riding toward home.

"Awfully," said Lynn.

"A charming man."

"Yes."

122

"The greatest tenor since Caruso —"

"I never heard Caruso," Lynn told her. But she had not been thinking of the child-like and entertaining Scarletti.

It was not very late when Lynn reached home. Jennie was out, and Lynn had the apartment to herself. She felt wide-awake; stimulated, almost overstimulated. She thought, self-scornfully, *Just because you've dined in a penthouse and listened to an operatic tenor free of charge, and prewar wine and played bridge with a famous lawyer! Laugh it off!* But she wasn't able to laugh it off. She observed herself in Jennie's mirror, for once entering that untidy bedroom without a feeling that she would like to go through it with a rag-bag, a vacuum cleaner, and about a million square feet of fresh air. She leaned her hands on the dressing-table top and surveyed her flushed, small face and very shining eyes. Her wrap dropped from her bare shoulders, and she regarded her reflection, "rose-quartz pagoda," satin cap of black hair, curved, half-smiling lips. She said aloud, solemnly, "Society becomes you, darling!"

The gardenias held their deep fragrance but were drooping, turning slightly brown and curling at the waxen edges as if they had

123

been put in a slow oven. Lynn unpinned them and went into the living-room to hunt for a small vase. She found one and put the flowers in water, carefully unwinding the cruelty of wires from their hard stems with little exclamations of compunction.

No, she was not sleepy. She turned the dials of Tom's home-made radio idly and listened to dim snatches of distant jazz, loud screams of local jazz, and the complaining voice of static for a few minutes. Finally, silencing the machine, she undressed lingeringly.

Such a happy evening. Such a gorgeous apartment. Such a delightful company of four. Such a charming host. Well, why shouldn't he be? she argued to herself, as if against some unspoken disloyalty. He has everything — position, money, brilliance, and the most enormous acquaintance and experience.

She slipped her striped flannel robe over her nightgown, tied the cord about her slim waist, and thrust her feet into slippers. She couldn't be hungry after that dinner! But she was. She was rummaging in the icebox when Jennie came in.

"Home, Lynn?"

"Yes — I'm out here — be right in —"

Lynn arrived in the living-room with a

glass of pale milk in one hand and a chicken bone in the other.

"For God's sake," said Jennie blankly, "didn't they feed you tonight?"

"And how! Darling, such food! Cocktails, caviar in blocks of ice, super-soup, sole Marguery, partridge, wine, hearts of lettuce, individual Alaskas —"

"Stop, you're driving me crazy!"

Jennie fled to the icebox, returned bearing a ravaged-looking bone, fixed Lynn with a reproachful eye. "And I had spaghetti and beer!" she said.

"Good time?"

"No. Yes. I've got to stop seeing Slim. He's serious and poor. I'm getting to like him, sort of. Darned if I know why. First thing you know I'll go soft on the situation and he'll have me living in a hen coop in Jersey yet. Not for this baby."

Lynn, not listening, said excitedly, "Jennie, it was a most marvelous party, really. Look, gardenias" — she gestured toward the little vase — "and bridge — And Scarletti sang —"

"How's the new boy friend?"

"Boy friend?" Lynn's eyes were wide.

"Drop the lashes over the baby stare. Dwight, the lad who gets 'em out of the hoosegow, for a price."

"Oh, he's a dear," said Lynn wholeheartedly.

"Huh," said Jennie, gnawing a bone. "Exit Tom."

"Jennie, don't be absurd — As if Tom could ever — As if Mr. Dwight — Oh, you're crazy," cried Lynn, entangled in odds and ends of sentences.

"Yeah. Crazy like a fox, that's me!"

"But Jennie, he's married, he's 'way over forty, he isn't the least bit interested in me. Besides, I love Tom!" Lynn reminded her, flaming.

"I know you love Tom," said Jennie soothingly. "But the rest of it doesn't make sense. Married? What does that mean? 'Way over forty — that's a good laugh, too! And of course he isn't interested in you; he sends you gardenias out of charity. Only, I'm telling you that Mr. David Dwight is just about as harmless as a serpent."

"He asked me," remarked Lynn, subsiding slightly, "to bring you to one of his parties."

"He did? Well," said Jennie, slinging the bone with accuracy into the scrap basket, "that's the best news I've heard since the stock market crashed and show girls lost their sables. How about catching a little sleep?"

Chapter Seven:

ON THE KNEES OF THE GODS

But it was a long time before Lynn slept. Jennie's idiocies were barbed. Absurd, impossible to think that Dwight was personally interested in her, Lynn Harding. Why should he be, with all the world from which to choose? She liked him frankly enough. But she hadn't a significant thought for anyone but Tom. Perhaps she'd been foolish to think this evening so important. It had gone to her head a little. It had been so different from anything she had ever experienced. If Dwight had made pretty speeches to her it was because his profession was, partly, speechmaking, and because he said just such things to every woman he met. Tomorrow night she would see Tom again, and tell him about the party, and for a little while she would remember it with pleasure, and then she'd forget it; and that was that.

She smiled, and, suddenly as a child, fell fathoms deep into sleep.

Blocks away, David Dwight was walking,

still softly as a cat, about his library. Wilkins, yawning, waited discreetly in the background to see his employer into bed. Dwight looked at a small gold clock on his desk. Not yet 2:00. He knew several all-night clubs. Not worth while to go there, he said to himself yawning, but he had never felt less like sleep in his life.

A pretty girl. But he had known girls and women far prettier. An intelligent girl. That didn't mean much either; he had known women of signal brilliance, and after a while they, too, had bored him.

But little Lynn — there was something tremendously appealing about her; something fresh and radiant and untouched; something quaintly serious. But she could laugh, as a child laughs, with spontaneity, and her eyelids would crinkle and there was the unexpected fingerprint of a dimple in her cheek. Her left cheek. He hadn't been as interested in a girl in months. Or was it years?

What about this sex business anyway? — he thought vaguely — stupid or ugly or beautiful or mysterious, depending upon how you viewed it and when you viewed it. Before and after, like the advertisements. Indefinable, no matter how much print was wasted on it. You met someone — and that was that. Unreasonable, unreasoning.

He must see her again. He would see her again.

He must walk as delicately as Agag. There was no immediacy about it. When a man left the careless twenties and the casual thirties behind him he grew to know the value of making haste slowly, of savoring the moments, as a gourmet swirls the Napoleon brandy in the great crystal glass, aware of its perfume, and permits it to slide, drop by burning, smooth drop, over his palate. This girl in her dusky pink frock was like spring. And you grew to value spring, to cherish it, to take each day in your hands as if it were breakable and infinitely precious, and exact from it the last drop of heartbreaking fragrance, the last atom of star dust.

He thought briefly of Sarah. Frowned. Sarah — Sarah might make trouble. But perhaps not. Still, he thought easily, he could handle Sarah.

He made no plans, uttered no definitions. He was not a seducer of innocence. Seduction was abhorrent to him. He called it by another name, by several names. Every love affair into which he entered had its special glamor, its exceptional romance; he loved like a boy, like a mature man, and for the first time; and loved the more ardently because it would not last, because in the nature of things it could not endure. Knowing this, he said, each time, *This is the last time, this will not perish.*

Therefore, he did not say to himself, in words, *This girl attracts me. I shall possess her.* Few men do.

Any love affair was, with him, upon the knees of the gods. No one, he least of all, knew what tomorrow might bring. Sometimes, the quarry run down, the capture effected, he would wake to find a woman in his arms; would wake, grateful, astonished, and superbly moved emotionally. Later when it was over, he would ask himself how it had happened. "I did not will it. It was not my fault."

The anchorite is not more mentally chaste than the true Casanova. For to the true Casanova every woman is the first, every woman is the last, love is as sentimental as an old-fashioned valentine, every love is the goal and the end of the road, each victory brings amazement.

These are the men who never grow up, who do not pass perceptibly from adolescence into maturity, who are forever seeking the impossible, forever demanding the static and the stable of something as variable as the seasons and the winds; who look to the pot of gold at the rainbow's end, and who say finally, *it is tinsel after all, but the next rainbow shall not fail me.* And who, insecure and somehow unsure of themselves, seek always to prove to themselves their own potence.

Of such men was Dwight, one of that charming, tragic, and misinterpreted company whose opprobrium is so much more than they deserve because they mean no harm, and so much less, also because they mean no harm, and whose day of reckoning is blacker than any rumor because the other days have dawned so bright with promise. This is the company whose end is the Kiplingesque one of "sittin' and thinkin'," who, having grasped the shadow for the substance, cry out upon life as a cheater, and believe themselves cheated — never knowing that it was always the other way about.

So David Dwight drew no mental pencil marks through his own and Lynn Harding's name, murmuring interrogatively, *Friendship, hate, indifference, love, kiss, court, marry.* Merely he went to bed thinking that he had spent a delightful evening; thinking that even though his extravagances had been notable during the past year or so, he was bound to win the Carson case when it came up on the calendar in the fall, and thus retrieve his slightly dejected fortunes; thinking too that he had never felt better in his life and that tomorrow was another day.

Girls should always have gray eyes, a little inquiring, a little mischievous, tremendously trusting and eager and shining; they should always wear a sleek blackbird's cap of hair with a dark arrow pointing the way upon a smooth white forehead. They should have a fugitive, elusive dimple, always in the left cheek, and a black beauty mark to tempt the beholder at the corner of a very young, very red mouth. They should be small and slenderly rounded, and they should always wear dusky pink, the color of afterglow in summer —

Such girls were always kind, of course, gentle but not docile, spirited but not shrewish. Such girls should be protected and befriended —

He believed it. So much so that a few days later, blessing the legal business which still brought him to the Seacoast Building, he waited at noontide, impatient as a boy, just outside the doors of her office, in the crowded corridor. And when she came out, brave in a spring suit as gray as her eyes, but with a small scarlet hat for gaiety, as bright as her lips, he said, feeling tremendously young and highhearted and excited, "Well, how about lunch?"

She was glad to see him; said so. Said, also, with a delicious small scowl of indecision, "I haven't much time. I have to be out of the office this afternoon. I've made an appointment" — she looked at her watch — "in just an hour."

"We'll go downstairs to the Gavarin then," he suggested. "That will give us more time, won't it?"

She hesitated, nodded. Tom came by, seeing no one but herself, taking her arm in his firm, unconsciously hurting grasp.

"Lunch, honey?"

She said, a little embarrassed, "I'm sorry, Tom, I didn't know you were going to be free."

Then he recognized David Dwight, standing there beside her, so sure of himself, so infernally well dressed — *Smells of money,* said Tom to himself with considerable heat — *damned fop!*

"That's all right." He spoke to Dwight; he said, "Good morning, sir," in accents that endowed Mr. Dwight with a long gray beard, a limp, and a rheumy eye. Then he was off, ahead of them, saying over his shoulder, "See you tonight, Lynn," and swinging that shoulder and its mate with some self-consciousness.

Dwight looked after him. "Good-looking boy," he commented. "I've seen him before, haven't I? I don't exactly place him."

Lynn explained, as they moved toward the elevators. "Tom Shepard, he's Mr. Norton's private secretary."

"Oh, yes," recalled Dwight, in a tone of complete dismissal.

She was annoyed. She was annoyed with herself for being annoyed. What right had David Dwight, no matter who he was, or any other man for that matter, to take that tone toward Tom — her Tom? On the other hand, why shouldn't he? Tom was, of course, nothing to him. She was somewhat bewildered by her small, sparkling flare of anger, like a little rocket; and by the bleak, blank common-sensical stick it immediately displayed, burned out, falling to the ground.

They lunched well if not elaborately; and talked a great deal about nothing in particular.

They had reached the salad course, and Dwight was lighting a cigarette, when Lynn took her eyes from his vivid face for a moment and looked up to see a girl whom

134

she knew through Jennie, slipping between the tables, smiling slightly, followed by a tall, thin, stooped young man with a sensitive weak mouth and fine eyes.

Why, it's Mara Burt, said Lynn to herself, and called out, "Oh, Mara!" and the other girl stopped a moment to smile and wave. She indicated with a gesture to her escort that she preferred a table farther back in the room. They moved on and sat down.

"That's an attractive girl," Dwight commented. "Rather the baby-faced type, but what lovely red hair. Bank employee?"

"No, but she works in the building, in a branch insurance office on the thirtieth floor," Lynn replied. "I haven't seen her for some time."

"I wish I could persuade a pretty girl to look at me as she is looking at her companion," Dwight sighed, "all 'ohs' and 'ahs' and big eyes. She is certainly making a play for that young man — lucky devil."

Lynn said abstractedly, "I don't think so; she's married, you know." And Dwight shouted with laughter.

"That's classic. Speaking of young men — and pretty girls — what about this Shepard boy?"

His eyes were intent on her own. Kind eyes, she thought, quizzical, understanding. Her own fell to the modest diamond on her right hand. He probably knew about her and Tom now; possibly Sarah had told him. She answered honestly, "We — we can't get married. Not now, that is."

A bald little statement. He understood it in all its implications. His eyes did not change, his face was impassive, but a little rat of anger sharpened its teeth in his brain. Of course! It would happen. He looked at Lynn with coldness veiled by an impersonal friendly interest. She was not nearly so pretty as he had thought her. A quite ordinary little girl, like millions of others, like hundreds, right in this suddenly oppressive building. And a quite ordinary boy, who had an average job and wouldn't get any further ahead, whose build was football, but whose brains were ping-pong. Two very commonplace little people planning a wedding day and a walk-up flat, dishes and babies, slippers, radio, the movies —

He said gently, "You're very young —"

"I know it" — she looked at him, gray eyes black, the pupils dilated — "and so is he. We — we've left each other free. It's better that way. I want to keep on with my job, I like it awfully. I'm crazy about it." Her small firm chin was set, held a little

136

high; she made a funny, hopeless little gesture with the hand which wore the ring. "Tom won't hear of my marrying him until — until he gets ahead. He doesn't want me to work. So there we are!" Her face was grave, even a little melancholy. Then she laughed up at him. "Sarah doesn't approve at all," she admitted. "Sarah doesn't believe in marriage. She's all for careers. I don't believe Sarah's ever been in love, ever in all her life!" said Lynn with unconscious brutality and patronage.

Ah, had she not? He knew, he knew very well. His heart tightened.

"How old is Tom?"

She told him.

"And you? You told me once. Tell me again."

She obeyed. He laughed, suddenly, very much relieved.

"Infants!" he mocked her.

Twenty-two and twenty-three; not planning to marry yet; tomorrow was another day. How had he ever thought her ordinary, even for a moment? How had he ever fancied her like anyone in the world, even so briefly? She was unique.

Competition is the life of several trades.

He said happily, "Never mind Sarah — suppose you bring Tom — and that model girl with whom you live — Joan? Betty?"

"Jennie," Lynn corrected, laughing.

"Jennie, then. Bring her and Tom to the house; we'll throw a party — for you. A very young party — not, perhaps, altogether in years. Whom would you like to meet? Gossip rehashers, otherwise columnists, stage or motion-picture folk, artists, writers? Or just people?"

Her eyes danced. She said, "Anyone you say. It will be fun."

"We'll make it so. We'll dispense with Sarah, I think," he decided, without regret. "She's not as young as we are," he said cruelly. "Yes, we'll dispense with her. That is, if you don't mind. We're old enough friends by now, are we not, to get along without the *tertium quid?*"

"The what?"

"Sarah," he said smiling, "and, besides, that was a cockeyed allusion."

He set the date; and later, paying the check, murmured, "You'll telephone me if the evening's all right?"

"Of course it will be," she told him happily.

Leaving, she looked back at Mara Burt and her companion, so evidently engrossed in each other. She wondered a little uncomfortably. She had met Mara in the rest room with Jennie. Jennie had given her Mara's history with a characteristic brevity. "Married, see, and Bill's out of a job. So she has to hold hers. She generally holds it by her knees."

"Do you mean on her knees?"

"No, *by* 'em. As far as I can make out she's only a fair typist and won't get much further. But the men in whatever office she's in like her. See?"

Lynn had been to Mara's apartment once or twice and had met Bill, a sulky, stocky young man, terribly aware that it was Mara's earnings and not his own that were paying rent and grocery bills. Lynn had come away feeling sorry for them both.

That evening while they were dressing to go out she spoke to Jennie of her encounter with Mara. Jennie nodded her wise, blond head.

"Sure. Was it a tall guy, sort of T.B.-looking?" And at Lynn's nod, she went on, "That's her boss's nephew, Frank Houghton. She told me about him. He's been out in Arizona with his wife and kids and now he's back, working for his uncle. Mara says his wife doesn't understand him." Jennie laughed. "Sure, that's what they all say. He's been giving her a rush on

Bill's lodge nights and all. His wife writes or something, and sticks around home — they live in Flushing — and looks after the kids."

"She must be crazy!" said Lynn indignantly.

"Who, the wife? Oh, you mean Mara. Crazy like a trained seal. She knows darned well she wouldn't get anywhere in business without the old S.A. and she doesn't give a whoop how she holds her job just as long as she holds it. I don't mean she'd go very far. She hasn't," Jennie explained scornfully, "the guts. She'll just shilly-shally around, and if she's ever asked to come across she'll faint, and when she comes to, she'll yap that she's a married woman, and 'Oh, how could you misjudge me so!' Bill's a sorehead of course, but I don't blame him. It isn't so keen for him, you know, hanging around the flat, waiting for her to come home with the weekly wage."

Lynn thought, *But all men who marry girls who keep on working don't take that attitude.* Yet she wondered. And after a moment, fluffing powder on her nose, inquired, "But suppose she really likes this Houghton or whoever he is?"

"Not she. She likes his pull, that's all.

Besides, what's it to us if she falls by the wayside?" inquired Jennie inelegantly.

Nothing, Lynn supposed. But she rather liked Mara Burt, the little she had seen of her. She wished somehow that she could be warned. For it was a losing game she was playing. Jennie would laugh at that. Sarah, if consulted, would remark merely, "Apparently the girl has no ambition, no intelligence; she is just ten mechanical fingers and for the rest — conscious sex appeal." Tom, who had met Mara and her husband, would shrug. She thought, *I wonder what David Dwight would say?* She would rather like his opinion; some day she'd ask him what he thought, as a purely hypothetical case.

Jennie was talking about Dwight's party. She was enchanted. She planned to put some money in the little number 543. "You know, Lynn, the one I told you about — alternate white and black ruffles, simple, swell, stunning. Hope he's asked a lot of very old men, lousy with money, who have reached the stage where they're perfectly satisfied to hold your hand."

"Lord," commented Lynn honestly, "what a terrible prospect!"

"You're young yet," said Jennie.

The party that evening with Tom was a

Dutch-treat affair at an unfashionable bar-room. Slim was there, and some of the UBC men. Slim took Jennie; there were other girls. Nice, happy-go-lucky crowd, not very noisy but very genial, talking inexplicable shop between drinks, food, and dances. Tom was perfectly happy. "Gee, you look sweet," he told Lynn, "like strawberry ice cream. I could eat you up!"

She wore the dusky pink dress. Strawberry ice cream — and a rose-quartz pagoda! She thought wistfully that it was a pity a person as young and dear, as thrilling and beloved as Tom, could not shape his exciting voice into the quaint conceits and phrases that were like little windows opening — as could, say, a man like David Dwight. But of course if Tom talked like David Dwight he wouldn't be — Tom.

Guileful girl, she waited to tell Tom of Dwight's proposed party until this particular party was halfway through, and Tom, his hair ruffled and his eyes bright had just sung, with several others, the bulldog song — "Wow! wow! wow!" sang Tom, slamming his glass on the table.

She had thought he would rebel at the idea. But now, when his humor was expansive, now was the time to tell him.

She did so. He replied casually, "Swell — soup-and-fish, I suppose? Well, with a sponge and press, I can get by."

So, after all, he wouldn't mind going. She was amazed to find herself slightly disappointed. Or was it that just at this moment and in this humor he didn't mind?

But next day he didn't mind either. Stopping at her desk — "Nice," he said carelessly, "of the old boy to ask me. Think how it will impress Gunboat."

He didn't mind because he'd be there with her. Together.

Chapter Eight:

AFTER LAUGHTER, TEARS

Resplendent, he arrived at the girls' apartment in time to escort Jennie and Lynn — in Dwight's car — to the party. He leaned back against the upholstery and muttered words of contentment. "This is the life," said Tom, and added glumly, "only when you get it you're too old to enjoy it."

Lynn said, laughing, "David Dwight isn't too old — He isn't old at all. You have such comic ideas about age, Tom. Anybody over thirty looks like Methuselah to you."

Tom digested this in an unhappy silence. She didn't think Dwight old then. Well, hell's bells, he wasn't, of course. But too old for Lynn.

Jennie shook out her black and white flounces. She looked very handsome, hair like daffodils, eyes like blue-bells, Lynn's old onyx and gold earrings swinging from her ears. She said, "We're in for a large evening, I think."

Lynn wore white. The "too innocent" white, upon which Jennie had passed on the occasion of Dwight's dinner. Jennie had grunted, observing her as, dressed and ready, she swung away from the mirror. "You need," Jennie had said critically, "something a little startling. If you tied a blue sash around you now, you'd look like first prize at a baby party. Give me your jewel box."

"I haven't any jewels," Lynn reminded her, smiling, "just the old stuff grandmother left me."

"That's just what I want. How about the garnets? Knock 'em dead. That's what you need, you'll look virginal, quaint, and sophisticated, all at one and the same time. Here they are. Try 'em on."

A garnet necklace set in intricate gold. Earrings, heavily encrusted, and two wide bracelets. "There," said Jennie, standing back, "that's what you needed. You looked like orange juice, straight, before. Granny's garnets put the kick into it."

She handed Lynn a bright, light lipstick, entirely artificial. "Tone up the little old mouth to match the antiques — in color —" advised Jennie, "and you'll lay 'em in the aisles like a row of prewar stingers!"

"Gee," said Tom, staring, upon his entrance, "you look swell, Lynn." He added, courteously, "and you, too, Jennie."

"Never mind me," said Jennie complacently. "I know how I look."

"Haven't you got a lot of lipstick on?" was Tom's next, and natural, remark, his eyes on Lynn's brilliant mouth.

Lynn said, worried, "Perhaps. More than usual anyway, but with this white dress —" She started for the bedroom in order to hunt for cleansing tissues; but Jennie caught her arm and swung her around.

"Leave the face as is," she ordered, "remember, Tom isn't married to you yet. You're just right — as you are."

So, lipstick and all, Lynn went to the party.

Wilkins opened the door, with a special smile for Lynn. The big room was more or less filled with people. The loveliest frocks, the prettiest girls. "I feel like a poor relation," Lynn whispered to Jennie as they mounted the steps to the temporary dressing-room, Tom having disappeared in Wilkins's wake.

The bedroom contained more women. Smoke, laughter, powder clouds, heavy perfume, the smell of cosmetics. Lynn pinched Jennie's arm until she shrieked,

"Hey, what's the big idea? When I get bruises I *sue!*"

"Isn't that Lillie James — over there talking to the tall girl in black?"

"So it is," agreed Jennie, staring, "thought she was in a sanitarium, nervous breakdown — boy or girl?"

"Jennie, hush, she'll hear you!"

When they had descended the stairs Dwight detached himself from a group around the fireplace and came forward to meet them. He took Jennie's hand in his and measured her with a cool, smiling glance, while Lynn murmured the introductions.

"Delightful of you to come, Miss Le Grande," he said formally, but his eyes danced a very little.

"Jennie to you," was Jennie's generous response.

"Of course, Jennie to me!" He turned to Lynn, and now his eyes were not smiling nor were they cool. "Where's the lucky young man?" he pleasantly wanted to know.

"There he is. Tom — oh, Tom!" called Lynn, turning to see Tom standing by the door, very tall, very broad, very young, somehow a little ill at ease, with the sulky expression of the small boy who finds the party not quite up to his imagination and expectation.

Tom came over quickly. Women turned to watch him walk across the floor, not with the feline tread of his host, but the light step of perfect balance and vitality. He and Dwight shook hands and murmured conventionalities. Tom said, with an engaging grin and the courtesy of the junior which so infuriated the other man, "Looks like a grand party, sir."

"It will be, now," said Dwight, smiling, his hand lightly on Lynn's arm. "Let's circulate, shall we?"

Lynn couldn't remember half the names of people. Later the theatrical crowd arrived, straight from their dressing-rooms. Yes, that had been Lillie James, the motion-picture ingenue who had shot into stardom and was now making a new picture on Long Island. There was Mark Manners, the illustrator, who attached himself to Jennie, to Jennie's later commercial interest. There was George Fane, juvenile lead in "Let's Be Silly," and Manse Marr, musical comedy star, and Babe Leonard, who wrote stark tales of the submerged millions and lived on Park Avenue from the proceeds. There were dozens of others, all very gay, all very friendly. There was Ike

Kirschbaum, the "new" song writer-composer, who, they said, out-Gershwined Berlin. There were many more.

There was dancing, singing, with obliging artists doing impromptu turns. There was Gwen Hammond singing her latest melancholy blues song, and "Brownie" Bird, star of "Mulatto Madness," singing her most famous version of "St. Louis Blues." There was, very late, Sonny Carter and his gold-plated saxophone and one turn of hired talent, the three adagio dancers who had held all Manhattan breathless in the recent "Roamers Revue." And, of course, an orchestra.

Things to eat, things to drink, things to smoke; couples out on the terrace whispering, swinging idly in the great swings, leaning on the parapet in the sweet spring night; laughter and the ceaseless murmur of voices.

It was two o'clock, and the party was just well under way when Dwight gently but firmly detached Lynn from George Fane, with whom she was dancing; and, after taking her twice about the room, stopped by the terrace doors and led her outside. "Sure you're warm enough — shall I send for a wrap?" he asked.

"No, it's heavenly out here," she said, looking over the terrace wall, drawing in deep breaths of the night wind, the subtle, small fragrance of earth and green, growing things.

"Did I annoy you taking you away from Fane? I annoyed him, that was very obvious."

"I hardly think so. He'll find another audience," she laughed. "He was telling me he couldn't get a break. 'The women stars are always so jealous!' "

"He's a conceited ass but a good youngster," Dwight told her, indifferently, "even if he does break all the feminine hearts across the footlights."

"He's not nearly as good looking as Tom," she said absently, and wondered where Tom was and if he were having a good time. She'd danced with him a little earlier. The orchestra was playing bygone hits by request. " 'I can't give you anything but love, baby,' " Tom had sung, holding her close — "and that's no idle jest," he had added abruptly. "There won't be any penthouses for a long time, Lynn."

"As if I cared!"

"You do care — for me?"

"Idiot!" And she had looked up at him, gray eyes shining between the dusky lashes, lips curved in reproach.

"I want like the devil to kiss you," Tom told her savagely, and a little sharp tremor of emotion troubled her pulses and sang in her veins and weakened her knees, very sweet, very disturbing. And she swayed a little closer to him and murmured, her breath catching, "Please don't look at me that way, Tom, I can't bear it."

A moment of pure desire, pure and perfect anguish, pure and ecstatic happiness —

Then Fane had cut in.

But something of that pleasant trouble, something of that burden of languor and painful, frustrated delight remained with her now, as she stood on the terrace and Dwight leaned beside her there.

In the room they had left they were now playing one of Gwen's great songs and she was singing to it, husky, sweet voice, the high notes fading like the subdued sound of smitten silver bells, drifting over the shuffle of feet, the voices, the piercing violins, the brassy yearning of the saxophones:

When my man's away,
*   there ain't no peace,*
I dunno what to do —
Can't sleep, can't walk, can't smile,
*   can't talk,*

Feelin' so doggoned blue —
When my man's away, I just sit and pray,
God, bring him back to me,
When my man's away, for a night,
* for a day*
There ain't no peace for me.

Trivial words and an important truth. The husky voice made magic of the dragging morbidity of the music, invested with the eternal glamor of human longing the tinsel-tawdry lyric. Only the truth remained, heartbreaking. "Hokum," commented Dwight at Lynn's side, "but like most hokum so infernally veracious —"

She said, in a dreaming voice, "It's — lovely, so real —"

"Women feel like that, I suppose," he told her idly, or with apparent casualness, "and, believe it or not, some men."

"Yes." She clasped her hands on the wall in front of her and stared out into the darkness. There were not many lights at this time of the morning. But the stars were big and very near.

"It's a pity things have to be so complicated," Dwight said, throwing his cigarette to the stone floor, crushing it under his heel. "Pity that love's so wilful. Other women's men, other men's girls, we don't

152

stop to think of that, do we?"

"I suppose not." She remembered Mara, for no good reason, and spoke of her. "A girl I know," she said, confident that he would understand.

When she had told the little there was to tell he said slowly, looking away from her, looking out to the velvet arch of the heavens.

"You can't do anything. Isn't she just like most of us, caught in a trap of her own contrivance, struggling, hurting herself, trying to manufacture a little happiness, a little escape? She calls it 'having a good time.' I spoke to you the other night of the skyscrapers, didn't I? Sometimes I see them from another angle. Tremendous traps, opening and closing on time signals. I watch the girls and women come out of their doors, evenings, hurrying toward their homes, happy or unhappy, but always preoccupied with the fear of losing their economic independence — if it is independence; leading such disseminated lives — the life of the skyscraper, ordered, patterned, the life of the home — whether it is a flat, a furnished room; whether it contains the family unit of parents, fraternal relations, or husbands and children.

"Possibly your friend is disregarding the

red light in order to make her life more bearable; possibly, like so many women forced to earn their livings and having little interest in the means, she is simply trying to bend one of the oldest forces in the world to her own small ends — in short, she accepts invitations from a man who may be able to guarantee her job to her. Yet perhaps she is only escaping. As for her husband, she probably loves him. But love, the strongest thing in the world, the poets say, is a delicate thing. It bruises with ease, it shatters at a touch. Love in a walk-up" — he laughed a little, quite low — "with lovers trying to budget love the way they budget finances, with little wives working, and coming home disheartened and tired, with bills to think about and a run in the last pair of stockings, with grouchy husbands and fatigued wives, with the smell of cabbage and laundry soap, with babies crying — Love nourished upon occasional routine embraces and stereotyped kisses — love has to be stronger than I believe it is to rise above that," he said.

Lynn drew a deep breath.

"I suppose you're right. I hate to think you're right. I won't believe it," she answered childishly. "Tom — Tom and I." She was silent. He did not disturb her, his heart beat thickly, he held himself in a close and calculated restraint; her voice went on, still dreaming, thinking aloud she was, and he knew it, "Tom and I are different. We must be different. Waiting's hard," she said with that unconscious natural cruelty of hers, "when you're young and love each other. Sometimes I don't know what to think. I can't see ahead. We'd be plain crazy to marry — now. Perhaps we'd be crazy to marry even if I kept on working. Yet I can't give up my work. And Tom doesn't want me, married and working —"

Dwight said, with deliberate lightness, "If I were Tom, even if I knew as much as I do now, I'd want you, I suppose, at any price, and at any risk. But possibly he's right."

He touched her hand. He said, on a deepened note, "Lynn, you're such a dear little person —" He felt her hand move under his, a startled gesture. In the darkness his mouth was ironic. He went on smoothly, "If I had a daughter —" That was damned funny too. He repeated it, savoring its comedy. He had a daughter. Two of them. Large, rawboned girls who had inherited their mother's plainness and who disapproved of him. Girls he would have disliked if he had met them as strangers, but without a break he went on — "a daughter like you." There he stopped, his voice effectively breaking. And why not? For a moment, superb actor, always living his part, he saw himself purged of any passional impulse toward this small girl beside him, visualized himself, perfectly paternal, indulging only in the soft, anxious, benevolent paternal emotions.

Now he laughed, withdrawing his hand. He said simply, "I wish you belonged to me."

She replied the perfect thing then; she said, turning to look at him, her little face pale, red-lipped, glamorous in the dim lighting of the terrace where Chinese lanterns, monstrous flowers swung in the gentle wind, "But you're far too young to have a daughter like me —"

She thought of her own father, gray, stooped, the X-ray burns on his hands, the shrewd, wise, kindly eyes. She sent him her love over the miles. He'd be on his way home now, with her mother. Suddenly she was homesick for them both.

"I'd like you to feel that I am your friend, your very good friend; that there is nothing I would not do for you. If you won't permit me a vicarious paternity —

how about an avuncular interest?"

She said sweetly, "I'd like a friend, best of all."

"You can always count on me," he told her; meant it, at the moment; not asking himself upon what she could count; not really knowing.

She put her hand in his. This was what she had wanted all along. He said, the control breaking a little, the veneer cracking, the theatrical backdrop forgotten, knowing himself on dangerous ground but risking the consequence, "A bargain, then — ? and — to seal it?" he murmured, bending toward her, "You will not misunderstand, dear Lynn."

Still he dared not risk too much. He kissed her lightly, briefly, and, with absurd adherence to fictional standards of a bygone day, upon the smooth white forehead she presented to him, his lips glancing over the dark and subtle arrow of the little widow's peak. *I point the way,* said the arrow, *to sweeter contacts —*

She was not afraid; not even warned. The night had its own spell, his voice another, she had spoken to him as one speaks to oneself — and was disarmed.

Now she smiled faintly, and stood apart from him; not that his arms had been about her, simply that she had moved close to him with the instinct of the animal seeking — what? Warmth, comfort, human affection?

Tom, in the doorway, looking for her, saw them. He had not seen the kiss, so absurdly, so delicately chaste. He saw Lynn move away. She was white in the glow of the lanterns, white in the dusky night shadows, white face, white dress; the banked fire of garnets flickering at her ears and throat and wrists, the fire of her lips burning, he knew, though he could not see them clearly.

But she had been too close to Dwight.

Tom went back into the room; and poured himself a drink; two drinks; three. Jennie, conducting her small but entertaining affair with the illustrator, cocked a knowing blue eye at him. *Sore about something, probably Lynn. Going to try and drink the cellar dry; don't blame him.* She then thought, deftly maintaining her conversation with the artist, *I must tip Lynn off.*

She did so later. She said confidentially, "I'm tight. But I can still walk. Why not? It isn't often I have a chance to get high expensively. But Tom's had enough. He's peeved about something. Watch your step."

Dwight had gone over to a group of his

guests. Lynn watched him a moment, with grateful, friendly eyes. He was a dear. He did understand. A lot more than he said. She went in search of Tom, troubled, but not very much so. She found him at a punch bowl, having made the rounds of the various other liquids, highball, cocktail, liqueur.

"It's late, Tom," she said.

"I didn't think you'd realize it," he told her, observing Wilkins's assistant serving the punch with a heavy silver ladle.

"Oh, but I do, I'm tired! Let's go home now," she coaxed him. "Several people have left."

"It's all the same to me," he agreed, without looking at her, a little drunk, more than a little drunk, but his voice still unthickened, his eyes clear, his step steady, marked by, perhaps, a more pronounced swagger.

Yet so different a Tom from the one who had held her close and sung — "I can't give you anything but love, baby."

He couldn't. That was what ate at him now, that was what all of Dwight's costly intoxicants could not blunt, that one vitally important fact.

Gloomily he watched Lynn slip back across the room to speak to Jennie;

gloomier still he observed her go up to Dwight, draw him momentarily aside. Her lips moved. She was saying, "We must go now, really." And Dwight was reminding her, "Tomorrow's Sunday. Little girls can sleep. Must you go?"

She must, she said; and he smiled at her companionably without, it seemed, a regret.

Tom made his way to the room set apart for the male guests. Jennie and Lynn, arm in arm, went upstairs and interrupted a long, hushed conversation between two girls, heads together, one very blond, one very dark. "Lovebirds," said Jennie to Lynn carelessly, as the other two fell silent, and one went to a mirror and titivated her oval, rather melancholy face.

"Good time, Jennie?"

"Swell. Even if no one insulted me and no immoral propositions came my way. However, I'm going to pose for Mark Manners. He's a stuffed shirt, but I'll pick up some loose change that way. Not too loose," she corrected herself. "How about you?"

"Me? Oh, the party! I loved it!" Lynn told her.

"Watch out for Tom. Warpath, firewater, feathers and all," Jennie warned her as they went downstairs.

"Taxi," said Tom, on the pavement.

"Mr. Dwight's car was to —" began Lynn.

"Taxi!" said Tom firmly.

Taxi it was.

On the way home, Jennie and Lynn talked. Conversation, at first quite spontaneous with constant interruption of "I saw" and "She wore," and "He said" and "Wasn't it funny?" and "Oh, golly the stuffed olives — anchovies, pearl onions, Teclas maybe, what the devil were they stuffed with?" became harder going after a while, in the face of Tom's obvious glumness. When urged to express an opinion on the party he merely said, "I suppose it cost a hell of a lot," and relapsed into grim silence.

They reached the doors of the apartment house. Jennie hissed in Lynn's ear as they waited for Tom to pay the driver, "I'll do a nose dive into the bedroom and shut the door. You make up with him. I don't know what's the matter. Maybe he's coming down with something. But never let the sun rise on anger," she said, "for it's pretty gosh-darned near sunrise now."

Facing Tom in the living-room after he had plodded heavily up the stairs with them and Jennie had vanished ostentatiously, closing the bedroom door, Lynn asked appealingly, "Oh, Tom, what's the matter?"

"What do you mean what's the matter? Nothing's the matter, nothing at all, what should be the matter?" he furiously demanded.

She moved her hands in her own little gesture of despair. "Please, Tom, don't take that attitude. You're angry about something."

"I'm not, I'm not angry at all. Why should I be? What's on your mind? Got a guilty conscience?"

"Tom —"

"Look here, Lynn," he shouted, "you make me sick! The whole party made me sick. You, most of all, cavorting around with those damned stagey pansies, smirking. I suppose you think you were the guest of honor. Honor. You make me laugh. And then necking out on the terrace with Dwight — Dwight — he's a fine guy, isn't he? What's the big idea anyway? Rich lawyer throws party for bank employee — that sounds swell doesn't it? I suppose he did it out of a fatherly interest!"

That went home. She accused him hotly, "You're drunk!"

"What if I am? I had to get something

162

out of it, didn't I?" he demanded. "I tell you I saw you out there, cuddling up to the big shot — after, after our dance together. Love! Women make me sick!" said Tom.

"You — you're being disgusting — and unfair — and vulgar. I — go away!" she commanded him, and dragged the little ring from her finger, and threw it on the floor.

Yet five minutes ago she would have sworn that if asked to explain her recent proximity to David Dwight, if asked to explain even the so innocent kiss, she could have done so sincerely, with all her heart — although, she would have said, it needed no explanation!

She turned on her heel; staggered a little, with fatigue, emotion, disappointment; yes, disappointment. She swung around to look at him glowering, his brows bent, his gaze riveted on the floor. She said sorrowfully, "It was such a nice party — now you've spoiled it, yes, you've *spoiled* it!"

Tears poured suddenly down her face, a crystal, miniature flood. Her face was childishly distorted with crying, she searched for a handkerchief, found none, stood there, desolate, forlorn, crying bitterly, catching her breath, sobbing in small gulps. In a moment, her little nose would redden, would require attention.

This was no competent young woman capable of earning $1900 a year, of maintaining herself, of interesting herself efficiently in other people's affairs. This was not Dwight's guest of honor nor yet his friend who had stood with him upon the roof tops, and talked of love and skyscrapers and friendship. This was a child whose building-blocks had toppled about her, who was looking at ruins — and crying about them.

The spirit had gone from her, the anger and the flame. Incalculable girl, garnets swinging at her ears, white frock billowing about her, tight at the little waist, smooth over the round small breasts, standing quite still, crying. Devastating effect —

Tom took two steps. White frock disappeared, girl disappeared. "Here's my handkerchief," he said, thrusting it, large, mussed, into her acquiescent hand. "I love you — too much — I'm a fool — forgive me —"

At their feet the little ring, a simple circle, a complicated circle, starred with a tiny diamond, and symbolizing eternity.

"Tom, I do love you, you didn't mean what you said —"

"Of course not. Look here, this can't go

on." He stopped, appalled at the sacrifice of pride, of principles that he was about to make. Nonsense, here she was, close in his arms, warmer than pride, more desirable than principles, terribly beloved. "We'll get married, Lynn," he told her, "as soon as possible. You — you can go on working, darling — and we'll be so happy," he promised.

"Tom —" She drew away from him a little, searched his face for truth. Truth was there, written on grave features. The liquor still sang in his blood but his mind was clear enough. He swept her back into his embrace, kissed her —

Jennie appeared in a negligee.

"Lord, I'm sorry; thought you'd gone," she murmured. She had reason. For several moments the room had been very still.

Lynn was radiant. After all, weeping had left no scar; nothing had left scars.

"Jennie, we've decided to get married —"

"Is that news?"

"No, but soon. I mean, I'll keep on working."

Jennie was glum.

"Nice for you, maybe. What about me? Back to the furnished room or driven to the streets," prophesied Jennie wearily. "Tom, for Pete's sake, go home and let us go to bed. Can't you set the date to-morrow — I mean, later today?"

But they had no eyes for her, clasping hands, laughing with a gentle madness, perfectly happy, perfectly secure, the future irradiated and clear before them.

Chapter Nine:

ON A NOTE OF HEARTBREAK

Tom had gone. He had closed the door, not gently, as a door is closed upon faint hopes, but with an exultant slam which reverberated through the entire flat and probably shook the old walls of the shabby building as well.

"Quiet little son of a gun, your future husband," Jennie commented, yawning, from the bedroom.

"He's happy." Lynn was wandering about in the living-room, getting ready for bed. "So am I. I knew he'd be sensible and give in," she announced.

"Oh, yeah? Well, here's something else you'd better know, too, and the sooner the better. He'll never stop reminding you that he did give in. When anything goes wrong he'll say, 'Remember I was against this, and you made me do it!' " was Jennie's sardonic warning.

"Oh, not Tom!" Lynn in robe and night-gown cantered into the bedroom and sat down on the edge of the bed. "Besides, what else could we do? We couldn't go on like this forever!"

"No, I suppose not. Well," said Jennie glumly, "I suppose you'll be pulling out of here any day next week —"

"Jennie, not quite as soon as that! We have to go house-hunting, and I've things to get. It will take ages, and then there's mother and father; they don't know a thing about it, I haven't told them. Oh, of course, I've written about Tom, but nothing to upset them. Sarah hasn't said anything, I'm sure. They'll want me to be married from home, I suppose — I don't see how I can be," Lynn added worriedly, "It would mean getting a leave from the bank. No, I don't see how I can or Tom either, for that matter. Perhaps they'd come on here. That's what I'll ask them to do. Oh, I wish they would!"

"Hey, hold on, whether you leave this dump next week or in a month's time it means I have to look around for someone to go in with me. Hell," said Jennie simply, "and we get along great."

"I know we do," Lynn told her, in compunction. "I'm awfully sorry, Jennie —"

"No, you're not. I don't expect you to be — Oh, well, maybe something will turn up.

For Pete's sake go back and get to sleep, I'm more dead than alive!" Jennie told her with a petulance which only partially concealed her own definite dismay.

Lynn, being in love, was normally selfish. She told herself that Jennie would find someone to share the apartment with her, and went to bed convinced that she would not sleep, and slept almost immediately, dreaming of Tom and preachers; of David Dwight and skyscrapers; of moons swung like lanterns over penthouse roofs; and through her dreams ran the thread of a forlorn and magic melody.

She and Tom spent the next day, which was Sunday, together. Tom, waking perfectly fit and entirely without the head he had more than half expected would be his misfortune in the morning, came to the apartment about noon, found Lynn up, dressed, and breakfasted, and Jennie yawning, rather half-clad about the flat, and cursing the impulse of family duty which had prompted her to promise this particular Sunday to her sister in Flatbush.

She would be gone all the rest of the day, provided she ever got started, and Tom, sitting beside Lynn in a motion-picture house, had a brilliant idea. Why couldn't Lynn come down to his place and cook dinner for him? The desolate Slim would be out somewhere, drowning his unrequited love in quantities of Scotch, and the third man who had recently been added to the small menage, an engineer in the broadcasting company, whom Tom had met through his friend there, would likewise be absent until late evening.

Lynn pondered this proposition for a few minutes. The conventions played no particular or repressive part in her momentary doubt. She had been at Tom's before this, generally with Jennie, always with other people; but going alone to his bachelor quarters did not impress her as being a defiant gesture, not in this day and age. Nevertheless, something traditional caused her slight hesitation.

"Come on," he urged her, while upon the stage the "flesh" show played itself out in a tap-dancing quartet and a "Mexican" soprano who had been no nearer Mexico than Hester Street. "Why not?"

It had once been agreed between them that he should not come alone to her apartment when Jennie was away or no one else was there. Nor did that restriction spring from convention, merely from the somber wisdom that here were two young people very much in love and without much hope that their love would be consummated with the customary legal and religious rites. Having come to a turn in the road marked "Danger," they had discovered that each could read. But now, of course, it was different, they were to be married very soon; that knowledge would lessen the tension; it is hope deferred that maketh the heart sick, and it is not easy to wait when there seems no end to waiting.

He wanted, he said, to show her the improvements in the newest of his home-built radio receivers. He urged, "Come on, do, it will be swell."

So when the spring night was slipping toward dusk, wearing upon its infinitely tender and fragrant breast the radiant message of a star, they went down to the Village, walking arm in arm from the bus stop, and halting at an open and thriving delicatessen to laden themselves with round and square and long packages, cold cuts, salads, tea rolls, spice cakes. "Not," promised Lynn, "that I intend to feed you this way after we're married."

"Woman, you'd better not!"

Down on Perry Street was the more or less antique apartment house where Tom and Slim and latterly Hank Mathews lived and had their beings. It was an imposing affair of dusty and shabby brick, flanked by magnificent columns of a synthetic and unashamed marble, in patterns of black and white. On the third floor, which was next to the top floor, was the lair of the three young men, an ample five-room suite which cost them $60 a month. There were three alleged bedrooms, a living-room, a kitchen, and a bath. Lynn, stepping across the threshold, as Tom unlocked the door, picked her way over collars, socks, and shirts. Articles of intimate apparel were draped over light bulbs, and there were unwashed dishes strewn about in a masterly pattern of confusion.

She said, standing quite still in the welter of dust and worse than dust, "I don't think I'll marry you, after all!"

Tom came up behind her and swung her about, his big arm closing around her firmly.

"Think again. This doesn't express my soul. I'm a tidy man really," he told her solemnly. "It's Slim — and it's Hank; and last week half a dozen others slept here, off and on, three to a bed, and the guy that didn't get a bed rated the floor."

"It looks," Lynn remarked, "like a Municipal Lodging-House. Only not as clean."

Tom dumped the delicatessen packages down anywhere.

"Darling, must you be so fussy?"

Lynn vanished into the nearest bedroom, screamed on a small note of horror, and flew out again. She added her hat and coat to the general chaos and went into the bathroom for a towel. Mutters arose. "*Why* do men use towels to mop up the floor?" was her plaintive question.

"Search me," Tom replied cheerfully, lighting a cigarette and sitting down before the radio. Discovering a speck of dust upon its chaste top he whistled and took out his handkerchief. Dust on a radio was not to be endured. Also Slim had deposited a glove and Hank a sock along with the dust. Tom flung these articles to the floor with an expression of outrage.

Lynn appeared, a comparatively clean towel tied about her slim waist. She rustled about in the kitchen and while Tom turned dials, smiled or frowned and surrounded himself with blue smoke, there was a running of water, a clatter of dishes, a sound of brooms and of slapping dust cloths.

"What's the use?" he demanded as she dashed in and out upon her errands of reconstruction. "It will look worse tomorrow!"

"I don't care how it looks tomorrow," she informed him severely, "I don't have to see it tomorrow; but if you think I'm going to spend my married life picking up after you, Tom Shepard —"

Tom grinned. He said mildly, "I wish you could hear this thing on a cold snappy winter night. Summer's not so hot, in a reception sense."

"Tom," she wailed, "you might at least put these pajamas and things away!"

She did so herself, and it is on record that Slim, some hours later, searching for his night garb unavailingly for ten minutes, cursed and went to bed raw.

"Let's eat!" suggested Lynn finally after her labors were completed.

"Happy thought!" Tom leaped up from his beloved obsession to assist her in clearing the long and battered table. After a time coffee bubbled upon the gas stove, and the clean plates were burdened with cold and pleasant fare, including fat dill pickles and the horseradish for Tom's beef.

"Gosh, this is great!" He viewed her across the table. "Come here —"

Replete, he pushed his plate away, pushed his chair back, and held out his arms. Lynn came and perched upon his knee happily.

There was a little silence. "It's as if we were married," he told her, after a moment.

"I know —"

Darkness outside and the glow of lamps. The still more or less untidy room took on an aspect of mystery and comfort. The noises of Perry Street, children crying, children quarreling, mothers shrieking, cars passing through, faded to a dim murmur, and their own heartbeats were louder than any alien sound. They were fed and warmed and roofed; and they had each other. "A loaf of bread," commented Tom, who always quoted Omar upon sentimental occasions.

"They were tea biscuits," she reminded him, "and we didn't have any wine. As for boughs —"

A dog barked in the street below. "There!" said Tom, in silly triumph.

They laughed together, absurd, young, happy; and recited their worn but never monotonous litany:

"Do you love me?"

"You know I do —"

"How much?"

"More than all the world; more than you love me."

"But that isn't possible —"

"Let's," said Tom, "let's get married soon — tomorrow!"

"Well, no, Tom, I've thought it all out. Mother and father, they'll want me married from home. I thought it couldn't be managed, but, if we ask to take our vacations at the same time?"

"Marvelous, dear Sherlock," said Tom, "we'll do that little thing. We'll put in our applications next week. Sarah's a good old scout, she'll let you — and perhaps she'll speak a word to Gunboat for me."

"We can go home," said Lynn dreamily, "and be married —"

"And go somewhere honeymooning — Where?"

"What difference *where?*" she wanted to know ardently; and, then, with recovered practicality, "But we mustn't go to an hotel or anything and spend money. We can't afford it. Look here, Tom, mother has a cousin who has the cutest little old place in Virginia. She goes to Maine summers. I think if I asked her, she might let us have her house for ten days or so — Wouldn't that be perfect?"

He agreed with her without words, but to the satisfaction of both of them.

The shadows lengthened. The radio was silent. The street noises grew less. The remains of the picnic supper still sat coldly, dismally, upon the table.

Lynn stirred in the clasp of Tom's arms — and the battered sofa upon which they had been sitting for hours protested. She said, pushing her hair from her heavy, bright eyes and laying her hand to a flushed cheek, "It's getting late, darling, I must clear up — and go home —"

"Stay a little longer."

His voice was very low; it scarcely rippled the surface of the spell in which she was slowly and entrancingly drowning.

"I *must* go —"

It was madness to stay.

She pulled herself away from him; sat upright, a little dazed, forcing herself back to reality with a finality which a little sickened her. She got to her feet and took the dishes into the kitchen. They clattered slightly, her hands shook so.

Tom rose and lighted a cigarette and went to the window and stared out of it, unseeingly.

Presently she returned to him, ready for the street. "Going to take me home?"

"Rather. As if I'd let you run around New York by yourself — you might get lost," he told her, "or be kidnaped or something. You're such a little thing."

They laughed together, shakily enough, and presently, locking the door, went down the narrow steps which creaked furiously in the darkness. At a turn he caught her, halted her, held her against him and kissed her.

"Some day, soon, we'll be coming home and — staying home, together," he said.

And so it was planned that sometime soon, they would ask for their vacations — Lynn first, in order to enlist Sarah's sympathy and aid.

She did so, early in the week, lunching with Sarah, looking at her with appeal, across the table.

"We've decided to get married, Tom and I." She hurried over Sarah's exclamation of dismay and went on: "Do you think, Sarah, I could have my vacation a little earlier? I know I wasn't supposed to take it until fall, but if I could, and if Tom would get off at the same time, it would be wonderful. I want to go home to be married," Lynn said.

Sarah's face was grave. She looked, quite suddenly, her actual age. She answered after a moment, "I won't attempt to dissuade you, Lynn, although you know how I stand on the matter. But of course I will do what I can. Still, I don't see why you are

178

figuring on vacations — if you intend to resign."

"Oh, but I don't!" Lynn answered radiantly. "I'm going on working. I — we couldn't afford to marry otherwise, and Tom's come around to my way of thinking."

Sarah said, torn between compassion for the younger woman and her own natural feeling of triumph, "But — I'm afraid it won't work out."

"Oh, why not?" Lynn looked at her unhappily. Was Sarah like Mara? Lynn had seen Mara the night before. Mara had said bitterly, "I think you're a fool. Any woman's a fool who works after she's married. Any woman's a fool because she doesn't know what that sort of thing does to men. It's your own business of course, but I think you're crazy and, believe me, I know!"

"Because," Sarah answered, looking away from the lambent gray eyes, the very red mouth, sobered now, the smile fading, "because the bank isn't employing married women, because they are letting out the married women they now have."

"Sarah, I don't believe it!"

"It's true," said Sarah stiffly, offended.

"I'm sorry. I didn't mean that," Lynn

said instantly. "But — why, Sarah — I can't understand it! I hadn't heard."

She hesitated. No, she hadn't heard. Yet now she remembered seeing during the last month three women whom she knew slightly, all of them married, from other departments. She had seen them, red-eyed or a little pale in the rest room or corridors and had not seen them since.

"Why? It's obvious enough," Sarah told her immediately. "Unemployment is on the increase. The bank is going to keep everyone it possibly can — single people, heads of families. But when a woman is married and her husband holds a position also, the bank has decided that the woman must go. If a married woman is the sole support of her family, is widowed, or has children, that is different. It isn't difficult to see the justice of this, Lynn."

Lynn was very white. Against the pallor of her face her lips were astonishingly bright. She asked, "You mean that if Tom and I get married I'll be — fired?"

Sarah answered, still looking away from her, "I'm afraid so, Lynn."

The red lips trembled, and the small pointed chin shook. Lynn said, low, on a note of heartbreak, "Then all our plans —"

Sarah's own heart was a battleground.

Her natural and loyal affection for the girl; her antipathy to Lynn's marriage at this stage of the business game; her own insistence on career rather than marriage for women, that hard shell of protection which she had built up around herself and suffering; her pity for Lynn, looking to her for help, for sympathy, for assurance that it wasn't, after all, true; and her own quite normal triumph that the course of true love didn't, in this instance, run smooth — were embattled factions.

She cleared her throat, absurdly embarrassed, and said, rather brusquely, "If you are not willing to marry Tom Shepard on his present salary — and I don't blame you for not wanting to — you'll have to wait, that's the only solution that I can see. I don't, of course, know for a hard and fast fact that the bank would take action against you, but it's my belief that it would."

Lynn ignored all this and seized on one sentence only. "Then we'll have to wait," she said.

It was difficult enough before, caring so much for one another and seeing no way out, quarreling over the only way out that appeared feasible, arriving at the impasse, trying to the best of their bewildered abilities to minimize the dangers and delights of propinquity — and then, all at once, coming out into the clear sunlight of a decision, which seemed to point, for better or worse, to a future shared. Having had that for a few days, it was harder than ever to return to the old status of readjustments, of waiting, of uncertainty, of the practically inevitable hostility between them brought about by the situation itself.

Sarah said, and curiously enough, meant it, turning her eyes to the small and stricken face, "I'm sorry, Lynn —"

But Lynn's usual instant response to a tender of friendship and comprehension was lacking today. She interrupted, almost harshly, "Oh, *sorry* — but where does that get us?" and brooded, looking with distaste at the remains of a luncheon, cool and light and appropriate to the day, which a few minutes before had seemed so delicious.

She picked up her tall glass of iced coffee. The day was exceptionally warm, but her small, even teeth chattered against the rim of the glass.

"If," suggested Sarah, distressed, "if you want to take the chance —"

"Do you mean, get married and not let anyone know about it except you — I

182

mean, here at the bank?" asked Lynn, life returning to face and lips in a revival of hope.

"No, no," Sarah answered slowly, "I didn't mean that. You know that you couldn't keep it quiet long. It isn't possible." She thought and Lynn knew, that her own loyalty to her employers would not permit her to be party to the virtual deception. "No, I meant if you and Tom want to go ahead and marry and then see —"

Lynn shook her head. "I don't think so. There wouldn't be much happiness in it, would there — waiting for the blow to fall, wondering every day if you were going to be let out."

Sarah argued no more, and as Lynn made no motion to finish her lunch called for the check.

She put her hand on the girl's shoulder with unaccustomed tenderness as they left the restaurant together. If something could be done — if for instance, David Dwight could help — He had, of course, a personal secretary of many years' standing, and would probably be unwilling to take on another, and Lynn, for that matter, had not had sufficient training. Tom then? But Tom couldn't hope for more money elsewhere than he was getting now. These things went through Sarah's mind as she and Lynn went upstairs, in a sort of vain search for some alleviation, some comfort, although she knew in her heart that to help Lynn out of her present difficulty would be against her own judgment.

Lynn worked late at the office that day. Returning, Jennie greeted her, "Shopping for the little old trousseau? Better let me help," offered Jennie generously, and sang a snatch of an old song, " 'I can get 'em for you wholesale.' "

"You needn't bother. I don't think we're going to be married."

Lynn pushed her small hat even farther off her forehead and sat down limply in the one big chair. "What?" asked Jennie, rising from the couch. "Haven't had a row, have you? What about? Margaret Sanger or the family budget?"

"No," Lynn smiled faintly. It was impossible to resist Jennie in her idiotic moods. "Sarah just told me they are letting the married women out, that's all. But it's enough to keep *me* single."

"Well, the dirty bums!" exclaimed Jennie sincerely. "You poor kid — all keyed up to the blushing bride act and now — bang, once more a spinster! Gee, I'm sorry,

Lynn. Couldn't you get another job?"

"I've thought of that. But it's too risky, Jennie," Lynn answered slowly. "You know people aren't getting hired by the carload. There might not be a place for me in another bank; employers are letting out, not taking in. And I'm not well enough trained for anything else — I mean, I couldn't get as much money. I'd get a darned sight less, I guess."

"That's so." Jennie nodded her yellow head. "Have you told Tom?"

"No. I haven't seen him. He's coming up here tonight."

"I'll ankle out," Jennie offered.

"It's not necessary," Lynn told her wearily, wishing that she would stay. Perhaps if she stayed it would be easier to "tell Tom."

"No, but I've got a date," Jennie told her importantly, "and boy, is it hot!"

"Slim?" asked Lynn with a flicker of interest.

"Not that kind of hot. A guy named Meyer."

"Meyer?"

"That's the moniker. Look." Jennie clasped her arms about her knees and her heavy-lidded, narrow eyes shone between the thick, mascara-ed lashes. "He's the merchandise man for Meyer and Carberg, the big department store in Chicago that's giving Marshall Field a run for its money. He's a partner, see, the son of the original big shot. He comes on now and then with his buyers to look the town over and see that they don't shoot too much of his wad. He used to be a buyer himself, when he wasn't a stock boy and a ribbon clerk and a section manager or what have you.

"He came into the place this morning with Raeburn, his dress buyer, and maybe Pearline didn't step around, and Madame herself was on the job. We had some of the good fall numbers. He sat behind the table and tapped on it with a pencil till I thought I'd go goofy. He kept looking at me, see. And when the buyer was talking to Madame this Meyer gives me a buzz. He told me I could model clothes like nobody's business and wondered why I wasn't on the stage. I told him I had been, thank you, but if I waited for a show job I'd be the best-looking woman on relief. That handed him a big laugh. He says, 'How would you like to show me the town tonight, Miss Le Grande?' and I said, 'Swell with me.' He's coming for me, in a car," Jennie concluded.

"I thought," said Lynn, troubled, "that you girls didn't go out with the buyers."

"We do and we don't. If we want to and like 'em, we do. Why not, you only live once? We don't have to, if that's what you mean. He isn't a buyer anyway; he's just about the whole works. I asked Madame about him afterwards."

"What does he look like?" Lynn wanted to know, quite normally.

"He's not as tall as I am," Jennie said regretfully, "but he's something of a swell dresser. Dark, little mustache, smokes gold-tipped cigarettes, has a platinum watch and doesn't wear rings!"

"Single?"

"I didn't ask, but of course not. He must be about forty-five. No one with his speed and his money is going to get to forty-five without being grabbed off by some little girl trying to get along. But that's no skin off my nose. Good Lord, I'll have to get busy! I want to set my hair — had it done day before yesterday in my lunch hour and my hair's as straight as a string, already!"

She departed for the bedroom, whistling.

Lynn rose after a time and took her outdoor things off. She'd get herself a glass of milk and some crackers, and then wait for Tom.

Wait for Tom? She knew that as far as loving him went she would wait an eternity. But that didn't promise that you'd be happy or content — waiting.

He came early, and she knew by the sound of his step on the stair that he was coming to her, happy, eager, full of their plans.

How should she tell him?

She did so quite simply, and to her unexpectedly, by bursting into tears when he walked in the open door, by running to his arms and burying her head on his shoulder to his dismay and astonishment.

"Hey, what's up?" he asked, concerned. "Here, easy does it. Lynn — darling — what is it? Not — not bad news from home?"

"No." She controlled herself a little; told him.

There was a silence. After a moment he said heavily, "Well, that tears it. I couldn't ask you to —"

She said, after a pause, "Tom, it isn't that I'm so selfish that I wouldn't be willing to live on your salary. But things — cost so much. We couldn't save. You'd be tied down and nervous and worried all the time; you'd never get ahead in the circumstances. You know that."

"If — Oh, you're right," he told her gloomily. He swore fluently for several seconds; said gruffly, "Sorry — but —"

After a moment she suggested hesitantly, "I could try — for another job."

"Sure, you could," he agreed, radiant. "If you could do that — get a job where they didn't have these dumb ideas about married women. Gee, that would be great! I *can't* give up hoping," he told her, low.

"Nor I —"

She forgot in his arms how risky it was to look for the jobs that seemed to be, nowadays, practically nonexistent; and how she had set her heart against the sort of position in which she would not be happy, to which she had not been trained; let, for this moment at least, ambition go by the board; a job, *any* job, that would enable them to live, and live together.

Two weeks went by. A Saturday came, and Jennie asked, crumpling a yellow telegraph blank in her long hand, "Lynn, you look rotten. What have you been doing to yourself?"

"Nothing. Trying to work and look for another job at the same time."

"Have you asked David Dwight to help you?" Jennie wanted to know. She unfolded the telegram again. Mr. Meyer of Meyer and Carberg would be in town over Sunday. Would Jennie dine with him?

Would she? She hadn't had as good a dinner as the first one he'd given her since she was born.

"I hadn't thought of him. Do you suppose he would? Oh no," said Lynn, "I don't like to ask him."

"Don't be a sap. He'll find something for you to do," prophesied Jennie carelessly.

"Is that wire from the Chicago boy friend?"

"It is." Jennie chuckled. Upon the first occasion she had gone out with Meyer to dinner, show, and supper, she had come home to tell Lynn all about it — the food, the liquor, the seats, the service, the favors. "Some spender. Married — but a widower. How's that for a break?"

"Jennie, you wouldn't marry him," Lynn had gasped.

"Why not? Do you think I want to model the rest of my life? Not that I could. I'd end up scrubbing offices. Not me."

"But you wouldn't have to marry —"

"Meyer? Well, no, and won't get a chance, more's the pity, I suppose. There are other men, of course. Poor men — and I'd go on working. Or I'd end in a walk-up doing diapers. Not this baby. When I marry, if I do, there has to be money and a wad of it," Jennie had announced.

There was no arguing with her. Lynn saw Jennie toss the telegraph blank into the waste basket. Then she forgot it. Odd that she had not thought of David Dwight. He had said — what had he said? That he was her friend; that she could count on him. And she had believed him. She had seen him once since the night of the party, one night when he had taken her to dinner and a play. She and Tom had had words about it. Then he had gone away on business — to Washington, she remembered.

She had told him nothing of her present preoccupation.

If he were back now!

She telephoned him at the penthouse that night while Jennie was dressing for her engagement. And he was in.

"Lynn?" his vibrant voice came over the wire. "My dear, how very sweet of you to call me. I'm just back."

She said hesitantly, "I didn't know — There is something about which I want to ask your advice. I thought perhaps if I could see you — next week? I could come to your office."

His offices were uptown, in an ivory tower, the builders of which had dedicated themselves to making America castor-oil and talcum-powder conscious.

"But of course. Shall we say Monday? After your work is over? I'll wait for you — and will you dine with me afterward?"

She hung up presently. Jennie, listening, poked her head in at the door between living-room and bedroom.

"You're going to see him."

"Monday."

"What did I tell you?" And Jennie, now attired, danced out to her duty, which was to make merry on a merchandising man's Saturday night off.

Chapter Ten:

TWO TROUBLED GIRLS

Dwight was very understanding. His face, like an actor's in that it lent itself readily to illusion, if without the camouflage of grease paint, was perfectly impassive as Lynn stumbled her way through her explanation. At intervals he said, "I see," and fingered an astonishingly small, round, gold clock that stood upon the neat and polished vastness of his desk.

It was the first time Lynn had been in his office. He was housed halfway up the great pyramidal height of the uptown business building. Save for the desk there was little of the office about his private room; it was more like a library, and into that atmosphere the desk fitted unobtrusively. There were paneled walls and built-in bookcases, but there was nothing somber about the draperies or the fine oriental carpet on the floor, nothing massively oppressive about the chairs, the occasional furniture. Frankly, a modernistic bar presided with charm over the working-quarters of a man at law. Within the desk itself a humidor had been built. Lynn watched him open the compartment and select a cigar. There were no photographs in the room, but over the fireplace, in which green boughs had been heaped in deference to the season, there was a portrait — not of a woman, curiously enough, but of the little son whom David Dwight and his wife had lost during the first years of their marriage.

There were flowers in the room, very gay and fragrant. "From my place on the Island," he had told her, when upon entering, she had exclaimed over their beauty, sparring a little for time.

His office force, save for his personal secretary, an elderly, narrow-lipped, dour-faced woman, had all gone home by the time Lynn arrived, directly from the bank, having hurried the few intervening blocks through the hot late afternoon, wishing somehow that she had not made this appointment.

But Dwight's reception of her had dispelled her formless doubts. Now she sat smiling at him faintly, from the depths of an armchair, and waiting to hear him speak.

If he had sustained a blow she could not

know it. He said gently, "I appreciate your situation. I could of course give you letters — a lot of letters. I know so many people, I have a finger in several pies. But as our Sarah has probably told you, as you doubtless know yourself, most concerns are cutting down their staffs. I can, as it happens," he went on, "offer you a job — a rather anomalous job — and with myself."

She demurred hurriedly, flushing. "Please — I didn't mean that — I — why, what," she asked in open astonishment, "what on earth could you find for me to do? I" — she thrust up her little chin — "I can keep on at the bank perfectly well," she said.

"Not so fast. You haven't had, I suppose, any secretarial training?"

"None. Just typing."

"I thought so. That's what I should be willing to offer you. You see, I'm writing a book." He smiled a very little. "I know it's a confession of weakness and I have no intention of publishing it now. It might be better, all around, if it were published posthumously. But I need someone whom I can trust to get my notes into shape, to do the first rough typing and eventually the revisions on this egoistical and naturally autobiographical expression of myself. I had thought of giving it to Miss Mays — my secretary — but she has enough to do as it is. Moreover, I have other things that a home secretary could do for me and which would not involve dictation as much as, say, bookkeeping, tact, and the ability to use the English language on one's own initiative. I should require you to work at the apartment, and perhaps on Long Island — not here at the office. And I would pay you what the bank now pays you, and a little more."

She asked, aghast, "But are you very sure — I mean, it doesn't," she added, with a flash of shrewdness, "seem reasonable!"

"It isn't unreasonable, is it?" he asked her, laughing.

She said after a moment, "If I accept it means —"

"Marriage?"

She nodded her dark head unsmilingly.

He said gravely, "I'm afraid I can't approve any more than Sarah does of that. But if your mind is made up —" He gestured briefly and then smiled at her again. "And I deplore the fact that by marrying, you will give up something of a career. Mind, I don't offer you that with me. There's no future in turning amanuensis to an egoistical lawyer, you know, but it would perhaps tide you over this time of depression and then, later, when business picks up and banks begin to take on bigger staffs there would doubtless be a place for you somewhere."

She said brokenly, "I can't thank you —"

"Don't try. Is it a bargain?"

She nodded. "As far as I am concerned. But I'd have to stay at the bank a while longer until one of the girls in my department could be trained to take my place," she answered.

"I understand that perfectly." He rose. "Come, the car's outside. Let's forget business for a time and take a drive through the park and perhaps up to the Clairmont for dinner."

It was a pleasant drive, a pleasanter dinner. Dwight was his wittiest self, he talked incessantly, almost nervously, always entertainingly. It was still quite early when he left her at the door of the apartment. She thanked him, saying good night, and as she did so, he held her hand a moment.

"May I be very banal?"

"You couldn't be," she assured him.

"Thanks, that's sweet of you. I wonder if Mr. Thomas Shepard knows how infernally lucky he is?" he concluded.

Lynn drew her hand away. "I hope so," she answered gaily. "I hope that he knows it and that he *is*."

Dwight watched her enter the clumsy door, stood there a moment, bareheaded on the pavement, climbed back into his car again and gave an address; not that of his apartment. As the car slid away through the night, he pondered on himself, ironically amazed.

Now, what exactly had he done? Offered to take the girl on for work which was practically nonexistent. He'd have to make an attempt to get the scattered notes of some of his big cases together. Of course, he'd planned to do a startling book at some future date — very future. In addition he was committing himself to a new obligation, an expenditure which he couldn't afford. He was up to his ears in debt.

Yet his cursed vanity had been unable to permit him to let Lynn down. Moreover he had offered Lynn Harding a situation in order that she might be in a position to marry that awkward young cub, Shepard, who was not yet dry behind the ears! Of all the sublime idiocies! Had he not offered her the job, she probably would have postponed her marriage indefinitely and almost anything might happen during that time. Married, she was lost to him. Yet was she, working with him, not in the allegedly impersonal surroundings of an office, but in his home? Married, once the first glamor had passed, she was, according to his own curious code, perfectly legitimate quarry.

He wondered if Shepard would make any objection, but dismissed him from his mind as negligible. Any man in his right senses would object, but a young man in love, and ardently desiring marriage, is not in his right senses. Yet one person there was of whom in his heart David Dwight was a little afraid. And that was Sarah Dennet. Well, he could manage Sarah, couldn't he; hadn't he proved that?

Lynn, running upstairs, burst into her apartment and was utterly astonished to find Tom sitting there glumly and alone, crushing cigarettes into an ash tray. At least from the appearance of the ash tray that was what he had been doing for some time past.

"Tom — how did you get in? Where's Jennie? I thought you were going to be busy this evening," she exclaimed, staring at him.

"Jennie let me in; she went out directly afterward. I did have a date — but Rawlson came down from UBC just before closing to tell me it was all off. I looked for you, but you'd gone," he accused her.

"I know; I left a little early. Oh," she said, "I'm sorry. Have you had any dinner?"

"With Rawlson," he answered.

"Oh!"

Lynn was silent. She didn't like Rawlson, who was one of the salesmen that came to her desk daily for the little blue cards. He was a slim, smooth, rather nervous young man, who, it was rumored, had "inherited money" and "didn't really have to work." Latterly, he and Tom had struck up something of a friendship.

"And where have *you* been?" he shot out at her.

She hadn't told him of her engagement with Dwight. If nothing came of it what would have been the use? Now that something had come of it all the laughter and excitement and satisfaction had gone. Tom's dejection was like something tangible in the room; it smothered and oppressed.

"I had an appointment with David Dwight; afterward, he took me to the Clairmont for dinner," she told him, and to her own bewilderment was unable to keep from her voice a note of pure defiance.

"Is — that — so — ?" Tom asked, spacing his words, "Isn't that *lovely?*"

"What's wrong about it?" she wanted to know.

Tom glared at her.

"Everything. I won't have you going out with him," he responded unamiably. "Damit, you're engaged to be married to *me*. I don't get any pleasure going out with other girls — and I don't go out with them, what's more! And I wouldn't get a kick out of smirking over a dinner table at a woman twice my age!"

"Tom!"

"Well, I wouldn't," he said doggedly. "I don't want to be with anyone but you. *I* can't trot you around in a limousine and throw penthouse parties and take you to expensive restaurants and send you gardenias and all the rest of it. But you knew that, right from the beginning. I *won't* have you going around with Dwight," he said again. "He's a damned-sight too interested in you."

"He's not!" Even as she said it she had misgivings. Absurd, couldn't a man be decent to a girl, offer her friendship, without premising a personal motive? "And I'm not interested in him."

"Then why do you make dates with him?"

"Well, if you must know," she flung at him, "I went up there to see if he could help me to get a job. So that I could work; so that we could be married. I think — I think you have a rotten mind!" she ended childishly.

"Look here, Lynn." He rose now and walked over to where she was standing, her small shallow hat perched on the back of her head, her clear dark skin flushed with anger. "Look here, I didn't mean that. But it hurts me like the devil to see you so friendly with Dwight — and, moreover, I don't think you should be, aside from me. He hasn't the best reputation in the world. He couldn't be *any* woman's friend," said Tom.

"Well, he can be! He's mine!" she cried. "He's offered me a job as his secretary."

"What!" Tom stood perfectly still, head lowered and thrust forward, his hair wildly disordered and his very blue eyes hot with suspicion. "Secretary! That's a good one!" He laughed, without merriment. "That's swell! He's got along without a secretary all these years, I suppose, and has just decided to take one with no secretarial experience, is that it?"

Lynn said, paler now, "You needn't waste the heavy sarcasm on me, Tom. Of course he has a secretary — several of them, for all I know. This is different."

"I'll bet my life, it is," Tom agreed darkly.

"It's to type his notes for a book he is doing, and other personal work," Lynn said, infuriated.

"Can't he get that done in the office?"

"He doesn't want it done in his office. He wants it done at home."

"That's practical of him," said Tom admiringly. "What are your working hours to be — ten p.m. to six a.m.?"

Suddenly, she was transformed into a small and flaming harridan. Years of training in social repression dropped from her; she was a child of the back yard, fighting furiously with the neighbor's brat, sick with disappointment, beside herself with anger.

"You shut up, Tom Shepard! How dare you say such a thing to me?" she raged. "You get out of here! I never want to see you again!"

Anger broke her voice and set her whole body trembling. It had, however, a wholesome effect upon Tom. Anger such as hers, argued a pristine innocence — or at least, to him. He advanced upon her and took her into his arms. She fought him like a cat, left the marks of her nails on his astonished face. He dropped her quickly.

"You little devil —" was his natural response.

He nursed the scratch, applying a rather grimy handkerchief. Lynn cast herself on the couch, reaction setting in. Sobs shook her. Standing there, the handkerchief to his face, he heard her say, through the storm:

"Just because I was afraid — of losing my job — if we got married — and he was decent enough to give me one — so that we could be —"

But Tom's impulse toward reconciliation had passed. He said coolly, "You needn't accept Dwight's offer in order to marry me. Because if you do, I won't marry you, see?"

She sat up on the couch. "Tom, do you mean that?"

"I mean it. I didn't want you to work after we got married. Then I gave in. You know why; or if you don't you're a damned sight dumber than I thought you were," said her lover baldly. "You know why right enough. But if you think I'm going to marry you on Dwight's charity you have another guess coming. Not me. It would be bad enough to have you working in the bank; but I'd be there, at least. But to have you working for him — in his house — under his eyes — within reach of his hand — You may think I'm crazy; perhaps I am — crazy about you anyway — but I'm not as crazy as that. Or too crazy. I don't care *what* you think!"

He put the handkerchief in his pocket.

She said, all the anger gone, "Oh, Tom, I'm so *unhappy.*"

That reached him. He went over and dropped to his knees beside her, and put his arms about her.

"I'm sorry I said what I did, honey," he told her. "You know I didn't mean it. I was sore, that's all."

She touched the scratch with her fingers, put her lips to it gently.

"I'm sorry too." She laughed shakily. "I didn't know I had such a temper. Why, if my own mother had seen me, she'd have spanked me and put me to bed —"

"I could do that," he told her confidently.

"No, don't — But, Tom, what shall we do? Oh," she told him hopelessly, "I didn't see any other way out. I was so happy, planning; and then Sarah knocked that house of cards to smithereens. And so I figured if I could get another job — and you agreed with me. And then I thought of Dwight — no, Jennie thought of him —"

"She would," commented Tom grimly.

"And I went there; and he was so nice, so awfully nice; and I thought, *It's the solution, I'm sure it is* —

"But it wasn't," she added, after a minute.

"I suppose you think I'm a fool?" he proffered.

"Yes, I do."

"Thanks — a lot."

"But a dear fool. Oh, Tom, why are you so stubborn? Why will you look at things this way?"

"Suppose I look at them another way. Suppose you're right, and there's nothing in the back of Dwight's bean except a nice friendly feeling and a desire to help us both and a real need for someone to type this book or encyclopedia or whatever it is — Well, when it's done, then what? You have always been so keen on a future. Where's a future there?" he argued, against his usual convictions.

"None. He told me that, too. But he said when business picked up I could go back into the type of work I had been doing."

"I see. He expects you to work all your life? Well, I don't."

"But I want to."

They were back where they started months ago. Tom sighed heavily and kissed her. He said, after a moment, "There'll be a way out. You see. I'll make a killing, somehow. Rob the bank! Start with a hundred in Wall Street and run it up to a hundred grand — not, however, in this market. I'll help an aged man across traffic and he'll leave me a million —"

"Oh, Tom —" She was laughing again. This was the Tom she knew best, boyish, absurd, young, *darling* —

"No, but seriously, I'll find a way. Rawlson was talking to me tonight. He says there are lots of ways —"

"What did he mean?"

"Never mind now," Tom told her solemnly. He held her close, kissed her. "You'll tell Dwight, 'Thank you kindly, wealthy sir, I don't want your job'?"

"Yes — it doesn't make sense any more," she told him mournfully.

"You bet it doesn't. Hello, here's Jennie."

Jennie came in, scattering her outdoor garments about and greeted them imperturbably.

"Hello, turtle doves."

"Where have you been?" asked Lynn.

"Didn't Tom tell you? I told him to. It's Mara. She phoned here in a fit or something. Wanted you," explained Jennie, walking around the room in search of a cigarette, "but as you weren't handy, I had to do. So I went up there, like a fool. Found the flat had been torn to pieces. It seems that her darling Bill has been feeling neglected of late. Missed his little wife. So he picks up with some synthetic blonde who runs a beauty shop in the neighborhood. Mara found out, and they had what the books call words. Words and music. And then he sprung it on her that he had known for weeks she's been seeing Frank Houghton, and the battle was on again. You never heard anything like it, the echoes of it, I mean. He wasn't there when I arrived. Gone to the beauty parlor for a facial, I guess. She is leaving him. He is leaving her. I don't know who's leaving who. Anyway, it's a hell of a mess. I gave her two aspirins and some spirits of ammonia before I left. She was going to sit up for Bill. No, thank you, said I, and cleared out — Marriage," reported Jennie, who had found her cigarette and was surrounding herself in smoke, "marriage is the bunk; I don't care what you two think. Marriage, unless it means a bank account and no questions asked, is a flop. I've seen plenty, and tonight was the pay-off."

"Oh, poor Mara," said Lynn, distressed.

"Poor, my eye! She's a fool. Where will this Frank Houghton business get her anyway? Houghton's got a wife and kids and a job that depends on his uncle, and if he has money in the bank it's just rainy-day savings; the first good thunderstorm will melt it. She thought she had to choose between losing her job or making a play for Frank; I got that much out of her. Wait till Frank has to choose between his job and her," prophesied Jennie, and ambled into the bedroom. "Marriage!" she said, disappearing.

"Gee!" remarked Tom in the silence which followed.

"I ought to go see Mara — call her up or something," said Lynn, worried.

"Keep out of it," he warned her, "and you'll be better off. I'll go now, Lynn; you look pretty tired." He added awkwardly, "I'm sorry as the devil that — that I can't see things the way you do."

"It doesn't matter." It did matter. "Perhaps you're right," she said faintly. She kissed him. "We'll have to wait," she said, and clung to him a moment — "We do love each other, don't we?"

"We do." It was like a vow, the way he said it. He bent his tall head to hers once more and kissed her sorrowful red mouth. "Go to bed, honey, see you tomorrow," he said gently.

When the door closed Lynn picked up her things and went wearily into the bedroom.

"About Mara — Should I go up there now, Jennie, and see what I can do?"

Jennie, creaming her face at the mirror, turned.

"Well, no! Are you out of your mind? There's nothing we can do for her except give her a bed if Bill kicks her out."

"He can't do that," Lynn reminded her. "She pays the rent."

"Well, maybe he can't. We'll see. Did you see Dwight? What did he have to offer?"

"He offered me a job with him. I'm not," said Lynn, over Jennie's exclamation, "going to take it."

"Well, I'll be a vestal virgin!" gasped Jennie. "Not going to take it? See here, does that mean you — or Tom?" she asked shrewdly.

"Tom, I suppose. He has — ideas. I

know he's mad, but what can I do about it?" asked Lynn, sitting on the edge of the bed. "He says that he won't marry me if I do take it — and as all I was taking it for was to get married — there isn't much use, is there?"

"*Men!*" said Jennie.

That night before she went to bed, Lynn got out her best monogrammed paper and wrote to Dwight. It was an awkward letter, without life or color. How could she tell him the truth? It sounded so conceited, on her part — so childish, on Tom's; she would never be able to meet David Dwight frankly again if she told him. She wrote that, after thinking it over, she had decided Sarah was right: it was better to stay where she was and also not to incur the possibility of dismissal by marrying immediately. She had talked it over with Tom, and he had agreed. After all, her position was excellent in the Seacoast Company; she had a chance of a future there — It had been so kind of Mr. Dwight, she appreciated it, etc., etc.

She mailed it on her way to work. It reached Dwight that evening, was waiting for him when he came into the penthouse. He read it twice, swore once, and then laughed.

Young Shepard, of course. Had more guts than he had given him credit for. All for the best, he supposed. He hadn't, Dwight hadn't, let her down; he had made good his offer of friendship. And things were as they had been; she wouldn't marry the youngster for heaven knew how long; and in the meantime perhaps she would change her mind. Women do. Yes, possibly all for the best, he thought, and wrote her a brief note regretting her decision but abiding by it, gracefully, and concluding with the wish that before the summer was over she would spend a week-end on Long Island as his guest. He would ask Sarah too.

For three days Lynn looked for Mara in the rest room, and did not find her. She disliked going to the insurance office, and tried several times, evenings, to ring up the flat. Twice there had been no answer; once a strange woman had answered and had hung up immediately; and the fourth time Bill had answered and had announced heatedly that Mara wasn't there — he didn't know where she was. On the third night Mara arrived with a suitcase.

Jennie and Lynn were at home. Tom was out with young Rawlson again, and Jennie for some reason seemed lately to have a scarcity of engagements save when Meyer from Chicago was in town. Mara came in, her red hair flaming under her hat, her face ashen under the rouge.

"I've left him," she announced, "for good!"

"Mara — !" Lynn sprang to her feet. "Here, let me take your things — and your bag — You can't mean it."

"I do mean it." Mara sat down on the edge of a chair.

Jennie, standing hand on hip, watched her and said nothing — eloquently. "I went home this afternoon — a little early. That woman was there — not for the first time, I suppose."

"What did you do?"

"I told her something. She left pretty quick. I told Bill he could leave, too. He said he wouldn't, the place suited him. I said I'd paid for it. He said the lease was in his name. If I wanted to go, I could; he'd stay on till the end of the month. I said I'd divorce him. He told me, go ahead — but on what? And that he had as much on me as I had on him —"

"Don't cry," said Lynn, after a moment. "What are you going to do?"

"May I stay here? I can pay my share. I won't," she said viciously, "have Bill to support —"

"Of course you must stay here till you find a place," Lynn told her, "that is, if Jennie doesn't mind."

"I don't mind," said Jennie, yawning, "I've a double bed. You can sleep in it if you want to — provided you don't snore or kick."

"Bill's a beast!" was Mara's only expression of gratitude. "Going around with that cheap woman behind my back!"

Jennie asked gravely, "Sure it was all his fault? You hadn't paid much attention to him lately."

"If you mean Frank," Mara said, flaring up, "there isn't anything to it — Bill hasn't any *right* — Frank's lonesome, that's all. So was I. Sick and tired of going home at night to a grouch. Nothing was ever right; I couldn't do anything to please him. Bill, I mean. Besides," she added, "Frank's got a drag. Nowadays, you need all the drag you can get. Well, why shouldn't I stay on the right side of someone who has influence?"

"You're riding for a fall," was all Jennie had to offer.

Later, when Mara was running water in the tub and making herself at home generally, Lynn had a word alone with Jennie.

"Look here," said Lynn, "this is a mess, isn't it? It isn't fair to you to have Mara

214

here. Of course we can put up some kind of a cot in the living-room, if she stays on — but it's putting you out, and you don't even like her very much."

"I don't mind," repeated Jennie. "No, I don't like her particularly. She's neither one thing nor the other."

"What do you mean?"

"Well, she isn't good or bad. Not that I think anyone is either, one hundred per-cent, but that's the nearest I can get to it. I don't blame Bill much. He must have felt pretty rotten, having her bring home the bacon and slice him his share, with re-minders. Then after a while I suppose he got used to it. But they've led a cat-and-dog life for months, as far as I can see. So I figure he turned around and made passes at someone who told him how wonderful he was and what a success he was going to be. Mara never told him that. All she did was tell him he was a failure. So he is, per-haps; but maybe it's partly her fault. Then, as to this Frank business — that's her own affair. Only the point is, it isn't an affair. She hasn't the nerve. You'd have to respect her if she had —"

"You don't really mean that, Jennie, do you?"

"Sure, I mean it. Personally I'd respect

her more if she was paying for whatever influence this bird may have, instead of taking it and giving him a lot of hope that doesn't mean a damn. I like to pay on the nail," Jennie explained, "if I get anything worth-while. So far I've only got dinners and shows and perfume and flowers and stockings. Well, I pay for those with my bright and cheery company — it isn't worth any more in the open market, see?"

Lynn laughed. "You're the limit," she said affectionately.

"I saw Millie Haines on the street today," Jennie told her irrelevantly. "She used to work with me for Canton and Stein, the wholesale coat-and-suit house. She darned near ran over me, driving a big sports Packard. She still works for Canton and Stein and she gets forty a week."

She shrugged.

"And I'm not mentioning some of the show girls I used to pal with; they still ankle across a stage, they still have an Equity card, and their penthouses would make your lawyer boy friend's look like a bird cage! Well, I wonder," said Jennie, "whether it pays to be a virgin!"

Mara came out just then, wrapped in a silk robe.

"You're peaches to take me in like this,"

she said, fully recovered, her small round face flushed and smiling.

"Just as long as no one else takes you in," said Jennie.

"I'll look for a room," Mara promised.

"Don't bother," Jennie said; she added, and for the first time during their acquaintance Lynn beheld her embarrassed, a little ill at ease, "I may not be here long — I've plans — I haven't," she added, "made up my mind yet."

"Jennie!" Lynn stared at her.

Jennie waved a lax hand in her direction.

"Don't get all hot and bothered," she advised carelessly. "I don't know yet. I'm working on a prospect."

"A job?" asked Mara, not very interested.

"I'll say so," Jennie agreed. "How about a glass of milk and some crackers or some beer? I'm starved," she added, casting one oblique look at Lynn's worried face.

She went into the kitchen, and Lynn started to follow. But the telephone shrilled loudly on the table near her elbow. Mara gasped and shrank back into her chair.

"It may be Bill. Tell him I'm not here. Tell him you haven't seen me. No, tell him I'm here and I'll stay here," she ordered uncertainly as Lynn turned toward the instrument.

It was not Bill. It was Tom.

"Lynn? Did I get you out of bed? Look here, I've got swell news. Pick out your site in Westchester and hire yourself an architect. We're going to be rich!"

"Tom, you're tight," said Lynn severely.

"Not very. I can't tell you over the phone. Meet me at the old crasheteria for breakfast — We'll have chops, on me."

"But, Tom —"

"I tell you, I can't talk more now. But all our worries are over," he told her triumphantly, "and I love you like nobody's business."

Chapter Eleven:

MARA'S WAY OUT

On the following morning, Mara's presence having complicated matters, Lynn arrived breathless, late for her cafeteria appointment with Tom. She had wasted time in argument, standing at the door of the apartment while Mara, a cup of coffee in her hand, inveighed against Bill.

"A girl who marries and goes on working is a fool; and a man who agrees to the arrangement is a worse one," she said. "I'm warning you!"

"But," Lynn had argued, "if a woman's job means a lot to her, if she feels she can work it up into something big, absorbing, why shouldn't she go on with it? On a fifty-fifty basis, a partnership. Marriage ought to be that way!"

"Try and do it!" said Mara.

Tom, waiting, watching the clock, reproached Lynn at her entrance. She ordered coffee and rolls, smiling at him, "Tom, I'm so sorry —"

"You'd better be!" He squeezed her arm in his big hand. "Woman, you ain't heard nothing yet!"

"But I want to hear —"

"No time now — I'll see you tonight. Jennie going to be out?"

"I don't know. Mara's there, Tom; she's left Bill," Lynn said dramatically.

"Well, I'll be a son of a gun!" But he wasn't very interested. "Get rid of the audience," he advised her, "and I'll spill the news."

She drank her coffee hastily. "Tom, we'll be so late!" She watched him pay their check ("This time it's on me," he said), and walked with him through the cafeteria. "Can't you tell me anything?" she begged.

"Just that I've a swell chance, that's all. We'll be on Easy Street yet," he told her.

That he had been working on an experiment in radio, she knew. She guessed, radiant, "Someone in UBC is interested in —"

"No," he interrupted. His face was grave. "It's not that, though old Hank has promised to get me a hearing. This is different. Big Business." He laughed down at her, left her at her own door.

Shortly before closing time Sarah came

into Lynn's office and stood by her desk a moment.

Lynn rose, smiling.

"No, sit down. I've been talking to David," said Sarah. "He wants us to come down for the week-end. Saturday afternoon. Can you go? He'll have a car for us."

Lynn said instantly, joyously, "I'd love it." Then she sobered. Tom would object, she realized with a sinking of her heart. She added more quietly, "I'd like to, a lot — but — must he know right away?"

"No, tomorrow will do," Sarah answered, and left the room, with her easy, rather striding step. Lynn stared after her. It would be heavenly to spend a week-end in the country somewhere. But there was Tom. *Why should he object?* she asked herself angrily, unseeing eyes on the blue cards strewn on the desk. It was idiotic of him to be so sensitive where Dwight was concerned.

She resolved to say nothing until she had heard his news, whatever it was. She racked her brains for the remainder of the day, trying to discover some clue to his excitement and confidence, but could find none. That night he explained.

Jennie was out. Mara was out. They had the little place to themselves. Tom talked, pacing the floor, words hurtling over one another. Lynn sat there, her hands clasped, listening.

It was very simple. The Seacoast Bank and Trust Company was planning a merger with one of the biggest banks in the world; if the merger went through, and it had every likelihood of so doing, the result would be the biggest bank in the world, without doubt or rival. Tom had learned of the impending deal through certain channels open to him, correspondence, for instance, and overhearing here a word, and there another. "All very secret," Gunboat had warned him. The directors' meeting would decide it, Tom supposed, but that wouldn't be for some time. Somehow, Bob Rawlson had got wind of the thing, too.

The Seacoast Company stock was at the moment at its very lowest, due to the general downward trend of bank stocks. This merger would send it sky-high. The trick was to buy as much as one could, in small lots, here and there, without arousing any curiosity or speculation, and hang on until the big news got out. Of course, Tom didn't have much — but he'd borrow, mortgage his future; there were ways and means; he could borrow upon the principal of the small legacy which would come to him eventually, and Bob was going to borrow all he could too; they'd pool their interests. It meant, by autumn, perhaps, a big profit. What did Lynn think of it? he asked exultantly.

She replied slowly, "I think it's dishonest."

"*What?*" He stopped, mid-stride. "You're crazy!"

"No, I'm not. You've learned this — you couldn't help learning it, in your position — and it's supposed to be secret. Like a trust almost. You've talked it over with Bob Rawlson. With me. Little by little it will get out, reach the ears of the market manipulators. You've no right to cash in on your knowledge even in a small way," she told him. "It isn't honest; and it isn't loyal."

"But it is honest," Tom expostulated, "and as to loyalty —"

"How is it honest?" she demanded.

"It's perfectly legitimate business," he protested. "You can't tell me that Gunboat and the others don't expect to realize on it."

"They are officers of the bank," she said, "and directors. That's different. You — you're just an employee. No, Tom, you've no right to do it."

"You mean to tell me I haven't any right to buy a few shares of the bank stock at the present low?" he asked her. "Why, they're always urging me to buy the stock, you know that!"

"Of course, I know it." Her chin went up. "And you're at liberty to buy the stock. The few shares you can afford to buy, outright, won't make any difference one way or another, and certainly wouldn't put you or anyone else on Easy Street, no matter how high the stock goes after the merger. But you're planning something else — you know you are. What is it?"

He said sullenly, "Rawlson thinks that if we get to the right people we can borrow all we want to —"

"You mean," she said quickly, "you can sell your information. And you consider *that* loyal, I suppose — and honest!"

"Well, why not?"

She got to her feet. She was small and defiant, facing him. She said, "If you do this, I will never speak to you again!"

He said, "But, Lynn —" He tossed his hands out in front of him in a gesture of hopelessness. "But I was going to do it — for you. So that we could get married, so that we needn't wait."

"I was willing to wait," she told him

hotly. "I care enough for you for that. But I won't marry you on the proceeds of any breach of loyalty to the bank."

"I don't owe the bank a damned thing," he said stubbornly. "What has it ever done for me?"

"It's given you a decent job," she told him, "and kept a roof over your head and fed and clothed you. I don't care what a person's job is, if it does that it deserves loyalty. Mr. Norton expects it of you. Your position with him carries with it certain obligations. Can't you see that you are bound to know a lot more than other people in the outside office? And bound to keep it — confidential? That's your job. Confidential secretary. I didn't think," she said, and her voice shook, "that you'd ever listen to or be influenced by people like — like Bob Rawlson."

"You never liked him," he accused her absurdly.

"No, I never have, and my hunch was right!"

"Oh, hell —" He sat down wearily in the nearest chair, leaving her standing. Conscious of her tension, she forced herself to move about, emptying ash trays, straightening blinds, doing the trivial and unnecessary things women do when they feel they have reached a crisis.

He said gloomily, "Gee, Lynn, I never thought you'd look at it in this way. I just said yes to Bob because it looked all right to me. It *is* all right," he argued suddenly, with returning confidence. "That's the way fortunes are made. It's perfectly legitimate, Lynn; can't you see it that way?"

"No," she told him stubbornly, "I can't and never shall. You haven't any right to use this information to further your own ends; and if you go into whatever scheme Bob Rawlson has cooked up, you'll find yourself in a lot deeper than you bargained for. The few shares you two could buy on your own, that would be nothing. He's got more than that up his sleeve and you know it."

"It didn't," confessed Tom very naively, "sound that way when he talked about it. Look here, do you mean what you said? I mean, that you wouldn't speak to me again if —"

"I meant it," she said unhappily.

"All right —" He rose, hands sunk in pockets.

"Tom!" She ran to him, put her arms around him, looked up into his gloomy young face, "Tom, you mean that, too. That you won't —"

"I suppose so. Lord, I hate to let Bob down," Tom said, squirming inwardly at the thought. "What a piker he'll take me for!"

He cares, thought Lynn furiously, *more for what that shifty-eyed person thinks than what I think.*

He didn't, of course. What she didn't realize was the curious twist of something called masculine pride, looking back to those talks with Rawlson, over dinner tables, planning, arguing, excited, not alone by the barely passable liquor they consumed, but by their gilt-edged plans. What she didn't realize was that, at 23, the word *piker* is an unpleasant one — and relates pretty closely to the *cowardly custard* of little boyhood. At 23 no man wishes to be accused of women's apron strings binding him to a promise of caution; at 23 every man is secretly a soldier, a pirate, a highwayman — gallant and dashing and very gay. And talk of honesty and loyalty, putting so different a complexion upon high and thrilling deeds, is to say the least sobering and depressing.

There was something, Tom reflected glumly, of the schoolteacher in Lynn.

But that was an authentic disloyalty. Here, here she was in his arms, very small and sweet and warm, and, so she assured him, entirely his own. But she wasn't his own; and it was to make her so that he had planned and talked and listened, across the dingy table to Rawlson's persuasive low voice — "Chance of a lifetime, Shepard —"

Lynn detached herself without any effort from Tom's arms. She said, walking across the room and picking up a cigarette with fingers that shook, "Of course if you think more of Bob Rawlson than you do of me!"

"Don't be an idiot," was Tom's immediate return. "I — oh, I'll tell him tomorrow that I'm not having any." But his voice was without enthusiasm. He was feeling as sulky, as sacrificial, and as wounded as the small boy caught the instant before committing some household crime and haled before the explanations and warnings of the judgment seat, stubbing his toe at a rug, and thinking, *Gee, I hadn't* DONE *anything, had I?*

"That's all right then," she said. But she wasn't sure that it was all right. She searched his face anxiously, every familiar and beloved feature of it. It told her very little. She said, suddenly conscious of weariness, of a growing headache, "If — do you mind going now, Tom? I'm awfully tired. I'd like to get some sleep before the girls get in."

That was her mistake. But everything seemed so flat, so let-down between them. A good quarrel might have cleared the air. Perhaps, if she had mentioned David Dwight's week-end invitation — ? But she hadn't; nor would she. Perhaps if she had let him stay, a little longer, had turned her mind and his from the recent disagreement, from her triumph, which somehow didn't seem a triumph now? But instead, because there suddenly seemed nothing to say, she lifted her face for his kiss and heard the door close behind him, heard him go clumping down the stairs, and then for no good reason, it seemed, turned her face to the back of the shabby chair and wept.

It wasn't Tom's fault of course, she admitted, lying awake, staring into the darkness, searching in vain for the good sleep she had offered as an excuse for inhospitality. No, it wasn't his fault. He was — gullible. He was enthusiastic and impulsive and sick of grubbing along on that fatal $50 a week with no future near enough to seize and look at and rejoice in; and Rawlson was older, cleverer. Tom wasn't, she told herself, not for the first time, a

229

business man. He was perfectly at sea in graphs and dollars and cents and tickers and market reactions and "big business." He was an engineer, an inventor; his mind was wholly mechanical, constructive. She thought, *he'll never make good — in the bank*. But what else was there for him to do?

Drowsily she wondered about Mara. Where was she? and with whom?

The door bell rang violently.

Tom?

She rose, fumbled her way into robe and slippers, and went out into the living-room. She opened the door. Bill Burt stood there, glowering at her. The normal exclamation, "Why, Bill!" rose to her lips, and he brushed it away as one does an annoying trivial insect.

"Where's Mara?"

"She's out," said Lynn.

"That's nice. With whom?" asked Bill.

She thought of her own mental query. Well, she knew nothing, and was glad of it.

"I haven't the least idea," she said, and started to close the door.

But Mara's husband was a stocky and determined young man. His foot was in the door. He said grimly, "Oh, no, you don't. I'll come in — and wait — if you don't mind."

"But I do mind. I'm alone here," she told him angrily. "I'd gone to bed. You can just wait until tomorrow!"

"I don't intend waiting until tomorrow," he told her, "and you can go back to bed. It may not be conventional but it won't hurt you once. I'm not here to see you. I'm here to see Mara. I intend to know what she's going to do. I haven't heard a word from her since she walked out on me."

"Since you threw her out!" cried Lynn furiously.

"Is that what she said? Well, it doesn't make any difference."

"You —"

But he had walked in and closed the door, spun his hat on a bookcase, and sat himself down in a chair.

She had rather liked him, unhappy, sulky, complaining though he had shown himself to her. Now she disliked him very much. She said, standing there before him, dark hair ruffled about her face, "Mara was perfectly right to leave you — If you think she's going to stand for the way you treated her and —" She stopped, conscious of delicate ground.

"Oh, so she's told you about Betty?"

guessed Bill, and grinned without mirth. "Well, what did she expect?" he asked defiantly. "If a man knows he isn't wanted he goes where he is — that's all there is to it. What about Frank Houghton?" he demanded.

"I don't know what you're talking about," said Lynn, "and as long as I haven't the physical strength to put you out, I suppose you can stay. I'm going back to bed."

She did, but not to sleep, followed by Bill's careless, "Suits me." She lay there, all the drowsiness gone, wondering if there were any way she could reach Mara, warn her. Of course, she couldn't. Equally certain was it that Mara was with Houghton. Would he bring her home?

She hoped fervently that he would not.

She heard the striking of matches as Bill sat there, smoking and waiting. If only Jennie would come. Jennie could handle him. But Jennie had said that she would be very late — "You and Mara better sleep in the bedroom," Jennie had ended.

There was no way in which to reach Mara.

If only she would come home — alone.

She did not. With a sick feeling, physical as well as mental, Lynn heard her come laughing up the stairs — with Houghton. It was long after midnight. They were talking. They thought themselves so safe. Lynn rose and groped for her robe and slippers again. She wouldn't lie here like a coward, her head almost beneath the sheet, she'd stand by Mara; she had to.

The door opened. "Good night, Frank," said Mara to the man with her. "Bill!" said Mara, and screamed — not loudly but loud enough for Lynn to hear.

Bill said, "Don't get all hot and bothered. I haven't a gun. Wouldn't use it if I had. Just wanted to know where you were — and with whom. That's all. I've found out now. Thanks a lot, Houghton — I suppose you *are* Houghton — for bringing my wife home safely. You can get out now," he suggested, pleasantly.

Houghton stepped forward, heedless of Mara's frantic — "Go now — *please* go, Frank."

"I don't like your tone, Burt. I see no harm in taking your wife to dinner. I'd be grateful if you'd modulate your voice and somewhat change your attitude."

"I'd be grateful to you, if you'd get out," Bill told him, rising and advancing toward the taller, more slender man. "I want to talk to Mara; and I'd rather do it in your absence. I'm not concerned about you. If Mara wants to dine — until midnight — with a man in order to keep her little tuppenny job she can do it —"

"To keep her job?" asked Houghton, bewildered.

"Sure, that's how they all do it," Bill told him, very ugly. "Good little old S.A. Vamp the boss — or the boss's nephew — and your job's safe. And now — *will* you get out?"

"Mara —"

"Oh, please go," she cried out. "Please — don't — don't believe him, Frank —"

"You'd better believe me," said Bill. "What good would it do you not to? You're a married man, I believe. Mara's married, too, although she appears to forget it sometimes."

Lynn said, appearing suddenly, "You'd better go — Mr. Houghton."

He went, withdrawing a shocked, bewildered face. Bill growled at her, "You don't have to be in on this either, Lynn."

"I don't intend to be," she said clearly, "but — I'm right here, within call."

Bill Burt laughed. "I'm not going to beat her up," he said. "She isn't really worth the effort."

Mara was crying, in the same shabby

chair in which Lynn had wept some hours since. She was saying — "Never been so humiliated —" and other incoherencies over and over again.

Lynn went back to the bedroom. There was nothing else for her to do. But there even with the door closed she could hear.

Bill stood over his wife. He asked, "How far has this affair with Houghton gone?"

"It isn't an affair — how dare you — just because a man is decent to me!"

"I see. Well, he needn't be decent any longer. You're coming home now. I've got a job out West. It starts in two weeks. You're coming West with me."

"Why don't you ask your beauty-parlor girl friend to go?" Mara wanted to know.

"She doesn't happen to be my wife. She'd make me, I imagine, a damned-sight better wife than you've made me," said Bill, "but I married *you*."

"If you think I'm going to condone —"

"You'll have to," he told her soberly. "Granted I was unfaithful to you — what of it? There are worse things than that where a man's concerned. Granted, if you like, that you've been unfaithful to me —"

"I haven't! I haven't!"

"No, I don't suppose you have. You're not the type," he said sincerely, "to come across. That doesn't matter either. We're going to start over again, you and I, on what's left. It wasn't my fault that I lost my job —"

"Nor your fault that you didn't find another?" she demanded.

"No. Do you think I liked it, sitting home day after day, waiting for you to come and remind me you were supporting me? That's a hell of a position for a man to be in. You might have made it a little easier for me, saved my pride a little, encouraged me. But you didn't. Every day it was the same —"

"Every day *you* were the same," she accused him, "growling about this and that, complaining, ugly —"

"I had to have something left, didn't I?" he asked her oddly. "What did you want me to do, run around and wash dishes and sing, 'Goody, goody, the wife's got a job, and I can stay at home and do the housework?' What do you take me for? It wasn't any easier for me to accept what you grudgingly gave me than for you to give. If my disposition was rotten — well — perhaps it wasn't all my fault."

"What about Betty?" she demanded. "Where does she come in?"

"Nothing. Nowhere. That's over and

done with. She was — kind. That's more than you were. It's over, I tell you. She understands. And you're coming West with me."

She cried shrilly, "I'm not. I'm not. I never want to see you again. I'll divorce you —"

"Better be careful," he warned her.

"I'll divorce you," she repeated. "I can take care of myself!"

Surprisingly, he said nothing for a moment. Lynn, in the bedroom, heard him walk to the door. There she heard him pause, and his words reached her clearly.

"Think it over, Mara. You've got ten days before I have to start. You know where to reach me."

The door closed.

"Brute. Beast!" cried Mara at the wooden barrier, and cast herself upon the couch and wept noisily.

Lynn did not speak or stir. She was not so sure. She thought, *Marriage can't be like that. But it was.* She thought, *How can they go on, after the things they've said to each other? Bill said, "We'll begin over again on what's left." What* is *left? They'll get together again maybe, hating each other, underneath, if that's marriage —* She halted, frightened. *But my marriage with Tom wouldn't, it couldn't be like that,* she thought. *Oh, if I believed for a minute that Tom and I could stand shouting ugly words at each other I —*

Somehow this business of Mara and Bill, who really mattered so little to her, made her feel insecure, soiled.

A little later Mara came into the room, and shivering in the warm night air undressed and climbed into bed. Lynn, pretending to sleep, lay still, far over on her side of the mattress. Mara said, "You *are* awake, aren't you? How you could sleep through that? — You heard what he said. Before I'd go West with him I'd — I'd —"

"What?" asked Lynn practically.

"I don't know," she admitted forlornly. "Lynn, what *shall* I do?"

"Do you — love Frank Houghton?"

"Of course not," replied Mara virtuously. "I'm married!"

To her own and Mara's astonishment Lynn laughed wildly. She said, "Sorry. Go to sleep, Mara; perhaps things will be different tomorrow."

They were. For when Jennie and Lynn entered the apartment together that evening they found Mara walking the floor. As they came in she turned on them angrily, and cried out, "I've lost my job!"

"Mara! How — why — ?" asked Lynn,

concerned, while Jennie, nodding her wheaten head, inquired, "Well, what the hades did you expect?"

"How? Frank Houghton, of course!" said Mara viciously.

"Frank?"

"Naturally. Frank. Because of what Bill said last night. Because of what I said today."

"What did you say?" asked Jennie, interested.

Mara flamed out at them both. "I had lunch with him. He said — he said he couldn't risk losing his job or letting down his wife and kids, but that I could divorce Bill and take a flat somewhere and give him a key!"

Lynn murmured something, but Jennie smiled a little.

"And you didn't like him enough?" she asked gravely.

"Like him enough! As if I'd ever like any man enough!"

"I don't think you would. Neither would I," said Jennie, "but that's not saying that I wouldn't accept, if the key were gold-plated and the flat had plenty of service."

"Well," said Mara flatly in the little silence that followed, "I'm not downright immoral like you, Jennie Le Grande!"

"No? I wonder what being moral is? Being *im*moral I suppose, is only a question of what you want to pay for things," said Jennie without rancor, and vanished into the bedroom.

"I hate Frank Houghton," said Mara after a moment. "If he thinks he can do this and get away with it — I'm going down to see the boss tomorrow!"

"I wouldn't, if I were you," Lynn advised her gently.

"I shall. I won't lose my job simply because I've been decent," said Mara.

She went the next morning to the office as usual. But Frank had taken, unexpectedly, a vacation. He was not there. His uncle was, however. The door of the private office shut upon Mara.

When she came out, she was very pale. No one spoke to her as she walked through and out of the office. She rode downstairs in the swiftly falling elevator. She walked into the street, and stood there, irresolute. The shadow of the skyscraper loomed over her, cold, dark, save for the aspiring towers, which were hot with sunlight, and soared into the blue.

She went back to the apartment and packed. She called a telephone number. "Bill," she said — and her voice was soft —

"Bill — I'm coming home —"

She left a note for Jennie and Lynn. Lynn reading it, exclaimed, "How can she?"

But Jennie turned her wise blue eyes on Lynn with something of pity in them. "She had to, don't you see? What else could she do? She probably spun a tall yarn to Houghton, thinking he'd say, 'Oh, goodie, goodie, let's all get divorced and change partners!' Not that bird. He wasn't even in love with her. Just crazy about having a woman make eyes at him and tell him how grand he was. Same thing with Bill and the other heart, see? Houghton got cold feet, I guess, and maybe spilled something to his uncle. So Mara's let out. And she goes back to Bill. It's all very simple," said Jennie, yawning.

It might be simple; but it made Lynn feel sick.

Chapter Twelve:

THE PERFECT HOST

In the end Lynn went off for her week-end without telling Tom the name of her host. She had not seen him since the night at the apartment except at the office, nor spoken to him save briefly over the telephone. This intangible estrangement on his part worried her while it bewildered her. She did not know of his awkward and embarrassed explanation to Rawlson — "Sorry, old man, I've thought it over and decided not to" — nor Rawlson's hot arguments and final, shrugged, "Well, if you won't, you won't, but I think you're a fool!"

No man likes being thought a fool, and that Rawlson did think it very sincerely, that it was with him no mere figure of speech, Tom was perfectly convinced. Now that he had thought it over, perhaps Lynn was right with her hair-splitting and woman's scruples. But that didn't make it any easier for young Shepard, facing his friend. If Rawlson thought him a fool, cau-

242

tious and unwilling to risk anything in "legitimate" business, he certainly felt like one; and he could give Rawlson no adequate reason for his about-face. Couldn't, of course, bring Lynn into it. He'd stand doubly condemned; first for having talked over his business with a girl; second for permitting himself to be so influenced.

The result was natural. A grouch. Tom, unable to forget that he had been adjudged an imbecile in the eyes of another man, and, if not "dishonest" and "disloyal," at least an incompetent in the eyes of the only girl in the universe, took to rebuilding his set as a man takes to strong drink, and to drowning his loss of self-esteem in summer static. Moreover, through Hank he had come to know one of the supervising engineers at UBC, and so spent his lunch hours in the tower, sneaking into the control room, or, en route there, pausing in the wide hall to look down through the windows into the great two-storied studio where orchestras played with ease, sound, and fury, of which no note penetrated walls or windows, yet whose music was miraculously and eerily released from the loud-speaker in the reception room not far away.

Hank said one evening, "Why not break

away from your blasted bank and come where your job will give you a kick? I think Noonan's quitting; you might make it there. You've got enough background, your engineering and the Y course."

"Lynn would never stand for it," Tom told him gloomily. "She's set on my becoming a sort of carbon copy of J.P. How much would I drag down to start with?"

"Forty-five. But you're not likely to become a millionaire," said Hank grinning, long legs on the mantel, while Slim, knocking the ashes from a rank pipe, said, "Not by a long shot. But then neither will I. Public utilities only make the stockholders rich."

Tom ignored this plaint. "Forty-five? Almost what I'm getting now," he murmured, "but, no, she'd never stand for it."

"Wimmin!" said Hank. Slim said nothing. It had been weeks since he'd seen Jennie. She had given him definitely the air. He'd been crazy about her, too. Crazy to think she'd ever look at him twice! And now here was Lynn, professing to care for his friend but blind to the urgencies of his nature. Not all a man's needs had to do with women, after all. A man had to have a job he was keen on, or he went empty-hearted all his life long, dissatisfied, a misfit. He tried to tell Tom something of this in his slow inarticulate way.

"Future? What's the future in that dump of yours?" he wanted to know. "All you do is keep an engagement pad straight and run around and yes people."

"I'm supposed to be learning the business," Tom grinned deprecatingly.

"Oh yeah? And when you've learned it, what then?"

Tom didn't know definitely. Between the $50 a week the Seacoast Company gave him, plus Christmas bonus and a chance for modest investments, and the straight $45 of the UBC there wasn't a hell of a lot of difference, he conceded; but if you went into radio the future was even more nebulous than at the bank. And then there was Lynn to consider.

"Put it up to her," advised Hank. "If she's the right kind of a girl she'll see your point. You could serve your time on the checkerboard and perhaps get into the lab. You'd like that."

He wouldn't *like* it. Research work, looking for something no other man had found, finding it perhaps, or working to perfect the vague dream of someone who'd gone before. Lord, he'd love it! If only you didn't have to think of money in this man's world. "Wish someone would leave me a million!" he said.

Yes, he'd ask Lynn. He'd been an ass, sulking for these last few days; it wasn't, after all, her fault that he'd listened to Rawlson's suave schemes.

He telephoned her eventually, all set to say, "I've a proposition; can I come up and sell it to you?" It would be this: that she would agree to his leaving the bank and getting into the UBC outfit; then, if when the depression passed there would be no question of losing her job, they could marry and work together. Because of his own dissatisfaction with his job and his longing, growing stronger daily, to be somewhere where he would feel perfectly at home, doing something he believed to be important and constructive, he was beginning to understand Lynn's attachment to her own work.

But Lynn wasn't in; no one was in that evening. She was, as a matter of fact, at Sarah's.

Saturday morning he saw her, not at breakfast — she didn't come into the cafeteria — but later in her office. Impossible to say much, with Miss Marple's shrewd eye on him, and the other girls turning to look, just, "Suppose I buzz up tonight?"

She said, "I'm sorry. I'm going away for the week-end."

His jaw dropped. "Week-end? You didn't tell me."

"I haven't talked to you — much," she reminded him.

"Where are you going?" he demanded, more abruptly than he realized.

She did the very natural thing; told the truth, or half of it; hedged. She answered a little stiffly, "With Sarah. We'll be back in time for work Monday."

That was that. He turned and left the room after a moment. She sat at her desk, staring after him, his height and breadth, the outdoors sort of walk, so out of place somehow in these surroundings. She felt small, ashamed. Why hadn't she said, "We're going down to David Dwight's; it will be fun; I wish you were coming, darling"?

She hadn't said it, no matter why. He'd been — different. Since the night in her apartment, she had waited to have him come to her and say, "You were right. I've told Rawlson. Let's forget it." But he hadn't said it.

Dwight drove them down himself in his small open car. There was another man with him, a polo player. Lynn found herself in the front seat with Dwight, the polo gentleman, politely bored, with Sarah in the back. It was a bright, warm day, too warm for comfort in the city, and the Long Island roads were crowded with cars, and dusty; even the trees were filmed with dust, blanketing their radiant green and drooping in the heat. "I hope you brought a bathing-suit," said Dwight.

She assured him that she had. He drove well, effortlessly, smiling, a little too fast but with perfect surety. He was hatless, and the faint wind stirred by their passage ruffled his thick gray hair. He was tanned, and his teeth were very white against the smooth brown skin.

"I'm glad you came," he told her. "I was afraid that young man of yours wouldn't let you."

"He hasn't anything to say about it."

"No? And he hadn't anything to say about the job I offered you, either?" he asked her.

She was silent a moment; then she replied, "Of course not," without conviction.

Dwight laughed. "What a very poor witness you'd make," he mocked her. "I could tie you into knots on the stand! Of course — yes. Of course, he said, 'I'd rather see you starve than working for that old reprobate!' "

"He didn't say anything of the kind," she denied indignantly.

"Well, perhaps he didn't put it quite as strongly. But whatever he said he was right," agreed Dwight cheerfully. "I thought it over myself afterward. I was ready to stand by my bargain, of course, but I realized that you are entirely too distracting to make a good amanuensis."

He had never spoken to her in that way before, as lightly, as caressingly. She rather liked it — but was warned. She said with equal lightness, "Well, you needn't worry, need you? As the distraction never materialized."

He leaned a little nearer, cut a corner, sent her suddenly against the side of the car, gasping a little. They rode on smoothly. He said, "I do worry."

In the back seat the polo player yawned and, by way of making idle conversation with Sarah, jerked a thumb toward the front seat in a fashion pardonable only to six millions and a string of ponies, and growled, in his usual manner, "Looks like old David was making a play for the youngster — What did you say her name was?"

Sarah hadn't said. Dwight had said it, in the unintelligible manner of all introduc-

249

tions. Sarah, her heart tightening, replied, "Her name is Lynn Harding. She's by way of being my goddaughter."

"Bet Dave would like to be her god-father," said the polo player, who was celebrated for things other than tact and brilliance. "Looks as if he were offering her about half of his kingdom this minute."

Sarah spoke of the scenery. But she was not happy. Was it possible that David Dwight's kindness to Lynn meant — anything? It wasn't possible. Surely he owed her, Sarah, too much to —

What did he owe her, exactly? A little belated loyalty perhaps; certainly, a sense of decency. She felt herself flushing with anger, glowing with it.

But to what had his kindness amounted? A party, luncheon now and then, dinner. David liked pretty girls. She'd always known that. That was why it had seemed so utterly incredible to her once, and still seemed so, that he had ever cared for her. But Lynn!

No, he wouldn't, he couldn't, he *dared* not — use her as a screen, as a convenience. Besides Lynn had no interest in him. For the first time Sarah felt a definite gratitude to Tom Shepard for loving Lynn, for being loved by her in his turn.

Why had she been so blind — if she had been blind? Was it because she, so unable to break loose from the old ties, the old associations, saw David Dwight through the eyes of twenty years ago? Saw him, perhaps, without love but still with illusion? He might do as he wished, possess a hundred women, cast them aside, be notoriously unfaithful to his wife, as he had, for the sake of his wife's money, been unfaithful to Sarah, and she would still regard him with the condoning and veiled eyes of what had once been pure passion and incredible tenderness.

He wouldn't do that to her, no matter how little he cared for her now; he wouldn't tamper with Lynn's happiness.

Thus she reassured herself. But the chance remark of a man whom she had never seen before and would never see again, once this week-end was over, had put her on her guard.

They reached the small, busy town, turned into the side road, and, passing between the gate posts of Dwight's property, eventually drew up before the house. Lynn took a deep breath. "Glad you like it," said Dwight; as the servants came forward to take the bags, to take the car to the garage. "I had an idea it would be becoming to you when I built it."

She was unwary enough to remind him — "But you didn't know me then."

"I knew I was going to know you," he answered, with his unwavering regard.

She was a little flushed, stepping out of the car.

The house was in the American farmhouse style. Part of it was quite old, as American farmhouses go; the remodeling, the additions had been done with reverence. It was shingled, painted white, and had blinds that were neither green nor blue but a faded mellow mixture of both. There were wide verandas and windows, all about it were gardens, and a small untouched orchard ran, laughing, down the slopes to the blue water.

They went between low hedges of box to the open door, which boasted a fanlight of great beauty brought from a house in Salem.

The door opened directly upon a wide long living-room, with furniture which, if for the most part antique, was comfortable and had achieved the perfectly right look of semi-shabbiness combined with beauty and stability. There was an enormous fireplace, and there were many flowers. The stairs leading upward were slender and polished, the banister hand-carved and lovely.

Sarah and Lynn had connecting rooms, each with a bath. They looked on flowers and trees and water, and the curtains bellied in a breeze that was soaked with salt and scented with roses.

"I've never been in a lovelier house," said Lynn, wandering into Sarah's room and watching her unpack. "What'll I wear?"

"He doesn't go in for formality," Sarah told her vaguely. "Sports things, I guess. There will be people for dinner. We'll change then. Yes, the house is lovely. Not, however, what I would have expected of David."

"You've never been here before?" Lynn asked her.

"No." Sarah realized with a start and with a return of warning that she never had been there before. Yet David had had the place — how long? — five years? Once he'd had a place in Maryland. She remembered that. She recalled it now and then, turned her mind from it with an effort of the will. No, she had never been asked here. She'd seen him all these years, off and on. Lunch, dinner, a play, parties. But he had never —

Why had he — now?

Lynn was back in her own room, discovering, exclaiming. "Such an adorable desk," her voice drifted back to Sarah, who stood perfectly still in the center of her room, unseeing eyes on the suitcase she had opened, a silk stocking dangling from her capable hand.

A little later Lynn and Sarah went downstairs. Lynn wore a tennis frock of yellow silk. She had brushed her hair until it shone; the black satin arrow was pointed upon her forehead.

Dwight and the polo player waited for them. "There are other people coming," Dwight said casually. "They'll turn up before tea. How about some tennis?" he asked Lynn.

She said doubtfully that it had been ages since she played; she'd probably make a mess of it.

There were rackets in the cupboard under the stairs. Dwight led the way to the court. "Never saw the sense of tennis," said the polo player, striding, bowlegged, beside Sarah, "too dam' strenuous!"

The court was on a rise of ground overlooking the water. The very high back stops were tapestried in late ramblers; there was a four-foot bed of perennials round three sides. There were metal, painted chairs, umbrellas. It had taken them only two hours to run down; it was not more than four o'clock now, and the pellucid sunlight lay in Dwight's eyes as he took his place across the court from Lynn.

He beat her, not too easily. She played a good game, lithe; her serve was almost vicious. But he played a better game. They played two sets, Sarah and the polo player — whose name it appeared was Travis — watching.

"I like beating you — by a slight margin," Dwight told Lynn as they left the court and went to join their small audience.

His eyes were friendly as he spoke; more than friendly. Lynn said: "Next time! You took an unfair advantage of me — I haven't played in so long. You play — a lot?"

"Now and then. Indoor, squash; have to keep fit," he told her, and added, dropping down at her feet on the grass, "I had thought it would be a love set. But you fooled me. Later, perhaps, you'll take your revenge."

Now he had meant nothing by that, of course. A natural remark; if he had meant anything, it would have been banal enough. But she did not reply.

He lay, propped on an elbow — there were his little piers, there his swimming-dock just below — and the speedboat at anchor. Over there the vegetable gardens, the farmer's cottage, the garage. "Rather lovely, I think," he said. "I like it."

"Has it a name?" she wanted to know.

"No. Names annoy me. When they're trite they're idiotic; when they're clever they're more so. I never named it, I never shall. I've a superstition about naming places."

His eyes flickered toward Sarah briefly. Sarah, sitting rather stiffly, very tailored, very correct, was unwelcomely conscious of the ghost of delight which never failed to stir her when she knew that David Dwight was, if fleetly, remembering. The Maryland place had had a name long before Dwight bought it for the proverbial song. He couldn't afford more than one verse and a chorus in those days. Latterly his taste in choruses had changed, become more concrete. The Maryland place, eight acres and a dear ramshackle house, had been called, sentimentally, Heartsease —

It was at Heartsease that they had once stayed, very far from all the world, at Heartsease they had parted, as lovers —

256

"Why don't you call it 'Nonesuch'? Wasn't there a house once — built for a queen — ?" asked Lynn, hazy on history.

"They never found its trace," said David. " 'Nonesuch?' That has," he said, "a melancholy sound, but sweetly secret."

Travis yawned. "When do we get tea? And I hope," he added piously, "I hope to God it *isn't* tea!"

A horn honked dimly.

"That's the Carters," Dwight said, and got to his feet, "and the host not there. Hurry!"

He slipped a hand under Lynn's arm, urging her forward. "Bet I beat you to the house," he challenged.

The others followed slowly. Travis shook his head. "You'd think he was twenty," he said in grudging admiration, conscious of the weight of his own 56 years. "I couldn't run like that from a fire!"

But Lynn reached the broad, winding walk first, and slowed down, unwilling to appear before strangers at posthaste, hair ruffled and cheeks red. There was a sports roadster in front of the door, and beside it a tall, languid man and a rather pretty woman. Thirtyish, both of them, very casual, the Collin Carters, of New York, Paris, Palm Beach, Newport — and originally Paw Paw, Virginia.

Now, with the introductions over, the house party was complete. They went indoors and, while the Carters vanished stairward, composed themselves to wait for tea. Tea was — tea, to Travis's disgust; but it was also thin tomato sandwiches and caviar on crisp crackers; and it was likewise cocktails and highballs, and Travis brightened. This chukker was going better than he thought it would.

Millie Carter was very pretty, after all. Reappearing, she wore lounging pajamas of black velvet and lamé, jade at her ears, jade on her wrists, jade as her symbol. She had proprietary airs toward her host. She had, she thought, a right to wear them, as gaily as she wore the cool green stones. Or at least, when they had been together, ages ago, he had been — interested. Was, it appeared, no longer. Millie drank three cocktails and pouted while her husband talked international matches with Travis.

Lynn was eating sandwiches with the zest induced by tennis, a naturally healthy appetite, and an early, hurried luncheon. David Dwight watched her, balancing a glass. He smiled at her lazily. He said, "I was going to suggest a swim — but I won't — not now."

"When is dinner?" she demanded.

"Eight-thirty."

"We've time," she said, and looked at a wall clock.

Millie was saying, "Bridge? I haven't had a game of bridge since — since Easter. I swore off. But —"

"Let's," said Travis.

Dwight touched a bell rope. Wilkins, the servant who had been with him in the penthouse, came into the room, with his astonishingly truculent air. He had, however, a special, almost fraternal smile for Lynn, who spoke to him by name. A bridge table was set up in a small glassed veranda. Dwight managed well. Sarah found herself facing Travis, Millie her own husband. "Oh, bother," said Millie, "why do I always cut you, Jack? You know we fight like cats and dogs and you never remember conventions!"

Neither did she, except at a bridge table.

Dwight asked, turning away from the table, "Swim? Sure you want to, Lynn?"

"I ate only four sandwiches," said Lynn, "and I didn't drink — oh, just one cup of tea. I never drink other things, this time of day; they make me sleepy."

"You must be charming — asleep," said Dwight, low.

But Sarah heard him — and overbid her hand.

Chapter Thirteen:

A SECRET BETRAYED

Later, Lynn in the one-piece affair of scarlet, belted in white, and Dwight, a bathrobe dripping from his astonishingly massive shoulders, were walking toward the docks, down the steps, together. "How well do you swim?" he wanted to know. "As well as you play tennis?"

"No. I lived inland so long," she answered, "about ten strokes is my limit."

He watched her wade in from the steps in shallow water and shiver with delight as the cool blue caress flowed about her. He dropped his bathrobe, appearing in trunks only, and dived cleanly from the end of the dock and swam around to join her. She was swimming in a little flurry of smitten water.

"Here, take it easy," he admonished her; and for ten minutes devoted himself to teaching, his hand just touching her, his eyes alert.

"If I had you here — for a long time —

I'd teach you," he said, and added, as if it were necessary — "to swim."

Returning to the house, he said carelessly, "I should have asked young Shepard, I suppose. But I'm a selfish beast. I must be, to put my happiness above your own!"

She ignored the implication; she had to. She said, "I'm perfectly happy — as things are."

She tried to believe that she was. She knew she was not. After all, she was not a little angry at Tom. Yet she would have given a year of her life — she could afford to be generous and reckless at her age — to have Tom with her now in this almost too perfect spot. Their courtship, their loving, had been in spite of surroundings; it had never had a setting of charm and ease and relaxation. Her face sobered, her eyes were miles away, Dwight, watching her, was uneasy.

"Yes, I should have asked him," he repeated.

"No — Oh, do we go through the house — like this?"

"We do. By the back way, through the back passage, up the back stairs. At least you do. I have my rooms," he told her, "in a small wing on the main floor. Here you are, there are the stairs."

It was a little dark in the passageway. He took her hand to guide her. She was close, she was sweet, in the red bathing-suit; she was fashionably, very nearly naked. She was suddenly conscious of it, conscious too of her companion's lack of conventional attire. She pulled her hand away.

"Is it very late?" Her voice was uneven.

"No, you've time to rest," he told her, "before dinner." His voice was exceptionally steady. He had made it so. He stood at the foot of the stairs and watched her mount them, her slim bare ankles and legs very white in the dusk.

He asked himself, turning away, *Are you going to make a damned fool of yourself — again?*

He was, of course; knowing it ahead of time made little difference.

There were other guests at dinner, besides Sarah in her black crepe and Millie in her turquoise tulle, too elaborate perhaps for the occasion but too flattering to china-blue eyes and ash-blond hair to resist, and besides Lynn, in the printed green chiffon. There was a Supreme-Court judge, who was a fine judge of old brandy and good prints as well as of legal tangles; there was his wife, who had money; there were two pretty girls, twins, from the neighboring estate, and two young men who might as well have been twins, perfectly resembling each other in innocuous good looks, manner, and clothes.

The dining-room was a comfortable, cheerful sort of place. Cream and yellow, mahogany and French blue. A plate rail. A chair rail. A good dinner, well served. "Everything off the place." The broilers, explained Dwight, cost him five dollars a pound, at least.

Cocktails before, and wine, during. Afterward, more bridge, the radio, the twin girls dancing with the duplicate young men. Millie, slipping her hand under Dwight's arm — "There's going to be a moon — do take me out to see the moon, Davie."

A perfect host, he did so; they returned very shortly; Dwight very unperturbed, the ash on his cigar at least two inches long, Millie, her respiratory action disturbed, a hard little spot of color under the delicate mask of cream rouge.

Lynn had been dancing with the judge, of all people. Large and pleasant, masking an almost mordant wit behind the fat, unlined screen of his face, he liked waltzing. Over the radio, from a New York roof garden, there came a waltz —

Now Lynn was listening to his honor's pleasant flattery. Dwight came up behind her, catlike, as always. "Bridge," agreed his honor cheerfully. He liked a game of bridge.

Somehow Lynn found herself out in the wide corner of the porch that overlooked the water. There were slatted screens, rolled up, vines, chairs, a lazy swing. She lowered herself into it and watched, with delight, the shimmer of moonlight on the water, the silver path leading to gold. Dwight, sitting beside her in a lounge chair, took out his cigarette case and offered it to her.

She smoked; the before-dinner cocktail, the Chambertin, the liqueur sang pleasantly in her veins; the exhilaration of strenuous exercise, of the swim, had left her glowing and pleasantly tired, open to the insidiousness of a perfectly planned dinner. She was sleepy, yet stimulated; her mental processes were a trifle blurred, not by anything as crude as an actual alcoholic intoxication but by the subtler intoxication of youth and health and bodily comfort. She swayed lazily in the soft embrace of the swing, touching the floor with a pointed toe, her arms clasped behind her head.

"Happy?" asked Dwight, low.

"Yes." But it was not true, she was not happy — not entirely. She turned the ring on her finger. Something disturbed her vaguely, ate at her consciousness, tunneling, undermining the physical languor, the sense of luxury and drowsy contentment.

"You're very quiet," he commented; and then, as if the undercurrent had reached him, he asked her, "Is anything troubling you, Lynn?"

"I don't know. A little, perhaps."

She fell silent, wondering. She couldn't, of course, tell him. Yet she had told him other things; had presented to him, for instance, Mara's case. She thought, *I wonder if I am being foolish, overscrupulous? Perhaps Tom was perfectly within his rights to contemplate —*

She could not, somehow, free herself of a doubt that was almost a conviction. Suppose Tom had not kept his word? Yet, caring for her, he must have done so.

"Can't you tell me?" urged Dwight, wondering in his turn. He smiled wryly in the darkness. Young Shepard again? Of course, young Shepard! Would he have to listen to her confidences, her confession that hope deferred maketh the heart sick? Well, he'd listen then, he'd let himself in for it.

"I shouldn't —" she admitted slowly.

Why not tell him, in part? She trusted him, he had told her that she might. A clever man, a brilliant man, perfectly versed in worldly knowledge, in legal knowledge —

Her impulse to seek advice, to find help, her relaxed feeling of physical well-being, all contrived to blind her to her indiscretion.

"It isn't my secret," she admitted youthfully, hesitating. "I can't mention names, or anything. You understand?"

He was becoming more and more puzzled. "Quite. We'll consider it — hypothetically," he agreed with gravity.

How young she was! How incredibly young! how more than incredibly sweet! He fought down the impulse to rise, to sweep her into his arms, to kiss the childish, hesitating questions from her desired lips, the impulse to say, "Forget it all, whatever it is, can't you? Let it wait — Love me, tonight. Tonight never comes again."

He went a little pale with the force of his emotion. He snapped open his cigarette case and lighted a cigarette with hands none too steady. The small spurt of the lighter's blue-yellow flame showed her his

266

face, against the background of darkness, grave, familiar, to be trusted. She drew a deep breath and began her explanation with, for the most part, a series of questions.

If, she wanted to know, an employee of a large and influential organization had access to advance, private information, had this person any right to use this knowledge for his own gain?

Dwight was immeasurably astonished. He had thought to hear a twice-told tale of love and frustration dictated by the heavy impatience of youth, which is, however, hardly youth's prerogative; he had braced himself against this in anticipation, conscious of the crying out of his own blood, the reaction of his own sensitive nerves.

Instead, it seemed he was being interrogated on the subject of business ethics.

He answered cautiously, "Could you explain a little more fully without betraying confidences?"

Well, then, it all had to do with a merger. The friend she mentioned was in a position to know that a merger was being planned. Nothing that this particular person could do, alone, would make any difference, of course. But he had been advised by an acquaintance to take advantage of the information. "I don't know," she acknowledged miserably, "just what — the plans are. But I think it amounts to selling the information, at just the right time, to influential people."

Dwight pondered the question, or appeared to, in silence. But he was thinking quickly enough. Shepard, of course, with his easy access to the bank's affairs. Lynn would hardly concern herself with anyone save Tom Shepard. The business was, of course, the bank's. Upon what other business would Shepard have advance information? What more interested Dwight was the "acquaintance." Who could it be? Lynn herself? He played with this idea a moment. Yes, it might be Lynn — afraid, after she had made her suggestion to Tom, wondering if she should withdraw her persuasion.

He replied at length slowly, "I don't know enough about it, Lynn. It's probably legitimate enough, that is, in the sense of being within the law. Ethically, that's another matter. I shouldn't worry about it, if I were you."

"But I do worry," she said, taken quite off her guard by his even, low tone, his unastonished acceptance of the situation, and her increasing sense of his interest, his willingness to help. "You see, he promised me that he wouldn't —" She stopped, and flushed, delicately in the darkness. Dwight could hear her little gasp, and then the sound of the swing being set into motion again; he kept his eyes turned from the pale blur of her face and listened intently, so intently that he could hear the blood beating in his own ears. "I'm being very silly," Lynn apologized, "and secret; I can't help it. But if you knew that someone you cared for were contemplating such a step? Oh, I *can't* think it's honest," she cried desperately.

Then it wasn't Lynn. Lynn didn't approve. He said cheerfully, "All's fair in love and business." He was to remember that statement, later. "You've told me that you have your friend's promise. Perhaps he'll keep it. Look here, Lynn, my advice to you is to forget this and say nothing to anyone. If — well, no matter how things turn out, you won't be helping your friend materially, will you, by talking about it?"

"I haven't talked," she defended herself quickly, "except, of course, to you."

That was sweet; he recognized it; treasured it; said gently, "Thank you, my dear. I won't ask anything further except to say that, naturally, it's Tom, is it not? I know

269

you wouldn't be troubled over anyone else."

She said that yes, it was Tom.

"Then he'll do what you want him to," Dwight assured her. "He'd be insane not to."

"I couldn't bear to have him disloyal, to have his integrity threatened," she explained, after a moment. "I told him that if — if he did this I'd never speak to him again."

"Then he won't do it," Dwight comforted her. "Forget it. I'll forget it, too. There! Look at that moon and see if you can keep your mind on troublesome hypothetical questions."

She turned and looked. It was sheer beauty. The pale diffused light was on her face. Dwight tossed his cigarette over the rail to the terrace and sunk his hands in his pockets. Predatory hands, he was aware of that. He thought, *If I take her in my arms?* But he could not, he must not; not yet; it was too soon.

Sunday was a repetition of Saturday, only more so. An hour of swimming, notable for Millie's suit, what there was to it, and tennis, a drive and lunch at a country club, and people for tea and more people for dinner, and then one episode of importance.

During the day Dwight found himself speculating upon what Lynn had, or had not, told him. What on earth? A merger? But that was impossible, there had been no rumor of it in banking circles or along the street which is paved with such very good intentions. Still, if there were to be a big merger — He owned some Seacoast stock; not very much. Nor could he buy more outright, on the off chance. He was very deeply in debt. The case he had counted on, which he had taken upon a contingency basis, had been appealed. If he won it would be a long time before he could get his money. If this vague thing proved concrete, and he were in on the ground floor — ?

But he would have to make sure. To whom could he go? Norton was out of the question, Shepard, too, of course. Who then was Shepard's "friend"?

He might ask Sarah — cleverly.

As it happened she asked him something first.

He had taken them all through the house, through his own suite, its bedroom and bath, its small library adjoining. Shown them too the passage leading from the back stairs. "How convenient!" Millie had said, and giggled. That was following their swim and before dinner. After dinner, that Sunday, he had walked with his guests in the gardens. It was a hot, still night. "I had them plant a lot of white," he explained. "A garden by moonlight is so blurred, white flowers alone give it character."

He dropped a little behind the others. The hedge was high, it grew in ordered circles. Lynn walking beside him in very high heels, turned her ankle, and cried out, for a brief moment, at the sharp pain.

He said, "What is it?" anxiously.

"Nothing — my ankle. It's all right now."

The others had reached the end of the hedge, had turned and were coming back on the other side, toward the water. "Take my arm," said Dwight. "Can you manage to get back to the house?"

She could manage. She set her foot gingerly upon the path and clung to him for an unpremeditated instant. They were quite alone, in the moonlit world of the garden. Near them a sun dial, wreathed in roses, was no reminder of the flight of time. Separated from them by the hedge, unseen, the others walked and laughed. But Sarah, missing her host, missing Lynn, paused a moment, anxious.

Dwight's arm was around Lynn. For a

heartbeat's space he held her, close — much closer than any turned ankle warranted. He said, softly and quite clearly, "Oh, my dear — you very sweet person —"

And Sarah heard.

A moment later they had rounded the hedge, and Dwight was calling to them, "Wait a moment, will you? Lynn's turned her ankle."

"But it's all right now," she protested.

It was all right. Right enough to dance later, with Dwight, with Travis, with Millie's weary husband. It was late when they said good night and went to bed. Sarah and Lynn must make an early start in the morning. Dwight was driving them and Travis up. Millie and Jack would have the house to themselves for a time: they never started anywhere before eleven, they protested.

Early to rise and late to bed. But sometime between retiring and rising Sarah, after Lynn slept, crept down the hall to the back stairs and put her feet cautiously upon them, listening to the creaking which seemed so loud, as loud as the beating of her heart.

Down the passage and to Dwight's door. She paused there, and drew the severe robe of heavy silk about her. Her heart beat so violently, it was as loud as her knock upon his door; louder.

"Come in," said Dwight, wondering what Wilkins wanted. Or could it be Millie? No, perish the thought. She wasn't *that* much of a fool.

Dwight's room opened on a terrace of brick, completing this small wing. He was standing at the French windows, in his pajamas, smoking. Sarah came into the room. Her eyes were enormous; her plain and pleasant face was tragic, it was old. And there was in it emotion that he had not seen for many years — from her. A bitter jealousy, with which she strove; a warning; a fear; and a question.

"Why, Sarah," he said, startled out of all poise. "Why, *Sarah!*"

Heaven knew what passed through his mind at that moment, what fleeting explanations, solutions, expectancies. He was sorry for them a moment later, a little ashamed.

She said, harshly, insistently, "Lynn — I had to ask you about Lynn — Are you in love with her, David — and if you are — what are you going to do about it?"

Chapter Fourteen:

DWIGHT GIVES HIS WORD

The French windows stood open. Outside, a red moon was falling swiftly through starry space to her close. Soon it would be very dark, and very hushed, before the pale prelude to the dawn. The room was scented with tobacco smoke, with the odor of leather, with the frail and tenuous persistence of roses. And it was so still that Sarah could hear the soft, enchanted murmur of water on the beach, the stifled sighing, in the branches, of a vagrant wind.

Dwight leaned against the window frame. He felt slightly ridiculous, in the long tunicked Russian pajamas of heavy silk. He said a thing, sparring for time, which was small and mean; which he regretted. He asked lightly, "Not jealous, are you, Sarah?"

She flushed, without beauty. She answered, her eyes on his, "No, I'm not jealous, David — I'm afraid."

But she was jealous; she knew it. She

could have scotched the little snake at her heart, set her heel upon its bright, dangerous, lifted head. She must destroy it. While he murmured, "Shut the door, come in, you can't stand there; what will people say?" and laughed a little, remembering, perhaps, as she forlornly remembered, a time when what people said — or thought — had meant so little to her, to both of them. She tried to destroy her enemy. She tried to think: *Of what am I jealous? Not, any more, of his love, or his desire for another woman. No, never any more.* Not jealous, in the common sense, of Lynn, whom she loved. Oh, not that. Jealous, it might be of all Lynn stood for, youth, grace, possible radiant surrender, laughter, life —

Jealous, too, of David's personal integrity, of the delicate balance of that curious unacknowledged relationship which was between them. So, she said, shutting the door, and coming into the room, a few deliberate steps, "David, you've got to be honest with me. You've always been honest with me before. You can't do this to — Lynn. You can't," she said, "do it to me."

He had not made a name for himself through being stupid. He had not earned — and flung away — and earned again, large, solid fortunes, by being insensitive and blind. He couldn't turn this off lightly, with a word of reassurance — "Sarah, don't be silly. There's nothing in it. Can't I be attentive to a pretty girl" — plaintively — "I *like* pretty girls, without your getting all worked up over it? Run along to bed, do, there's a darling."

No, he couldn't say that. Instead he said, and reached for a bathrobe of brocaded silk, belting it about his slim waist, "Sit down. We'll talk this thing out."

She sat down, docilely enough. He took the chair near her, at his small, fine desk. He was tired, he discovered suddenly. Yet a moment before he had been so far from tired. Wilkins? He hoped to heaven Wilkins wouldn't come in now with his unservile — "You should be in bed." Through the door on the little library he could see his bedroom, the bed turned down, waiting, the carafe on the night table, the book he was reading, the soft light on. What had possessed him to wander about the library? to write three letters to Lynn which were now destroyed and in the waste basket? and eventually to lean against the window frame and look toward the dreaming garden and the flowing water and wish impossible things, impossible even if they should come to pass? —

It struck him as enormously comic, as tremendously tragic, that he and Sarah Dennet should be sitting thus, at this time of night alone, shut in, in the quiet of the big friendly house, a lamp burning, and the fragrance of summer in the room. Once, a thousand years ago, it had been heaven to be with her thus, alone, enraptured, alien from the world.

Why not now?

He thought, fleetingly, that the question contained most of the love tragedy in the universe.

He turned his attention to Sarah. She was sitting wearily in the deep chair, in a strangely humble position, somehow, for one usually so almost irritatingly erect, sure of herself. Her hands were lax at her sides. He thought. *There isn't much use lying — to her — She always knew when I lied, there, toward the end.* He thought, *If one could put her in the wrong, get at this from an angle disadvantageous to her —* It was not unkindness nor even self-protection. He was merely not a lawyer for nothing, as his clients very well knew.

"Sarah" — his voice was low, restrained, a shade reproachful — "aren't you taking a rather unfair advantage of me?"

She knew what he meant, shrank back against the chair, cowered, as if the touch of padded upholstery meant safety. They hadn't, for years, spoken of the days gone by. They had agreed to that. No use. No use stirring embers; and when embers have become ashes even more futile to blow upon them and watch the gray wisps drift upon uncaring air.

He had liked that about her so much. The only woman he had ever known who would not say, long after love had perished, "Do you remember — ?"

She answered, as steadily as she could, "I didn't mean to — you know that. Lynn, Lynn means a great deal to me. Oh, why can't you leave her alone, David?" Her big fine hands writhed, twisted, "Why can't you leave her alone? — She's so young —"

"And I'm so old?" he murmured wryly.

"No, I didn't mean that." She didn't. She stared at him, eyelids torn wide open. Old? Dwight? Not by any standards.

"What did you mean?" he pressed her.

Her hands were quiet again.

"She doesn't know much about life — She's pretty innocent, David."

"Lynn? Lynn?" His voice was tender, he couldn't, for his life, prevent it. "How old is she — twenty-two? Twenty-two-year-old girls, nowadays, dear Sarah! —"

"Oh, why do you twist the things I say?" Her voice rose a little.

He said, "Hush!" compellingly.

She quieted, went on, dully, "Can't you see what I mean by innocence? I don't mean an ignorance of pitfalls. Lynn's modern enough, sane enough, for that matter. But she doesn't know what life can do to — to a girl. David, she's happy, she's in love. Tom Shepard's a decent sort of boy. They'll quarrel and be reconciled a hundred times before they marry. Can't you let her alone, leave her to him? She belongs to him."

"Does she?" His eyes were unpleasant. "If she does, then why worry? She won't be hurt. No one will be hurt, except, perhaps, myself."

A tacit enough acknowledgment. She felt with the most curious warning agony of compassion and protection that she did not want him to be hurt, she couldn't endure it, she would sacrifice anything, herself, Tom, Lynn, even Lynn.

But that was madness. With the balanced cells of her brain she knew that David Dwight would not be hurt; not really; or thought she knew it. She said, "You do love her then? But you won't be hurt,

David; you — you've cared for women before."

"Yes. And had them for the most part," he agreed cheerfully, brutally, "and lost them, somehow; and been hurt, for a time. But —"

"Don't say it!"

It was on his lips to say it — *But this is different.* She had heard that before. For a moment they stared at each other, across miles, across years.

She said bitterly, "I've been a fool. All my fault. I never thought, never dreamed —"

"Why not? You knew me, Sarah, you have known me for a long time," he reminded her.

"Yes — but Lynn? My friend — my" — she stumbled, she said it bravely — "my almost daughter, the daughter I might have had."

"Sarah, do you realize you're talking like a very bad play?"

"Oh, perhaps. Life," she said uneasily, "is like a play — a very bad play, I expect. But to use me as a *convenience* —"

"Is that where the shoe pinches, Sarah?"

In part, it was. But she had herself in hand now, and answered, "No, not altogether. I can't have you taking Lynn's happiness from her."

"Are you sure it's happiness?" His mouth twisted. He said violently, "What can that cub give her that I can't?"

"Life. Youth —"

"Oh, youth!" He dismissed it with a gesture. "What does she want from life, a home, shelter, love, passion? I can give her these things. As well as Tom Shepard. Better."

"*He* can give her marriage," Sarah said.

There was a species of sick triumph in her eyes. Marriage — David Dwight had not been able to give her marriage; at least, he had not wished to be able — And now, for a long time, his rather legendary wife had served him as a protection —

In the scant minute which elapsed before Dwight answered, he thought and realized a number of things. Marriage — with Lynn? It had not occurred to him. Why should it have done so? At first, a pretty girl, a desirable girl; one played with the idea of pretty girls and then, perhaps, with the pretty girls themselves. Later, with the intrusion of Tom, one resigned oneself to a waiting game. Waiting for what? Seduction was an abhorrent word, a word not in Dwight's working vocabulary. But if a girl turned to one on, say, the rebound, of her own free will, was that seduction?

No, not exactly. If he had had that goal, an end to waiting, in his mind, he put it aside now. Marriage with Lynn. His breath quickened at the thought, his heart pounded, he clenched his hands in the pockets of the dressing-gown. To teach Lynn to love, to show Lynn the wide reaches of this very glorious world, to be guide and mentor and lover, to slip back into unthinking youth again through the elixir of her youth, to dream, perhaps of a child, of children — not of the rangy uninteresting girls who bore his name, whose blood was tinged with his own, but of boy children, sturdy, brown babies, with Lynn's gray eyes —

That the present and only Mrs. David Dwight might be persuaded to release him he knew; none better; he had known it for a long time; but the idea had not appealed to him, had far from suited his book. But now! He laughed, a short, excited sound, curiously brutal, curiously exultant. There sat Sarah, the faint, sickened triumph still in her eyes. She thought she had him. She was wrong. He had her; he had, on the instant, everything that made life worth living. "*He* can give her marriage," Sarah had said. Well —

"That, too, might be arranged," said Dwight, coolly.

She shuddered away from him. "No!"

"Yes. Mrs. Dwight," he smiled maliciously, "is rather bored. Or so I've heard. She might be persuaded, for a consideration —"

Yes, he knew she could be persuaded. But the consideration must be very large. Far, far larger than he could afford. His thoughts turned back swiftly to his conversation with Lynn on the previous night. If there were anything in it — by all the unholy gods, what curiously poetic justice!

That there had never been rumor of Dwight's wife freeing him before this, Sarah knew. She looked at him incredulously. The arrangement had, so far, been an exceptional convenience to him.

"Marriage," he went on, enjoying himself, loathing himself, a veritable battlefield, "marriage, by bell and book, a home, children. Can your candidate do more?"

"No." But now suddenly she thought she had conquered; she said, again, in triumph.

"She loves Tom. She doesn't love — you."

"No," he said frankly, "she doesn't love me — yet."

"You think you can make her love you — all you stand for? David, it wouldn't be love, it would be glamor, enchantment, it would be — betrayal of the most material sort —"

He rose, faced her, smiling very slightly.

"Sarah, we are getting nowhere. We are, I take it, enemies?"

"Enemies," she agreed, low. She too rose. They regarded one another warily, they were duelists, dealing with clumsy words, yet they bore invisible weapons, weapons of the spirit, which nevertheless drew blood.

"An armistice?" he suggested, after a long minute. "As long as Tom Shepard is in the picture, I'll keep out. Does that satisfy you?"

She thought she had won. She thought that this was his way of telling her so. Her hands went out to him, and drew back, fell at her sides.

"Your word of honor, David?"

He was a little pale. He had his code. He asked, "Must I?" and then nodded gravely enough. "My word of honor then, as long as Tom is in the picture," he said.

She told him, "You keep promises — honor promises. I know."

He knew too. He opened the door, held it for her. For an instant their eyes met, for an instant that unspoken, vanished thing was living, flashing between them for a second's fraction.

"Sarah, Sarita," he said, and sighed, "life plays us idiotic tricks. Try to think that it wasn't wholly my fault, my dear."

It had been years since he had called her Sarita, the silly, the sweet nickname. She was crying silently as she stumbled back along the passage and up the stairs, careless of how they creaked under her hurrying tread.

Dwight went back to his room and stood again at the windows. He had given his word. As long as Tom were in the picture. But he had not promised to withhold his erasing hand — *I told him if he did this I'd never speak to him again.* He smiled and went, catlike, into his bedroom.

Chapter Fifteen:

JENNIE'S BARGAIN

In the morning they drove to town. "Sarah," asked Dwight, "will you do me the honor?" and held open the door for her. Grimly, looking twenty years older than her age, she climbed in and sat beside him.

"Here's luck," Travis hailed Lynn, his eye brightening as she took her place beside him.

"Enjoying yourself?" Dwight asked Sarah as the miles unrolled beneath the wheels, while back at the place which had no name Millie and Jack Carter regarded each other without pleasure across their breakfast trays.

"Please —"

"I'm sorry, Sarah," he said instantly; and was.

Because of their early start and the scarcity of traffic, they came to the Seacoast Building on time. Lynn said delightedly, holding out her hand, "It was — gorgeous. I can't thank you enough."

He replied coolly, smiling at her, "It was pleasant of you to come," and turned to Sarah. Lynn, a little taken aback, watched them. Incalculable man! One moment he was your friend, dependable, you had only to reach out your hand for comfort. Nice, that feeling. Then, the next second he was less than your friend, more than your friend, caressing eyes and disturbing voice. That frightened you a little, but was — pleasurable. And then, again, as now, he was a hundred miles removed from friendship, an acquaintance merely, courteous, a little bored.

Not that it mattered — much.

He had said nothing of when they would meet again. It was the first time he had not given her a meeting to look forward to.

She went in to work, a little hurt, more than a little puzzled.

But he lingered, detaining Sarah. "Will you lunch with me tomorrow?"

"Why?"

"You know why. We'll talk of — cabbages," he promised, "and kings."

"Well," asked Tom, appearing at Lynn's elbow toward luncheon time, "did you have a thrilling week-end — with Sarah?"

He was ugly, definitely so. He had seen

the car draw up, had seen the people in it. Lynn replied defiantly, "Very. And you needn't take that attitude, Tom Shepard. I *was* with Sarah and you know it!"

"Sarah and who else?"

"We were at Mr. Dwight's country place."

"Very jolly," admitted Tom, and departed without further word.

She had half expected it, of course. But — oh, everything was spoiled a little today. She slammed her desk drawer shut.

"Blue Monday?" asked the blond Miss Marple, understandingly, "well, I feel that way myself. Boy, I haven't gotten over Saturday night yet. Was that a party!"

Lynn rose. She didn't want to eat alone. She didn't want to *be* alone. Mara was no longer available. Mara, home with Bill, planning to go West — "Not that I want to go, Lynn, but what else can I do? He says — he says he's sorry."

Could people really be "sorry" and begin all over again with the memory of things they had said between them, terrible things, terrible memories?

Jennie? Perhaps Jennie would be free. Suddenly Lynn wanted Jennie and her astonishing acceptance of things as they are, her unenglamored eyes, her slangy, salutary cynicism that was not cynicism at all but a hard, poised ego as blunt as an old knife, impervious to the usual slings and arrows. She would go upstairs, she thought, and look for Jennie.

In the express elevator she rose, swift as a bird but without volition, and watched the small green numbers flash above the door as they passed each floor. She had been once or twice to Madame Fanchon's with urgent messages for Fanchon's "best" model. Now she went into the gray, ivory-paneled room, empty at this hour sacred to luncheon. Fanchon herself, in a bright long tunic and a brief crêpe-de-Chine skirt, came out and frowned at her a moment, puzzled.

"If I might see Jennie?" asked Lynn, smiling.

"Oh, Jennie's little friend. But, certainly!" She stepped to the curtains at the door of the models' room, thrust her dark birdlike head between them, spoke; and returned. "It is nearly autumn," she told Lynn. "We've been very busy."

Mr. Pearl drifted by. Lynn had never seen him before but she recognized him at once. He was like a lily, walking, vague flutterings of pale hands, probably pink-tipped. He looked at her with nearsighted curiosity. No, she was not a buyer. He smiled with an entirely academic appreciation of pretty girls and wavered into the stock room.

Jennie came into the room, with the step that would have been ambling had it not been for her integral grace. She looked, Lynn thought, somewhat taken aback.

" 'Allo, keed," she greeted her in her idiotic idiom. "What's wrong?"

"Nothing. Jennie, have you had lunch?"

"Not yet."

"Come downstairs and eat with me. I want to talk to you."

"Oke," agreed Jennie, shrugging.

Later, as they made their way toward the cafeteria, Jennie touched Lynn's arm.

"Not there. Let's go to the Gavarin," she suggested. "It's on me, this time. And I've graduated."

"Jennie, did you get a raise?"

"Maybe." Jennie's face was imperturbable. They went into the Gavarin and ordered. Jennie leaned back in her chair.

"What's under your hair, infant?"

"Nothing — but —"

"But what? — dandruff? Come on, spill it; mamma's listening."

Lynn found herself talking furiously. Her quarrel with Tom — she did not mention the cause, "We just disagreed about something" — the week-end — "Such fun, Jennie, such a perfectly grand place"; Dwight's subtly changed attitude, Tom's exhibition "barging into the room and calling me down!"

Jennie commented slowly, "It looks like your girl friend to me. Dirty work at the crossroads."

"Girl friend?"

"Sarah the Stately. Sure she hasn't been putting a bug in Dwight's ear, on your account? Look here, was he — all over the place about you, down there?"

"Of course not." But she hesitated, colored up a little. There had been, after all, a rose garden by moonlight, an ankle turned, an arm about her, a voice — *"sweet person —"*

"Hum," said Jennie, "don't get mixed up with him; that's all I have to offer. You steer clear. You'll make it up with Tom, all right. Don't feel yourself falling in another direction, do you?" Her words were light, but her eyes were anxious.

"Jennie, no, not in a million years!"

"Make it two million. The first million pass so quickly," murmured Jennie. "Watch the traffic lights, Lynn; you aren't the type to cross against them."

"What do you mean, the type? Who is?" asked Lynn.

"I am," said Jennie, and turned her eyes away.

Lynn stared at her. Jennie was different, somehow, less sure of herself, ill at ease.

"Look here," said Jennie, "I've been away for the week-end, too."

"You have?" Lynn took it blindly enough. "Jennie, where?"

"Where do you think? Atlantic City!" Jennie laughed, herself mordantly amused and aware of the sly humor of the situation. "It's always Atlantic City, isn't it, where girls go, good, and come back —"

"Jennie!"

"This is the time to call me by my right name," Jennie advised. "Say, 'Jane Smith!' with expression. Register horror. Leave your lunch. Leave the room. Leave me, sunk in sin, to pay the check!"

"Don't be an idiot," Lynn advised her crossly. She pushed her plate away and leaned forward, arms on the table. "Jennie, did you go to Atlantic City with — ?"

"I did. Meyer. Jake. I — he's not a bad guy," said Jennie wistfully, "and he's liberal. Suites. You know." She put her handbag on the table, opened it, and thrust her long hand inside. The hand

293

came out again and dripped, down on the sedate damask, several glittering objects; a plain gold wedding ring; a linked bracelet of diamonds; a solitaire.

Lynn stared, tore her eyes away, dropped them and stared again. "You're not — married?" she asked, hoping, but very faintly, against hope.

"No," answered Jennie. "Be your age. Of course I'm not married. All that glitters is not wedding rings." She pushed the gold band aside disdainfully. "The usual scenery," Jennie explained.

"But," Lynn said helplessly, "he isn't married — He can perfectly well —"

"No, he can't. Money. His wife's money, tied up in the firm. When he marries, if he does, it will be someone they pick out for him. Eighth cousin, twice removed. Nothing doing. His wife knew," said Jennie, "when she died that she had him where she wanted him; in perhaps the next best place to the grave. He — I'd like you to know that he told me — before I went. He's decent, that way."

Lynn thought, *I'm not shocked: I ought to be shocked. But I'm not. I'm* AFRAID, *that's all. For Jennie.* She asked, low, "Jennie, do you *love* him?"

"No," replied Jennie judiciously, "I don't

love him. I like him. I like him a lot. I like his money. What it can buy. We made our bargain. I'll play square, see. No two-timing. I owe him that much, don't I?"

"Are you — going to Chicago?" asked Lynn, sick at heart.

"Well, no. He has too much sense. I'll stay here; he'll come on, once a month, maybe twice. Then there'll be vacations, carefully managed —"

"I see." But she didn't. "Jennie," she cried, "why — *why?*"

"You wouldn't understand. Here, go 'way," she said petulantly to the hovering waiter. "When we want you, brother, we'll let you know!"

"Try and make me," said Lynn.

"I'm not like you," Jennie told her somberly. "I don't give a damn for jobs. I haven't any ambition. The stage, modeling, all the rest, a way of earning my way. As for marriage — I haven't any ambition in that direction either. You knew about Slim. I'm not saying I did not like him. But I had sense enough to quit seeing him. As a housewife, with a couple of kids and an electric washing machine, I'd be a flop. I can't help it if I was born with that breakfast-in-bed feeling, can I? I don't want to do anything but eat three, or maybe four, square meals a day and have good clothes and facials, and a decent flat somewhere. All right, go on, say it, I might get those things by myself. Don't be dumb! I wouldn't last ten days on any job but the one I have now, and that wouldn't buy birdseed, let alone a gilded cage. Men? If there are any men wandering around with money and looking for a nice blond wife, I haven't seen 'em.

"We girls have to have opportunities to meet men, don't we? They don't float in at the window with the influenza, do they? You don't find 'em on your doorstep with the morning News. In my job I meet men. But they aren't having any. See? Now and then a guy like Slim comes along, all set to go to the minister. That's something else again. He'd hate me in a year; I'd hate him in a month. I'm sick of seeing the girls I know run through the lights — when they do it in a Rolls. If you've got what people call character and ambition and all the rest of it, I suppose it pays to stay what people call good. If you haven't, it doesn't. Not, at least, as far as I'm concerned. I expect to be faithful to Jake Meyer. I'll amuse him, I'll entertain him, I have looks, a figure; he can hang me with clothes — and no whole-sale numbers either — and jewelry and take me out and be proud of me. Men are, you know; they throw expensive junk like this at you" — she touched the bracelet — "and show you off. 'Listen, world, I made her — and what she is today is none of your damned business!' "

"But, Jennie — do you think you'll be *happy?*"

"I don't know. I suppose so. Why not? I'll be safe," said Jennie.

"No —"

"Yes, I'll make it my business to be, see? Salt it all away, as much as I can. A girl's a fool who doesn't." After a minute she questioned, "I won't be seeing much of you, I suppose?"

"Why not?" asked Lynn with indignation.

"Tom — That's why."

"Oh, Tom — ! Do you think I'd tell Tom?"

"No, but he'll find out. Kid, if he does, give me the gate. You have to play safe too. I'll understand," said Jennie, with the closest approach to sentiment Lynn had ever seen in her.

Lynn's eyes were misty. Jennie said, "I'll pull out of the flat, of course. I'll pay my share there until you find someone to go in with you. That's only right."

"Jennie, I couldn't — it wouldn't be fair — and besides —" Lynn floundered.

"You don't want to have Jake's money helping pay your rent?" asked Jennie shrewdly. "Scorn the wages of sin, what?"

"I didn't say it —"

"You didn't have to. Well, it won't. I'll pay my share, till things are straightened out, out of my earnings as usual."

"You're going on working!" gasped Lynn.

"Sure. Why not? I'd go goofy sitting around all day alone, nothing to do but cut coupons and shine up the diamonds," Jennie said, with her slow, wicked grin. "Jake would rather I worked."

"I'll never understand you! You said, you practically said, that it was because you didn't want to work —"

"Check," agreed Jennie pleasantly. "Not when work was all I had to look forward to. But if you have a side line" — she cocked an eyebrow at her friend — "then the sort of stuff I strut is fun. Besides, it won't hurt Jake. I can tip him off, you know, when the hot numbers come in."

"But Madame Fanchon?"

"It works both ways. She'll know, but she'll never say so. She'll be glad to keep me on at present rates, knowing I won't ever hit her for a raise. She'll think I'll keep the home fires burning as far as Jake's firm is concerned. She'll be right."

"When," asked Lynn very forlornly, "when are you — leaving?"

Jennie grew constrained. She said hesitantly, "I thought you'd want me to go — at once. I figured on taking a room in a hotel. But Jake's got to go West. He said we'd fix it up about the flat after he came back."

Lynn said stubbornly, "I don't want you to go — until —"

"Thanks." Jennie looked down at her untouched plate. With astonishment she saw before her food which she was not eating. She asked, "When are you going on vacation?"

"September."

"Going home?"

"I suppose so."

"Before you go," said Jennie, "maybe you'll find someone to live with you. When you come back, I'll be gone."

And all Lynn said was, sincerely, "I'll miss you so, Jennie."

But back at work her mind was on anything but the blue cards. Jennie, how wrong, how mistaken, how entirely mad! Jennie, how rock-bottom decent. Decent, that was Jennie's own word. What was the matter with her anyway? What did she lack? Moral sense? Could a girl lack moral sense who was so integrally true to her friends, who had her own small yet inflexible code?

Lynn thought, *It's economic; it has to do, somehow, with the entire economic system. I don't know, I can't understand.*

Other girls, like Jennie, hundreds of them, thousands of them, good fellows, brutally frank, brutally on the make, willing to pay for what they wanted. Other girls, not like Jennie, struggling along, fighting, existing, earning their livings —

Something awfully wrong somewhere.

Her head ached. It seemed to her as she bent over her desk that the entire weight of the massive building was upon it, that she was oppressed, burdened, hemmed in. The stone and steel closed about her, there was no air, no light, no way to get free, to get clear, to soar upward spiritually with the defiant and escaping towers —

Tom came that night, repentant, more than a little sorry. Jennie was out. "Believe it or not," she told Lynn, "I'm going to sit up with a sick friend!"

Tom said, "Lynn, I'm sorry. I'm an ass. Why shouldn't you go to Dwight's with

Sarah? This summer's been hard on you, hot as the devil, no chance to get away."

She said, instantly responsive to his mood, his authentic plea for pardon, "That's all right; I should have told you before. Only, Tom, you've made me so self-conscious about David Dwight. There's no reason for me to be, you understand that, don't you?"

She was soft, appealing; she went to his arms and clung there, seeking, perhaps unconsciously, haven, protection. Jennie's decision had shaken her terribly, more perhaps than she knew. She felt ignorant and lost and miserable. Things were not clear-cut. Things were not black and white. If only she could feel that they were; could feel that Jennie was pariah, outcast, could dismiss Jennie from her life, all that she stood for, and forget her!

But she could not. Her liking, her actual affection, for Jennie was not altered.

If things were black and white, yes and no, right and wrong, life would be so much simpler; *was* simpler for people who could see things without compromise, without appeal, without mitigation.

"I do love you so much, Tom."

"Enough to — do something for me?"

"Of course! Anything. You know that."

She looked at him, eager, radiant, gray eyes shining.

"It isn't doing anything exactly. It's agreeing with me. Lynn, I can get forty-five a week at UBC. I know it's not much, I know you won't think there's as much future in it as in the bank. But, God, Lynn, I hate the bank! I'm bored with it, the whole outfit drives me crazy. I want to work at something I'm" — he remembered Hank's words — "something I'm keen on. If — Would you be terribly disappointed in me if I gave up my job with the Seacoast, and went — upstairs?"

She said, "No," slowly. She would be, she had counted on Tom's making good in the banking business. But if he were un-happy?

"No," she said again, "you must do what you like, of course —"

If she were not enthusiastic it was because she was thinking. Why *now?* Why is he suddenly so eager — to leave? She said, on the heels of suspicion, "Tom, you did see Bob Rawlson, didn't you?"

That was a sore spot. *And how!* thought Tom. He mumbled awkwardly, hastily, "Oh, sure, I saw him, that's all right. We fixed it up."

Never let Lynn know the humiliation of

pride he had undergone seeing Bob. The remembrance of it shifted his eyes, thickened his tongue.

Lynn looked at him, terribly uneasy.

He said, hurriedly, "I — gee, Lynn, I hoped you'd get to see things my way. I took out my license, you know, down at the Sub-treasury. You've got to have a license; it's better, you see, in case you fool about with transmitters. I — gosh, I'm glad. I'll go to see Hank's buddy today."

His subsequent embrace was all boyish, if bearlike, gratitude. In his arms she thought, confused, *He has seen Rawlson, he said so —*

He had seen him. But someone else was to see him in a day or so. Dwight, talking with Sarah over a luncheon table. "It was good of you to come with me, Sarah, to prove that if you haven't forgiven me it's at least armistice. I've been something of a fool," he confessed, deploring it insincerely, and believing it not at all. "I — I'd do anything rather than quarrel with you — We've been through so much —" His eyes were gay and wistful, imploring her to forget, forgive.

Her heart tightened. She couldn't believe, she couldn't trust, and yet — She told herself angrily, sorrowfully, *It's like a spell, an enchantment; I can't get away from it —*

"People of my age," he said lightly, "dream in impossibilities." He loathed saying it, even for a purpose, even to disarm her. It brought things too close. He smiled, shrugged. "Let's talk of other things. Or, rather, of young Shepard. Sarah, you must believe that, despite appearances, I have Lynn's welfare at heart as closely as you have. This boy, you really approve of him?"

"I didn't at first," she replied, reluctant yet forced into it. "I have been anxious for Lynn to make something of a career for herself. Not that that matters after all," she said half to herself, her mouth falling into the bitter lines of retrospective failure and starvation. "Marriage is bound to interfere. But — if they love each other —"

"Of course, if they love each other," he agreed instantly. "But has the boy any future, where he now is, in the bank? Has he — influential friends? Or any friends, in fact? Where does he hail from, who are his people? You see I know very little about him," he admitted.

She answered, readily enough, telling him all she knew of Tom Shepard. No, as far as she knew, Mr. Norton was his only friend of "influence." As for friends his own age — had David meant that? She knew he traveled with some of the UBC men, lived with a couple of engineers his own age or a little older.

"He appears to be a boy who would make friends everywhere, as well as in his job," Dwight said thoughtfully.

"Not in the job," she told him, "as much as outside of it — except for young Rawlson, one of the salesmen in our department. They are together a lot. I've seen them going out, quitting time, arm in arm. Rawlson seems a clever boy," she went on idly, "and has, I believe, a little money of his own. His uncle is a director in First Citizens'."

She went on talking, thinking only on the surface of what she was saying, thinking instead how pleasant this was, how Sunday night seemed a nightmare, seemed something that could not have happened. Yet it had happened. But she should have known better; to force Dwight into a corner was always to bring out the worst in him, it always led to making him say things he couldn't possibly mean. Out of her experience with him she had learned that only, it seemed, to forget it. And he had given her his word of honor Lynn was safe.

Dwight listened, his eyes bright with

courteous attention. He too was thinking, beneath the surface Rawlson, eh? It should be easy to meet him.

Chapter Sixteen:

A GNAWING SUSPICION

There would be some delay, Tom found, in assuring himself of the UBC position. There, in the tower, with its countless visible and invisible wires, its network, at once so concrete and practical, yet so symbolic, the mills ground slowly. Tom had said nothing to Mr. Norton about resigning. Life had, perhaps, taught him very little caution, but it had taught him enough to make sure of the bird in the bush before you cast away the bird in hand. It was several weeks before his application and interviews bore fruit. But when it was finally settled that he was to have Noonan's coveted place and salary, he approached Mr. Norton in some trepidation, his ears ringing with prophetic admonitions, warnings, and expressions of disapproval.

"Could I have a moment of your time, Mr. Norton?" he asked, in the doorway between Norton's room and his own little antechamber.

Norton had just returned from a luncheon conference. His usually austere but pleasant features were troubled, and his eyebrows twitched in the way they had when he was irritated or annoyed over something. Tom realized that this was hardly a propitious time to approach his superior. His gay heart sank. Norton — well, he wasn't his guardian or anything by a long shot, but he had taken an interest in him, he had done his best for him. To pull out of the association gracefully would be harder than he had anticipated.

"I was just going to ring for you. Come in. Shut the door behind you," Norton replied.

Tom crossed the intervening space and stood beside the desk. He was smiling, an engaging sort of grin, from sheer nervousness. Mr. Norton pushed his chair back, leaned his head against it, placed the finger-tips of one hand against the finger-tips of the other with delicate accuracy and looked up.

"I wanted to tell you, sir —" Tom began.

"That can wait," Norton said abruptly. He launched the bolt. It distressed him to launch it, therefore his tones were dryer than ever, more devoid of humanity.

"Tom, have you been so indiscreet as to talk over the affairs of the bank with outsiders?"

Tom answered quickly, without thinking, "No, sir."

"Are you sure?"

"Yes." He recalled Rawlson. Norton, watching him, saw the hot color creep up the strong young throat, stain the lean cheeks. He shook his head and felt his own throat tighten. Lying — ?

"Better think again."

Rawlson? Rawlson was not an outsider. Lynn? He had talked to Lynn. Lynn was not an outsider. He said painfully, "I — haven't talked outside. That is, other people in the bank know, Mr. Norton; they've spoken to me about it. I haven't said a word to anyone else."

"Someone has." Norton's voice was low. "There are indications — on the Street, in brokers' offices. Indications of a leak somewhere. More than anyone not actually concerned in this matter you have been in my confidence."

Tom thrust his chin out. He looked belligerent. He also looked guilty. In a sense he was guilty, and felt it — because he might have been the means of a "leak," and an important one. In another sense he was actually and practically guilty; but he did not know that.

"Do you mean that I —"

"What am I to think, Tom?" asked the older man. He added, under Tom's stare and little gasp: "There's no one else. Unless — it's someone you've talked to — Do you think — anyone in the bank — ?"

Tom shook his head stubbornly. He thought Rawlson — But, no, Rawlson had intimated that he would "do nothing further." It wasn't likely to be Rawlson. Without him, Tom, Rawlson couldn't operate accurately anyway, couldn't gage the exact moment, hadn't his finger on the pulse of this affair. It couldn't be Rawlson.

Norton in common with almost everyone else in the trust department had not been unaware of Tom's and Lynn's attachment. He spoke of Lynn now, a little hesitantly.

"There is Miss Harding — You are, I know, close friends. If, through something you said to her — Oh," he added hastily, as Tom's eyes grew brilliant with anger, "I assure you she might talk, outside, inadvertently, not realizing the mischief that she would cause, if she talked to — the wrong people. Women are like that," said Norton dourly.

"You can leave her out of it," Tom told his superior truculently.

Norton didn't care to be spoken to truculently. He was, he assured himself, making every allowance for the lad, trying hard to get to the bottom of this. The information which had come to him in the last few hours had caused him to lose a good deal of face. Someone very weighty had said, "What about that confidential secretary of yours, Norton?"

He could have — and had — replied, "What about yours, Wright?" But it so happened that other confidential secretaries were time-proved and tested. Tom was the youngest, in any branch of the bank; the newest; and, Norton had acknowledged to himself with a sigh, the least responsible, the least genuinely interested in the business of banking.

He said, "Very well, we'll leave her out. But you have admitted that you've talked. To whom, please?"

"It doesn't matter," Tom said, white. "Not to anyone who — who —"

He broke off. Rawlson? No, again, that was impossible.

"You haven't," Norton argued, "shown much interest in your work. I've given you every opportunity — The fact that you could go out of this office and discuss the private affairs of the bank lightly shows me that you do not hold your part here in deep concern. You spend a good deal of your spare time fraternizing with the young men upstairs in the tower. I had hoped, when I placed you here, that you would want to get ahead, that you would study, would fit yourself for a more responsible position, would interest yourself in every phase of the work. But unfortunately you show no such inclination."

"If my work isn't satisfactory —" began Tom, very white now.

"It has been satisfactory, as far as routine goes," Norton assured him, "but no farther. Tom, do you refuse to tell me with whom you have been discussing the projected merger?"

"I haven't discussed it," Tom shouted, goaded into a pyrotechnic display merely because, but for the grace of God — of Lynn, he would have been as guilty as hell, facing the quiet disapproving eyes of the elder man — "except — except to mention it to people within the bank, who hadn't — who couldn't —"

He had floundered long enough. Norton took a measure of cold pity on him. Lynn Harding, of course. He had talked to Lynn, she had talked to — heaven knew whom. It was distinctly traceable. Yet he wasn't so sure. Lynn had always seemed a most level-headed girl to Mr. Norton; Miss Dennet thought highly of her —

Well, it didn't matter. It was possible, probable even that, if Tom had talked, his talking hadn't affected things one way or the other. But the point was that, having talked, he proved himself unworthy of trust. Norton said so now.

"Never mind, I'll take your word for it, I have to. But whether or not you've done the organization harm by your conscious or unconscious indiscretion is beside the point. The point is we can't afford to have young men who gossip connected with us. The job of confidential secretary is just that. I'm sorry, Tom, but —"

"I'm being fired?" Tom asked quietly.

"I'm letting you go," Norton substituted the more courteous term. "You aren't particularly happy with us; why should you be when you're not interested in the work? And this incident has proved to me beyond question of a doubt that you take your obligations far too lightly. I'm sorry, Tom," he said, and sincerely. "I wanted to see you make something of yourself, I tried to help you —"

Tom admitted that, stiffly enough. He was sore, bruised, in his mind and in his pride. He couldn't, he thought, ruefully say now, "Take your damned old job, I've got me another, I was going to resign when you sprang this on me."

If he resigned as an anticlimax Norton would believe more than ever that he'd had it up his sleeve, as a way out, in case he was caught; or that it was a lie to save his face, out of bravado —

Somehow, he got out of the office, with Norton sitting there, like a judge, staring at him, sighing a little, eyebrows twitching.

On the following Monday Tom went to work for the UBC shooting skyward in the express elevator, passing the hivelike activities of the first six floors with a sense of discomfort.

Once in his new job he was to accustom himself to curious hours. The checkerboard — that square of ruled cardboard upon which, as neatly as any problem, the hours on duty of the men in the master-control room had been worked out — was an elastic affair. Tom might get to work at eight, cease at eleven, return at three, and work until night. Or most of his work might be afternoon and evening. For this reason he was to see rather less of Lynn, calling her up at odd times to report progress and peace of mind, running in to see her evenings, between programs as it were.

He had not told her that he had been let out. He thought, walking from Lynn's office, *if I tell her she might believe that I did — spill the beans.* He consoled himself with believing that she wasn't likely to find out. Norton wouldn't be apt to discuss it with her — or would he? And she had known that he, Tom, was going to "resign." Let her think it, as long as possible. Then, if he had to tell her — but perhaps he wouldn't, he thought — turning craven at the idea.

It was Sarah who told her, after being called into a conference with Norton, a conference that concerned Lynn herself. Coming out of Norton's private room Sarah was deeply troubled. Idiotic of Norton to feel that Lynn might be involved! She had spoken to him on the subject and so strongly that he had admitted it had been only a fantastic guess on his part.

"You know her better than I do," he had said, "and if you consider her loyalty impregnable —"

"As much so as my own," she told him. "No, Mr. Norton, you'll have to look elsewhere for your traitor — As for Tom," she had said, sighing, "I don't believe he would do such a thing consciously."

But she felt she must speak to Lynn. She waited until they were dining together one night in Sarah's apartment. They were alone. After dinner, listening to Lynn talk of Tom's happiness in his new position, she asked gravely, "Lynn, has Tom ever spoken to you about a rumor of a merger between the bank and the First Citizens'?"

Lynn put down the cigarette she had picked up. Her heart was racing. Instinctively, in a perfectly natural impulse to protect Tom, if he needed protection, she replied instantly, "Why, no, he never has. Why?"

"It has been," Sarah explained, "kept extremely quiet. For several reasons. There had been a rumor of a merger there," she said, "and it didn't go through. Depositors felt that it meant the institution was unsound. There was a run on the bank and its branches, one that no bank could withstand. So it was thought wise that all the details of this particular proposition be worked out, and the thing made absolutely certain with no chance of a slip-up, before anything was said. But something has been said. It's been reflected on the Street. That is to say, stock in both companies is being bought up quietly, in small blocks. For quite a time, and very cleverly. It may not mean anything; we'll see how long it goes on. But it is beginning to cause talk — and it looks very much as if there had been a leak somewhere."

"But," asked Lynn, and her voice sounded small and thin to her own ears, "what on earth could Tom have to do with it?"

"Nothing — I sincerely hope." Sarah looked at the younger girl. This was the first time they had talked together alone since Tom had left the bank. "But he was in a position to know, he couldn't, you see, *help* knowing."

"Well, if he did know," argued Lynn, with a laugh which was entirely unnatural, "you couldn't accuse *him* of buying blocks of stock — on fifty a week!"

"My dear," said Sarah amazed, "of course not. I merely asked you a simple question. After all, you must have known that he left the bank's employ under a cloud, and I wondered it —"

"What do you mean, 'under a cloud'?"

Sarah answered gently, "Mr. Norton accused him of being responsible for the leak. Of course he had no proof, and naturally Tom denied it. But he had to be let out just the same."

"Let out!" said Lynn in a whisper.

"What did you think had happened?" Sarah asked her, astonished.

"He *resigned*," Lynn told her. "He told me he was going to resign. He wanted to, he hated the work, he wanted to take a job with the UBC people. He had just put off quitting downstairs and going up to the tower because he didn't think I'd approve."

"He said nothing of that to Norton," Sarah told her.

"Perhaps he didn't have a chance," Lynn flared up. But she thought, *Could he have known? and covered himself by telling me he was going to resign?* She put her hands to the dark head with a distracted gesture. "Suppose he did say something," she asked, returning to the original discussion, "but without realizing it was important?"

"He couldn't help realizing it was important," Sarah reminded her. "At first the quiet purchase of the stocks went unnoticed. Lately all sorts of rumors have been current, during the last few days in fact. It is evident, we think, that some one individual or group of individuals is trying to buy up all the available shares. Naturally officers and directors are not beside themselves with pleasure."

Lynn said stubbornly, "It wasn't Tom."

Sarah was silent.

Lynn said defiantly, "He just wasn't happy in the job, that's all."

Sarah nodded. "I suppose that's the main thing," she said. She thought, *Norton may be all wrong*. Strangely enough, it didn't particularly matter to her whether or not Tom was the cause of this muddle. Nothing much mattered but that Tom and Lynn be happy — and safe. She realized with a slight shock that she had not, after all, changed with the years. Her principles, her judgments went by the board when in conflict with her emotions. She asked Lynn now, "You're happy in your job, aren't you?"

"Of course I am. I'm crazy about it. Not that I want to be there all my life; I want awfully to go on."

"I think you'll have an opportunity," Sarah said carefully. "I don't want to raise your hopes prematurely, but I can tell you this much. Since the particular sort of promotion I've done in my department has been so well received there is a chance that I may, at some future date, be transferred to the advertising department, in charge of advertising. If I do, that will leave my position empty. I will be given a chance to recommend someone. And I'll recommend you, Lynn —"

"Sarah — you angel!"

"Don't look so wide-eyed. You must

have known for some time that you would one day take my place. But you'll have to work."

"I will. Oh, Sarah, I'll work — so hard. I — I've been thinking for quite a while of enrolling at Columbia for some night courses — now that I don't see Tom much, now that his work keeps him busy and at such off times."

"An excellent idea," Sarah agreed relievedly, and turned the conversation to talk of books which would be useful, of classes which she herself had managed to attend, of the successful lectures on finance to prospective women buyers, of the bank's facilities, which she herself had arranged and managed.

"I can enroll after vacation," Lynn decided.

She left Sarah's early, determined to ring up Tom. If he were at home she'd see him at once, if he could come around, and get this thing straightened out. She told Sarah so in a brief reference to the topic as she was leaving. Sarah said nothing. She was already sorry she had spoken to Lynn. The last thing she wished to do would be to cause trouble between Lynn and Tom Shepard.

Tom was not at home. But Hank was.

Hank told her that Tom had been sent out to Long Island to learn the ropes at the UBC's great station there. He'd be gone several days, Hank thought, and would live out there for the time being. "He tried to get you," Hank explained, "between throwing things in a bag, but no one answered at the apartment. He's getting on swell," Hank said, "best thing he ever did in his life was leaving the bank. He wasn't cut out for a J.P."

So Hank too thought Tom had "left." Perhaps, perhaps Mr. Norton hadn't told Sarah the entire truth; perhaps Tom had gone to ask that his resignation be accepted, and Norton, angry and disappointed, had flared out at him about this other business. But that, she admitted, wouldn't hold water either.

Chapter Seventeen:

"MEN MAKE ME SICK!"

Lynn did not, as it happened, go home for vacation. Her mother wrote her that there was an infantile epidemic in town, her father was driven day and night, and they had decided it would not be safe for her to return. "Perhaps," she wrote, "when it is all over we can take a little holiday trip to New York to see you."

So Lynn remained in town, enrolling for all the classes she could manage for the fall term and for a tail-end summer class before the regular session. She took her two weeks' vacation literally in a classroom, and during that time did not see Tom at all, his apprenticeship on Long Island lasting longer than he had expected. He telephoned her now and then and wrote her short, illegible, happy notes.

The fact that Jennie was leaving worried her. Would she be able to swing the apartment alone? She thought not; not yet, at any rate. And of course she wouldn't permit Jennie to pay. She spoke to Sarah, a little self-consciously.

"Jennie's leaving the apartment," she said. "I suppose I'll have to look for a room, or go to the club again." She shrugged her shoulders. "It isn't a pleasant prospect; in the last few months I've become pretty accustomed to freedom."

"Where's Jennie going?" Sarah wanted to know.

"Oh" — Lynn was vague — "I don't know; she's tired of housekeeping, I guess."

Sarah raised her heavy eyebrows but forbore to press her further. She said, after a moment, "There's a little apartment on the ground floor in this building. Just one room and bath. The tenant is sailing on October first for Europe. She has a long lease. She told me that if she could rent it to someone reliable she would be willing to let it go for very little, less in fact than the rent. I — you'd be alone, of course, but in the same building with us."

"Sarah, that sounds grand!"

"Have you a lease where you are?"

"No, just one of those month-to-month things. Gosh, I'd love it," said Lynn. "Could I see it?"

Having seen it, she told Jennie, "It's just

the thing, awfully cute. You couldn't swing a cat in it, but I haven't a cat and wouldn't swing one if I had. It's fitted up as a living-room you know, one of those studio couches, and there's a sort of electric-plate affair in something not as big as a clothes closet. I can't stay on here alone anyway, Jennie; and I don't know of anyone I like well enough to ask to come in with me."

"Sounds all right," Jennie admitted after a moment, "if you're willing to be under Sarah's eagle eye every minute of the day and night."

"Oh, she won't interfere with me," Lynn said easily. "It would never occur to her."

"I'm not so sure," said Jennie. "Lynn, you haven't told Tom — anything, have you?"

"Of course not," Lynn replied indignantly. "What do you think I am? Why?"

"I didn't think you had. But Slim's been getting all hot and bothered about me lately. I — I just won't see him, that's all," said Jennie, setting her small jaw firmly. "I can't afford to. Suppose I get fed up with Jake — and Slim's handy? God knows what I'd do. And I don't *want* to do any-thing," she added ambiguously.

"Oh, but Jennie," — Lynn flushed and stumbled a bit — "if Slim should find out he wouldn't — I mean, you wouldn't have any more trouble with him."

Jennie slid her long eyes around at her friend.

"Oh, yeah? Well, you're all wet — that is, if you mean that Slim would cut me off his calling-list. He wouldn't, naturally, have honorable intentions any more but —"

"Oh, Jennie, not Slim!"

"Why not? He's a man," said Jennie definitely.

Tom came back in high feather, enthusiastic to the boiling or bursting point over his work. But Lynn, the first time they were alone together, paid him scant attention. She came straight to the point.

"Tom," she said, "why didn't you tell me Mr. Norton let you out?"

He looked excessively uncomfortable. Of course he might have known she'd find out! Everyone knew, he supposed. He answered awkwardly, "Gosh, it was all so darned stupid. I — I didn't want to tell you. You see, I walked into his office, all set to tell him I was quitting — and I can prove it too, Lynn, by the date I interviewed 'em up at UBC and was taken on — and then he sprang it at me. About firing me, I mean. Lord, you could have knocked me over with a — a cobweb!"

"But *why* did he fire you?" she demanded, believing that much of his explanation, impossible not to believe him; he was so entirely eager and honest.

"Oh, I wasn't 'responsible.' I didn't take my 'obligations' seriously, or so he said."

Now was the time for her to say, "And didn't you? Did you — did you break your word to me about Rawlson?" But she couldn't say it. She had missed him so much, she had him back again, he hadn't lied to her, she knew he hadn't lied, perhaps Sarah had misunderstood Mr. Norton, perhaps she had taken this talk of obligations and responsibilities to mean a dishonorable discharge.

She said irrelevantly, "Oh, darling, I'm so glad to have you back. Don't let them send you places again, will you? I've missed you so much. I wish," she said, low, "that they hadn't fired you — I mean —"

He kissed her. "So do I," he said cheerfully, "but if I'd said, 'I'm quitting, anyway,' he wouldn't have believed me, Lynn, I would have felt like a fool."

She asked, "I suppose you know Bob Rawlson has your job?"

He looked so perfectly aghast that she knew he hadn't known; knew, too, with a relieved throb of her heart that he hadn't been seeing Rawlson.

"Rawlson!" he exclaimed.

"Yes. Sarah told me that Mr. Norton had given him this chance, as he was dissatisfied where he was. Tom — do you think," she asked, "that — that it was wise — of Mr. Norton?"

"Wise?" He frowned, puzzled, then understanding, he laughed. "Sure! Thinking of that jackass idea he — I mean we had? Get it out of your funny little head. Pipe dreams, that's what it was. Nothing to it. Rawlson's forgotten it long ago, I guess."

She thought, *Then he doesn't know there's been talk on the Street.*

She decided not to tell him. What was, after all, the use?

By the middle of October Jennie had moved to a Riverside Drive apartment, to her own amused chagrin.

"Jake," said Jennie, "is old-fashioned. He thinks that if you're going to keep a woman —"

"Please, Jennie, don't talk like that."

"Why not? Is there a prettier name for it?" asked Jennie, and continued imperturbably — "that you have to keep her on the Drive. I held out for Park Avenue or at least, the East Side. But nothing doing. Still, it's a nice dump," she conceded carelessly, "and has all the works, including a maid."

She added, "I don't suppose you'll come see me."

"Why not?" asked Lynn, in her turn.

Tom, learning that Jennie had moved and Lynn was moving, was insistent in his demands for an explanation.

"What's the big idea? I thought you liked the place and that you two got along like a house afire."

"We did, we do, but Jennie's — Jennie's had a raise," lied Lynn desperately and futilely, "and she's had a chance to go into a bigger place with — with someone else."

"Who?"

"Oh, just someone she used to know."

"Look here, what's wrong with you? Come, spill it, what's it all about?" asked Tom.

"Nothing. Whatever it is, it's Jennie's business," said Lynn, "and I haven't inquired into it."

Her tone warned Tom that he was not to inquire, either; but for the rest of their time together, while Lynn in a brave endeavor to follow his jargon listened to his tales of the new job, his mind was busy with speculations. A talk with Slim enlightened him not at all and only served to puzzle him more. But one day, reporting for work at noon, he saw Jennie leaving the building with a short, dark, dapper man, and protecting herself against the slight autumnal chill in the air by a three-skinned Russian sable slung about the collar of her tailored suit. "So that's it!" said Tom, staring.

He told Lynn, when next he saw her, "I'm wise to Jennie's game. Look here, you'll have to cut her out."

Lynn said stubbornly, "I don't know what you're talking about."

"She isn't," explained Tom, "wearing sables — and such good ones that even I could tell 'em — and isn't living on Riverside Drive — oh, Slim knows that much — on whatever she pulls down upstairs. Don't make me laugh. You — you can't afford to see her, Lynn."

"Is that so? Well," said Lynn furiously, "you can't dictate to me about my friends — I'll see her as often as I want!"

Tom took his troubles to Sarah, braving all curious looks to stop in at her office one day and sit down beside her desk. Sarah listened patiently, making little dots and circles on the blotting-paper with her fountain pen.

"I thought it was something of the kind.

Don't," she advised slowly, more anxious than Tom could know that he and Lynn should not quarrel, "don't antagonize her, Tom. She's very loyal. No matter what Jennie does or has become, she won't desert her. And you'll only make her angry. Let me talk to her instead."

She did so, at the first opportunity, coming right to the point.

"You mustn't blame Tom," she concluded, after she had explained.

"I don't. Yes, I do! Men make me sick!" said Lynn violently.

"I know you're fond of Jennie," Sarah told her gently, "but can't you see that she has cut herself off from all companionship with you by this step?"

"No. She was honest with me about it from the very beginning. She was perfectly willing that I should, as you say, cut her off. She wanted me to, rather. But I won't. She's lonely — in a way. I — I don't go there when — anyone else is there, Sarah," Lynn told her.

"I see. That's wise, of course." Sarah was silent for a moment. She thought, *What a rotten hypocrite I am! What right have I to preach to Lynn about Jennie's morals? Even if — if it was all over years ago, it happened, didn't it?*

There is caste in everything after all —
No man kept me, she thought further, her
chin lifted — *That was a free gift; this is a —
business arrangement.*

She said aloud, "I'll not say any more,
and I don't think Tom will. It's up to your
own judgment, Lynn."

Now, when Tom came to Lynn's new
apartment, she took him as a rule up to
Sarah's. It was tacitly agreed between them
all that this arrangement would be the
better part of valor. But he came sometimes at such curious times that they
couldn't inflict themselves upon Sarah,
and so they took to going out again for the
brief hours belonging to them.

There were not many such hours. With
the opening of the fall term Lynn was busy
four nights a week.

Tom asked, dissatisfied, "What's the big
idea of killing yourself?"

She answered, "It isn't settled yet — but
if Sarah does change her position, I'm in
line for hers, you know."

"Gee, that's great!" He said it sincerely,
but his eyes flickered anxiously over her
small face, a little pale, a little thin. "But
you mustn't work too hard. You can't
stand it." And then because Sarah had
talked to him, advising, warning, he said

awkwardly, "You're not fretting about Jennie, are you?"

She said, "I suppose so, a little." She touched his cheek with her hand, leaned closer to him in the motion-picture house where they were sitting, heedless of the stage show. "It seems such a *waste*. I'm so sorry for her."

Tom said glumly, "So am I, in a way, but it's her own funeral. Slim's started to hang around her again. I'm worried about him, too."

They were silent, as the curtain fell and the house darkened and the film started to unroll, holding each other's hands, like children, for comfort.

Lynn had not encountered David Dwight since the house party, save once when she had seen him outside the bank. His car was driving away, and someone else walking briskly into the bank had presented to her abstracted view a back and a set of shoulders which reminded her of Bob Rawlson. She had seen Dwight only as a figure, leaning back against the upholstery of his car. He had not seen her. She admitted to herself that she was a little hurt, and more than a little bewildered by his apparently deliberate neglect. Before the house party, if she had not seen him often, she had at least heard from him occasionally; a note written from Washington, Chicago, Cleveland; flowers; telephone calls.

He was, she decided, probably dreadfully busy. Courts were in session, he would be away perhaps most of the time. Still, it was odd —

She even spoke of it to Sarah, frankly enough. Sarah, her eyes guarded, said, "He's occupied, I suppose. I saw in *The Times* the other day that another case had gone against him, on appeal."

Lynn thought, *I wish I hadn't spoken; she must think I'm crazy; as if I mattered to him — at all.*

The football season was on. Tom was sent out, with the announcers, to learn the business of the outside hookups. He returned from these expeditions full of enthusiasm. He liked such work even better than the master control room or "cranking gains" in the various studio control rooms — which meant, he assured her, simply monitoring the broadcast from the studio, in the studio control room, en route to the master control room.

It was, she decided, much too deep for her. But that he was happy was perfectly obvious. His work had changed him, even in this brief time. He was more sure of himself, not in his cocky, boyish way, but maturely sure. He had grown in poise, in stature almost. He was never bored now, but eager and ardent, looking forward to the next day's work.

"You'll get over it," Hank told him.

"Not I," said Tom. "This is like Christmas every day, as far as I'm concerned."

Lynn at his insistence came now and then to the studio and was permitted to observe the programs through the glass windows and to sit in the reception room and once to go through the control room, which filled her with the blank amazement and slight terror of the layman confronted by the mysteries of science. The various apparatus for sound effects amused her more than anything else, and she endeared herself to the gentleman in charge of them by asking what he called, with some astonishment, intelligent questions. She thought that afterward when her work permitted it, she would get books "and things," talk more seriously with Tom, try to learn a little more about this astonishing phenomenon which concerned him so closely and deeply. He could understand her work, but she couldn't understand his; and she wanted to, if only the better to comprehend him.

Lynn was by no means entirely satisfied with Tom's explanation of the way in which he had left the bank. But she forced herself to be. She had no proof, nothing upon which to base her occasional quite dreadful doubts of him. She had no proof that he ever saw Rawlson. But it was unfortunate that at this tag end of the season, at a time when little cars were going into cold storage and town cars replacing roadsters in the city, Tom took it upon himself to buy a car. It was not new, it was second hand, even third hand; but it had had, as he said proudly, "a sweet paint job," and it looked smart and shining as he brought it one evening to a flourishing stop in front of the apartment house, and, dashing in, invited Lynn to step to the window and gaze upon the chariot under the light of street lamps.

"But where on earth did you get it?" she demanded, feeling suddenly sick.

"Made a killing in the Street," he offered cheerfully, his arm about her shoulders.

She moved away from him.

"Tom — ? Please be serious."

"Robbed a bank," he went on. "Hey, what's the big idea of going over there? Won't it be swell when spring comes — provided either of us has any time — we can go picnicking. Bought it," he said amiably, "for a song."

"But I don't understand," said Lynn miserably.

"Bigger and Better Business, baby. I figured if I had to take to apple-selling I could load 'em in the rumble seat and park on quiet corners."

She said steadily, "Tom, you'd better tell me the truth."

"You won't like it," he warned her, sobering.

Her heart was very heavy. She said, "It doesn't matter whether I like it or not, does it?"

"Oh, it isn't that bad," he told her cheerfully, "only I know you hate speculation. No one on a small salary," he intoned gravely, "has a right to speculate. Well, I did — a little. And there's the answer," he said truthfully.

He flicked a finger toward the car. "Get on your things and we'll try it," he suggested.

"No, Tom, come over here and sit down."

He obeyed, wondering.

"Tom, are you — are you telling me the truth?"

"Sure, I am. Say, look here, Lynn, what's biting you?"

"But there's been a leak," she said steadily, "about — the bank merger. I heard about it some time ago. I didn't tell you — I thought — but now — Tom, you promised me — you swore you'd tell Bob Rawlson you'd have no more to do with that scheme of his. You said you had told him."

"Of course I promised. And I told him," he told her, bewildered. "What's all the shooting for?"

"Someone has been buying the stock," she said, "someone knows. And — you were let out."

"Well, it wasn't me," he said, "even if I was fired."

She was silent. He said again, "I didn't do it. Good Lord, Lynn, I bought that car for three hundred and fifty dollars. If I had done what you think — I wouldn't be buying second-hand cars."

She said, "I'm not so sure. You wouldn't, of course, make the profit other people would. You haven't," she said bitterly, "enough business sense."

He got to his feet and stood over her. "Is that so? Do you mean to tell me that you think I went back on my word?"

She said wretchedly, "I don't know *what* to think."

"And I don't know what to think of *you!*"

He was angry; and he was innocent; and it is a curious fact that a combination of anger and innocence wears often the very face of guilt. His hasty words carried, to her ears, absolutely no conviction. "I thought you were pretty fair-minded — and loyal. Sarah said you were. She said about Jennie — no matter what Jennie has done or become, she said, you would stick to her, wouldn't hear anything against her. That goes for Jennie. But because you hear some fool rumor you immediately jump to the conclusion —"

"I didn't jump to it," she told him. "You will have to admit that you thought of making a profit out of such a breach of confidence, not so very long ago."

"Well, what if I did?" he asked sullenly. "I didn't actually do it, did I, and that's what counts."

"Yes, if you didn't. But, Tom," she wailed, "I'm not *sure*. Was — was Mr. Norton sure —" she asked.

"To hell with him. If *you* don't believe me —" He stopped. He walked to the door. He was shaking with anger, with a wounded astonishment, and with a self-pitying sense of his own innocence, all the more innocent because once his conscience had not always been so clear. "If you don't believe me," he said again, "I'll go away — and stay away — until you do —"

The door slammed behind him.

Lynn sat where he had left her. Her knees were water. She could not have risen, she thought dully, to save her life. She thought, *He means it. He'll go away and never come back unless I tell him to — And I won't tell him. I'm not sure — I said — I said I'd never speak to him again if — if he broke his word. He has broken it. He must have broken it —*

She heard the car drive away from the curb. She put her hands over her face and wept aloud, as unself-consciously as a child.

In the morning things were no better. A dozen times she reached for the telephone on her desk. She knew at what hours Tom might be at home. A half-dozen times she started toward the express elevators. She would go up to the studios, she would wait until he could come out and speak to her — But that was absurd. He would be unavailable for hours, he might not be there at all; meantime she had her own work to do —

Surely he would come, would telephone? Surely he would come crashing into the little apartment, looking much too big for it, take her in his arms, kiss her eyes and her mouth and tell her, "Darling, you're mad. Of course I didn't do it. How could you think so for a moment?"

She might believe him, in his arms, close to his heart.

Apart from him, she could not believe him. She tried to think it out. If he had done this, what had he done? Committed a breach of ethics, of loyalty? That was all, was it not? He'd not stolen or —

But he had promised. He had given her his word.

Tom, up in the tower from whose slender pinnacle the invisible cords stretched around the world, was working furiously, inaccessible even to his friends. He and Hank saw little of each other, their free time not coinciding as it happened. Slim, leaner than ever, chewing upon an unlit pipe, had troubles of his own to occupy him. He said one evening, "Women are the devil," and Tom nodded, for once in perfect agreement.

What right had she to condemn him, practically unheard? Of course he couldn't prove anything to her. Other people besides himself had known of the proposed reorganization. Rawlson for one. Rawlson, now confidential secretary to Norton and much, much more confidential than Tom had ever been, dressing the part, speaking the part, being the part. Others besides Rawlson, too. Why should she pin it on him, just because for a little while he had dallied with the rather exciting idea of making a little money, with safety? A fat lot she loved him if she could send him out of her apartment, dismiss him from her life because of some imagined misdemeanor! He couldn't prove her wrong, could he, short of dragging Rawlson down there and facing her with him? And he couldn't do that. He wouldn't. If she loved him, if she wanted him, she could say so.

They were both very young.

Sarah said, when two weeks had passed and she was making plans for Christmas, "And Tom, of course."

"Not Tom." Lynn looked down at her slim ringless hands.

"Not Tom?" Sarah's face would have been comic had Lynn been in a mood for comedy.

She said, "He'll work Christmas Day."

"Surely, not all day?"

"No, I suppose not. But don't count on him, Sarah." Sarah thought a moment. She had not seen Tom lately. She asked shrewdly, "Have you — quarreled?"

"No."

"Then why —"

"Oh, don't ask me," cried Lynn, and flung out both hands. "It's *over*, that's all!"

Sarah said nothing. She had heard people say, *it's over*, before. But she was worried. She tried to reassure herself. *They'll make it up, silly infants, they're always bickering about something.*

She thought, *Dwight's away, I haven't heard from him — I hope he's away.*

As long as Tom were in the picture — According to Lynn, he was in the picture no longer. But if David didn't learn it?

It was Tom himself who gave Dwight the first hint of how matters stood, the suggestion for which he had been waiting. Dwight, making an appeal for the Community Fund over the UBC facilities, spoke, after his broadcast, to the program director.

"I've a young friend here," he said; "at least, I heard recently he was here. One of the engineers. His name is Shepard."

Tom was sent for, and was able at the moment to appear in the reception room. As a matter of fact, had Dwight known it, Tom had been at the controls of the studio control room, battling successfully with his temptation to do violence and distortion to Dwight's smooth, low voice.

By the time Tom, ready to go off duty after Dwight's broadcast, had been summoned to the reception room by a page the program manager had explained matters to Dwight, and Dwight held out his hand to Tom smiling. "I understand you put me over," he said. "Funny coincidence, isn't it?"

Tom grinned sheepishly and said something intended to be pleasant. "You went over fine, Mr. Dwight," he said.

"That's good. Haven't seen anything of you for a long time. How's Lynn?" asked Dwight casually.

His eyes were veiled and very keen. Tom answered, looking away, "She's all right, I guess." And then, defiantly, "Sure, she's fine."

They parted. Dwight went on downstairs, smiling faintly. He stopped in to see Sarah, studiously avoiding the other, more attractive room; more attractive, that is, to him.

She might as well know now. She'd know, soon enough. He sat down by her desk and presently cast a challenge; one looked to see the glove fallen dramatically between them upon its smooth and polished top.

"Where did you come from?" she wanted to know.

"From the tower. I've been broadcasting, pity you didn't hear me," he said lightly. "I had all the stops pulled out."

"Community Fund?"

He nodded.

"I ran into young Shepard there," he said. "I had heard he'd left the bank." He refrained from mentioning the source of his information. "I understand that he and Lynn are — well, *aren't*, let us say."

Sarah said hastily, "How ridiculous! They're always quarreling — about — nothing."

"Are you sure it's nothing, this time?"

"Why?" She looked at him, looked away again.

"Just for the sake of argument. Only, last summer, when we were all together Lynn honored me with her confidence. That is, she mentioned no names, but being a normally astute soul I guessed. I am not at liberty to repeat what she told me, but I will say this much. She and Tom disagreed upon a matter of, shall we say, business ethics. If Tom followed his inclination in the matter, she was through with him. I take it, he has followed his inclination," said Dwight, and rose.

"David." Sarah rose also. She stared into his eyes, being almost as tall as he, and held them, regardless of the people moving about the room, the people at near-by desks. "David — what are you going to do? You promised —"

"I think," he said, "I have been absolved of my promise."

"No — No —"

But he had gone, stopping in at Norton's room a moment, greeting young Rawlson with a casual nod, to wish Norton the usual holiday greeting. Sarah stood where he had left her, looking after him.

Many things were not as yet clear to her. But a nebulous theory was forming in her mind. That night she went to Lynn's apartment, and found her consuming bread and milk and cocoa, before rushing off to a class.

"Sit down," invited Lynn. "I'm almost through."

"No. Lynn, please tell me the truth this time. Did — did Tom know about this merger proposition, a long time ago, and speak to you about it? Did you disapprove of his attitude?"

After a moment, Lynn nodded.

"And you think — now — ?"

"Sarah — what am I to think?" She flung

her hands out. "The rumor — the stock buying — Tom's new job — his new car — He has broken his word," she said definitely.

"Are you sure?"

"He hasn't," said Lynn, "been near me since I accused him of it." Her lips shook. "Sarah, Sarah, don't — you're not planning to go to him, are you? to ask him? I couldn't bear that. You might," she said, "spare me my pride at least."

Sarah went back upstairs. Lynn had spoken to David Dwight of this last summer. Dwight knew. Dwight, it was possible, might be in a position to know more, to know definitely that Tom Shepard had broken his word.

But what was more important to Sarah was that Dwight had told her, as definitely, that he was absolved of his own.

Downstairs, in the apartment she had left, Lynn was putting on her hat and coat. How Sarah had come by her information she did not know. Possibly Mr. Norton had been talking to her. The telephone rang. Tom? She did not move. It rang again. *Tom.* She ran to the instrument, lifted it with hands out of all control.

"Lynn? This is David Dwight."

She said, after a moment, "How on earth

did you get my number? It isn't in the book."

"I saw Sarah today," he answered truthfully.

That was odd, Sarah had not spoken of him to her, yet she had given Dwight her telephone number. Lynn dismissed it from her mind. As a matter of fact, the telephone number, neatly typed, had been in plain view on a card of numbers lying on Sarah's desk. Dwight remembered numbers. He said now, "I've missed you. Will you have dinner with me — tomorrow night?"

Chapter Eighteen:

FAREWELL TO JENNIE

There is a curious little roadhouse not very far from Yonkers. It has an "authentic," romantic setting, and is perched on a cliff overlooking a deep ravine, from which the spruce trees aspire, very tall, with dark, straight trunks. The inn itself is bright, of evenings, with Japanese lanterns, and is run by two gentlemen from the Orient. But if you wish it, good American and better French food is served there, and of recent years the Cherry Blossom has found it expedient to stay open at all seasons and to engage one of the best colored orchestras in Manhattan.

For a long time, not so very many people knew about the Cherry Blossom. They serve a cocktail there of that name, a glorious rosy red in color, which cherry blossoms are not — but those who did know made use of its varied facilities often, gave large, expensive parties, thus assuring the smooth and smiling owners of a long old age, a gilded twilight, in the Far East on the proceeds. Lately, however, the enterprising UBC, always hunting for excellent sustaining programs, placed a semipermanent installation in the roadhouse, and on several nights brought the turgid or violent music made in an oriental setting by the possible descendants of African kings, into the homes of what are optimistically termed millions of listeners.

In this inn the long arm of remote control reached out and touched Lynn, figuratively speaking, on the shoulder.

Dwight had taken her there, the evening of their reunion. She had loved it, viewing it from an entirely surface angle. He had been very amiable that evening. And Lynn, determined to have a good time whether or not she felt like it, had with the ebullience of youth accused him of vast arrears of attention.

"It wasn't altogether my fault; and not my inclination. Sarah" — he stopped and raised a whimsical eyebrow — "Sarah, poor dear, warned me that I was rushing in where Shepards feared to tread — Nice Christmas metaphor, that," he concluded in mild astonishment.

Lynn said unsmilingly, "She needn't have bothered. That's — over, you know."

"No, I didn't know. I'm sorry. No, that's

a lie. I'm not sorry personally. But — if you're unhappy, Lynn, then I must be sorry," he told her.

"It's hard," she said rather simply, gray eyes on his own. "I — please don't talk about it," she said suddenly, vainly trying to control her lips. "Let's dance, shall we?"

Later, driving her home, he said, "Christmas won't be so very merry this year, will it? Suppose we celebrate together. I'm lonely too."

"You lonely!"

"Why not? Acquaintances, friends even, can't make up for — other things."

She thought he spoke of his broken home, his children; she touched his hand and said, "I do understand." She didn't, of course.

After a moment he drew his hand gently away. He had to, or crash to the ground the delicate structure of confidence he was assisting her to build.

"You're rather a darling," he said lightly. But he had not thought of his flat-footed, flat-chested wife; nor of his ungainly youngsters. At Christmastime he dismissed the latter from his mind by opening his checkbook.

"I have to have Christmas dinner with Sarah. In the middle of the day," she told him.

"Then give me the evening? We'll be very foolish. We'll do all sorts of absurd and childish things," he promised her. "Is it a bargain?"

It was a bargain. She made her excuses to Sarah, not very well. Sarah commented only, "I hoped you would stay with us."

"I promised — someone," Lynn told her.

Afterward, she wondered why she had not told her all the truth. But it seemed obvious at the moment that she could not. Sarah wouldn't approve; Sarah moreover had been interfering, just as Jennie had said she would.

Jennie sent perfume for Christmas, a great box of it, tied with holly and red ribbon, crystal bottles, silver-topped, brimming with costly fragrance. *Good luck,* read the card, *and happy days. Come see me on Christmas, if you can.*

That meant that the mysterious Jake was at home with his people celebrating, after his paradoxical fashion. Lynn took a bus early Christmas morning and went to Jennie's. Jennie, in a negligee, opened the door to her friend. "Gave my maid the day off," she explained.

Jennie had trimmed a Christmas tree. She displayed Jake's gifts — "Not that he believes in Santa Claus" — an ermine wrap, stockings by the dozen, a wrist watch, candy, flowers, fruit. "He's a good egg," admitted Jennie, yawning.

The apartment was just as you'd think it might be; more long-legged dolls and frilly cushions, decorator's drapes and uphol- stery, jade ash trays and quartz buttons, bell ropes, lots of furniture, the best radio money could buy. Jennie, in lace and chiffon, trailed about the place dissatisfied.

"Has Tom said anything about Slim?" she asked.

"Not very much," Lynn answered care- fully. "I — I haven't been seeing much of Tom lately."

Jennie nodded. "So I gathered from what Slim said." She pointed to a little package, clumsily tied in red paper, "There's what Slim sent me," she told Lynn. "Give it a glance."

A pair of gloves — "wrong size," Jennie explained, some handkerchiefs, a funny little pin fashioned in the shape of a perky Scottie, and a Christmas card. "Sorter sweet," said Jennie, low.

But, in a moment, as Lynn laid the things back in their box, "Drink?" asked Jennie, moving toward the cellarette.

"Heavens, no — at this hour of the morning. Jennie, you're not going to —"

"Believe it or not, I am! Look here, Lynn, I'm bored to blazes. I even look forward to going to work," Jennie admitted.

The long blue eyes were tired. The wheaten hair, pressed into the deep waves of her new haircut, had lost some of its luster. She was thinner than ever, a little haggard.

"You and Tom been fighting again?" she inquired.

Lynn stiffened. "No — It's over and done with, that's all."

"Damned shame." Jennie stared at her, at the angry hurt gray eyes, the set of the pointed chin. "Well, it's not my business," she conceded. "Sometimes I think it's a mistake for two saps to love each other a lot. I mean so that nothing else matters. What do you get out of it? Precious little pleasure for the rest of the trouble you have to wade through." Her eyes were moody.

Lynn asked quickly, trying to divert her from the subject of Tom and herself, "Is it Slim, Jennie?"

"Yeah. Damn him anyway," Jennie said, without anger, "with his long legs and his eyes like a hungry kid's and his coat sleeves that are always a couple of inches too short. I could laugh him off — before.

When I was on my own. Free. That's funny, isn't it? But now, hanging around this dump alone, nights — lonely, it's different. I've got to watch my step," she said, more to herself than to Lynn.

Lynn left her presently. Standing at the door, Jennie said, discontented, "Wish you wouldn't go. I'll stick around here, go out to dinner, come home and wait for a long-distance call — not that it matters. Lynn, what do you do with yourself now that Tom —"

Lynn said, "I've my work up at Columbia. I see Sarah a lot. Lately David Dwight has been taking me out. We've been to a funny little place out of town, the Cherry Blossom —"

"Yeah, I know it. I saw you there once."

"You *did?*" Lynn stared. "Were you out of your mind? Why didn't you come over and speak to us?"

"Fat chance! Lynn, you *are* a kid! I was with — oh, a gang. We had a private room. Do you think I wanted to let you know I was there so you could help carry me out?"

"Jennie —"

"Run along and eat your turkey," said Jennie, and gave her a gentle push, "and don't fret about me. I'm oke — everything," she said, "is Jake. That's pretty good, isn't it? That hands me a laugh!"

She was still laughing, lonely, forlorn laughter, as Lynn closed the door.

Christmas with Sarah was a rather falsely merry affair; a small tree and presents, and a heavy dinner; not much conversation. There was an empty place at the table. Lynn saw it; Sarah saw it.

Afterward, she was glad to escape. Dwight sent the car for her, and it took her directly to the penthouse. She went upstairs, wondering a little; not at the unconventionality of her visit, things like that didn't matter any more, but at what he had in store for her. She had been like a child always, greedy for a surprise, for a secret, and she was wondering if she could recapture that. She thought not. Christmas Day. Tom had not even phoned. He might have phoned. But flowers had come, without a card. Could it be possible — ?

Where was he?

He was in Child's with Hank, gnawing a turkey bone. Later he would be back at the studio, working savagely to insure the success of a new, important, sponsored program.

Dwight asked, "Did my flowers come?"

She thanked him, sick with disappointment. She might have known.

"Are you warmly dressed?"

"You told me to be."

He looked her over from head to foot. "Go upstairs," he said secretly, "and look in the bedroom. But not now; look at your stocking first."

It was of wool, it dangled from the fireplace. She took it down and opened it, under his amused and eager eyes. Perfume, lipstick — a gold one — soap, handkerchiefs —

"How — dear!" she said sincerely. But her eyes were absent. If he had planned to send her flowers why hadn't he included his card? She'd rather have known at once than hoped — and prayed.

"We're going riding," he said, "somewhere where there's snow. Down, in fact, on the Island."

"Oh, but —"

"Don't talk," he ordered sternly. "Go on upstairs and see what Santa brought you."

She ran up the stairs under the friendly eyes of the man Wilkins. In the bedroom she found a suitcase, fitted, stamped with her initials; and in the suitcase a winter sports outfit, stockings, sweater, scarf, beret, coat, amusing trousers, gloves.

"Oh —" her voice floated down to him.

Wilkins put his head around the door.

"Carry it for you, miss?"

She went downstairs laughing.

"Commander Byrd," she hailed him, and smiled, "shall I put them on now?"

"It's not Antarctic, but it's something of an expedition," he warned her. "No, wait till we get there."

Presently the suitcase and one of his own were put in the car. They drove out of town swiftly, through the twilight. It was a white Christmas. The trees shone lighted from the windows of apartments and houses and from the yards of churches. "It's beautiful," said Lynn, listening to the chimes.

They had left the town behind them. There was little traffic and Dwight drove fast and securely. Beyond Great Neck he turned off, and into a long snow-rutted lane.

Trees laden with snow, frosty, gleaming, bordered it on either side. A turn, and there was a house waiting, a house from an old-fashioned Christmas card. Every window was lighted, they wore wreaths of holly, there was holly at the door, and two lighted trees outside. The house stood high, on a hill. And as Lynn got out of the car she heard voices, laughter.

But where — ? Who — ?

"Friends of mine, you'll like them. Lulu and Mike Hayward."

She did like them. Their hostess, a fat woman, extraordinarily pretty, with the skin of a child, the wide blue eyes of a child — she'd once been the prettiest show girl in town. The host, her husband, lean, bronzed, smoking a foul pipe. Other people, all in sports clothes. The Carters.

Yule log, punch, a bedroom to change in, the toboggan on the hill, the first wild essay with skis, her feet helplessly slipping from under her, Dwight, laughing, picking her out of a snow bank. And at midnight, supper, dancing —

At nearly three o'clock in the morning they turned out of Hay- wards' drive and spun through the deadly quiet of the waning night. It was light when he left her at her own door.

"Tired?"

"No."

"But you'll have to work in the morning — this morning."

"I'll manage."

"Happy Christmas?" he asked her.

"Awfully —"

She smiled up at him. He took the sprig of mistletoe from his buttonhole and held it over her head; he kissed her, under the startled eyes of a lone and cold policeman. Not with the light kiss — that other kiss.

358

She drew back, afraid. Not repulsed, but afraid. Not afraid of him but of her loneliness, of her youth, her warm blood, her awakened senses, her longing for creature comfort, for human warmth.

"*My* Christmas present," he said, and drove away.

Trembling a little, she went into the house.

Sleep was out of the question. She thought, standing under a shower cold enough to make her tingle all over, *I ought not to see him again — Jennie was right — about its being dangerous — But why?* she argued. *I like him a lot, I — admire him — but I don't* CARE *for him — really care — It's Tom, always Tom — only —*

Only what? Only that she was unhappy, that she was lonely, that she had become accustomed to the speech and the caress of love.

I won't see him again, she decided.

But she did.

One morning in January the telephone on her desk shrilled loudly. She answered, astonished to hear Jennie's voice, broken, roughened with some unknown anxiety, "Lynn, can you come up here and see me — quick? It's — awfully important."

Lynn looked at her watch. It was after eleven. "I'll take my lunch hour early," she said. "What's wrong, Jennie, are you ill?"

"No — oh, *step* on it!" cried Jennie, the self-reliant.

Lynn went into Sarah's office.

"If I'm late getting back from lunch, will it be all right?" she asked. "It's Jennie; she's in trouble of some sort."

"That's to be expected," Sarah told her tartly; then, softening: "Of course, it's all right, Lynn. You don't often ask official favors."

She smiled with a little effort. She had not seen much of Lynn lately. Even without proof it was impossible not to conjecture with whom the girl had been spending much of her free time.

She thought: I must speak to her, warn her.

But could she?

She was torn between her loyalty to Lynn and her illogical loyalty to David Dwight. She was frightened. She was miserable. And she was ageing under it.

An oversophisticated maid admitted Lynn to Jennie's apartment. Jennie was walking around the living-room half-dressed. Her face was gray-white, her eyes had dark circles beneath them, as black as bruises. For the first time Lynn saw Jennie's face bare of make-up, the lips pale and dry. Somehow that startled her. Jennie, when they had shared a home together, had never permitted her face to "go naked." Carefully removing her make-up at night she would apply it again, if more lightly. "Because," she had explained, "there might be a fire, or something. Or a handsome burglar. Or I might get up in the night and see myself in a mirror and drop dead of fright if I weren't dolled!"

"What's happened?" asked Lynn, as Jennie stared at her as if she did not know her.

At the sound of her voice Jennie pulled herself together. "Plenty," she replied briefly. Lynn cast a look at the vanishing back of the maid. "It doesn't matter," Jennie told her wanly. "She'll listen at the door anyway. She knows enough as it is."

"Tell me — heavens, Jennie, you look awful!"

"I feel worse. It's Slim. Oh, I was a fool. It was easy, when — when I didn't know as much as I do now. But since — since Jake, it was different somehow. I was bored, too, fed up, couldn't call my soul my own. Lonely. And Slim, he hung around. Last

night he came here. Not the first time —
the third. Don't look at me like that, for
God's sake, Lynn! I can't help it, I
couldn't help it! Anyway, Jake showed up.
I don't know if he just took it into his head
to come on, or whether someone had
tipped him off. Everyone knows everyone
else's business here, and that girl's in his
pay, I suppose. Or was. I pay her plenty
more now. Well, the night elevator man
tipped *me* off. Held him down there, while
I got Slim out by the freight elevator. It
was — pretty bad. If it hadn't been for that
night man — he's always liked me, sort of;
I've paid him for doing errands for me and
he had it in for Jake. Jake bawled hell out
of him one night for no good reason —"

"But," asked Lynn helplessly, "what do
you want me to do?"

"See Slim," Jennie besought her, "tell
him to keep away. I don't care about myself. I can go back to living on my salary.
Tell him I'm going to Evanston. Jake said
last night he wouldn't be getting to town
very often; he wanted me to come and live
— nearer. I said I would."

"Jennie, don't! Let him go; live, as you
say, on your salary; there'll be Slim —
you'll be happy."

"Not me. Slim's sick at himself already.

I'm sick of myself too. He — he wouldn't marry me now, you know. He's funny that way — old-fashioned," Jennie told her with a futile attempt at wisecracking, and laughed. Lynn shivered.

"Lynn, see him, please see him. Tell him I'm going away, tell him I never want to see him again."

"Jennie, don't you care for him at all?"

Jennie turned, in her ceaseless pacing, stopped and looked at her friend. Her eyes were a little mad.

"Lynn, get wise to yourself. Of course I care. If I didn't, I'd stay on and two-time payroll. Or give him the air and become a working girl again — with a sweetie. But it can't be, don't you see that? I'd just — drag him down. I've done it already. God, what a fool I've been!" she said bitterly.

After a moment during which Lynn said nothing, there being nothing to say, Jennie said, low, "You'll see him, I count on you. I'm pulling out of here, as soon as I can get packed. Jake will stand for the broken lease. He'll be good to me. He doesn't really give a damn for me, you know. But men are funny."

Lynn said, feeling as it her mind had been beaten black and blue, "Then — I shan't see you again?"

"No, probably not. Don't let that worry you." She put her hands on Lynn's shoulders and gave her a little shake. "You're a good kid. Look here, whatever's wrong between you and Tom, make it up. It doesn't pay not to. You don't know how lucky you are. I do."

"You don't understand."

"No, I suppose not. Slim told me something, though. Said Tom was sunk. Said he couldn't find out why, all Tom would say was that you'd let him down, believed something that wasn't so. Don't be that way, Lynn. I don't know what you think he's done or hasn't done. I don't care. Only, if he's your man and you can make a go of sticking together the rest of your lives, what does anything he's done matter? It wouldn't to me, murder, arson, robbery — Lord, if a good guy loves you and is *yours* — I sound like a torch song. But I mean it. Don't you suppose I'd lie or steal for Slim now that I *know?* But I was always the dunce in my class, I always knew the answer too late. Well, I'm doing the next best thing for him."

She asked again: "You'll see him, won't you? Swear you won't tell him what I've told you. Just say — 'She's leaving town — and you stay on your own side of the fence.' "

Lynn promised. A moment later she was out in the corridor. The door had shut. Jennie was whistling — what was it? — the blues song they had heard at Dwight's, so very long ago. Lynn's cheeks were wet, whether with her own tears or Jennie's she did not know. She stopped and stood irresolute before that closed door. If she could persuade her — ? But she could not. She went on, alone.

That afternoon she telephoned the house on Perry Street. If Tom answered! But he wouldn't answer. He'd be working. She prayed he'd be working. She prayed he would not be working. Waiting, listening to the operator ringing, she felt faintly ill with fear — and with hope.

Slim answered.

"Slim? This is Lynn. I want to see you; it's important. I have to go to a class uptown. Could you ride up a ways with me? I wouldn't ask you, but it means a lot."

He replied, thinking, *she wants to talk about Tom,* "Sure, I will, Lynn, glad to; I — had sort of a date, but it's off now, I guess."

He's been trying to phone Jennie, she thought.

He came along presently; she was waiting outside the apartment. They boarded a bus, found an empty seat.

"What's on your mind?" he asked her.

"I've seen Jennie."

"Oh." He flushed, looked away. He said, with an effort, "I suppose she — told you?"

Sparing him as much as she could, she denied it. "No, nothing. Except to ask me to see you at once, and tell you she's leaving town. She's going — West, Slim. She wanted you to know it."

"Leaving town?" He was silent a moment. He said presently, "Running away, eh? I suppose she thought I'd follow her. She's wrong."

"She doesn't want you to follow her, Slim," Lynn told him.

"No, I suppose not. I don't blame her. She's picked the sort of job which matters most to her; she doesn't want her shabby friends hanging around, interfering."

He was cold with anger, hot with shame. He thought of the freight elevator. He moved away from Lynn. He said, "Nice of her to let me know."

"Slim, you don't understand. Don't be so hard on her. She —"

Lynn stopped. She'd promised. Besides, it would do no good to tell him, to try to interpret Jennie for him. It might do harm.

What was the use, anyway?

Slim said, against his will, "I was crazy about her. I wanted her to marry me — once. She wouldn't."

He was silent. There was nothing he could say of the things crowding and wounding his mind. He had loathed the whole situation. It hadn't been his fault, he told himself. Jennie knew he was crazy about her. She must have known how he felt when — when she moved uptown. Sick, disgusted, hating her, hating everything. But love, or love's little sister, hadn't died, couldn't. She'd known that too, phoned him, asked him up, made things easy enough. Everything was wrong, everything was spoiled. He hated her now, more than ever; and himself. But — men are funny.

Now she was leaving, sending this untender message. Well, good riddance; she'd played hob with him, all right! His throat swelled, closed. He asked thickly, "Is — is there anything more?"

"No, Slim, that's all," Lynn said.

But her eyes pleaded although her mouth was mute. Tom? How was he? What was he doing? Did he miss her? Slim, Slim, tell me about Tom!

Despite his preoccupation, his harsh

anger and harsher grief, her unspoken longing reached him. He said awkwardly, "Gee, Lynn, I'm sorry about you and Tom — He doesn't say much but, gosh, he's shot! He's working hard, making good. They like him up there. Hank says he'll do something big some day; he wants, you know, to get into the laboratory end of things. If — shall I tell him I saw you?"

Now her mood had changed. She answered briefly, "I don't care what you tell him, Slim."

"I see." He was silent a moment. Then he said, pressing the button near him, "Well, I'll be getting off here. Thanks for calling me."

She said, as he rose, "Jennie — shall I tell her — ?"

"Never mind telling her anything," he said.

She watched him, tall, overlean, walking to the door, getting off, crossing to the curb, without a backward look. She leaned back and closed her eyes. Why had she been so obstinate? Couldn't she have asked first, "How is Tom?" Couldn't she have said, "Why doesn't he call me up?" Damn pride anyway; hers; Tom's; Slim's, which wouldn't give Jennie the comfort of a word!

She called Jennie at the first opportunity. "I saw him," she stated.

There was silence on the other end of the wire. Then Jennie's voice, subdued, hoarse with unrestrained crying, "Did he send me — any message?"

"No, Jennie."

After a moment Jennie said, "That's the payoff. Sure, that's fine!"

"Jennie, I'll see you before you go?"

"No, if you don't mind," Jennie said carefully. Then she cried out over the wire, "Lynn, you're such a darned swell kid. I'd like to think of you — happy. That would help, a lot."

"You'll write me, Jennie?"

"Oh, sure, I'll write. Good-by," said Jennie faintly.

But she wouldn't write. Lynn, hanging up, knew that. Farewell to Jennie — farewell.

Slim, reporting to Tom, was taciturn.

"Jennie's leaving, she's going West — with —" he swallowed unpleasant words — calling names didn't help — "with *him*."

Tom commented, tinkering with his newly built set, "Oh yeah — well, what did you expect?" He kept his eyes away from his friend. Men don't go into hysterics of sympathy often. "Oh yeah?" asked Tom, very hard-boiled. *Damn all women!* he thought.

"It's oke by me," Slim said, magnificently indifferent.

"Did you see her?"

"Jennie? Hell, no. I saw Lynn."

Tom almost dropped the new tube he was testing out. He repeated almost inaudibly, "Lynn, eh?"

"She called me up."

"Don't suppose she mentioned me, did she?" Tom asked carelessly.

"Nope."

Silence. Then Hank, in a corner, rising, knocking out his pipe, "They're all alike. Look here, Tom, we've time for a glass of beer before we trek uptown. Let's go to the Hole in the Wall."

Slim had seen Lynn. *How did she look, is she well, is she happy, has she forgotten me, she can't have forgotten me!* But Tom, shrugging himself into an overcoat, spoke no word. He thought, *Funny, isn't it? Comic, that's what! I'd give my right hand to see her — and Slim, who doesn't care if he never sees her again —*

Not long afterward Tom saw her, at the Cherry Blossom.

Chapter Nineteen:

SARAH TAKES ACTION

He had gone up, with his two black bags and the announcer, to supervise the broadcast. He was busy behind the screen, testing the lines, waiting for signals, waiting for the broadcast to go on. It was a gala occasion, an anniversary broadcast. The dance music had been very well received; there was a chance it might be continued as a sponsored, rather than a sustaining, program. Tom was highly oblivious to everything but his work. Nemo programs interested him particularly. It was his job to regulate the levels, to see that everything was going as well as possible. The announcer did his routine part; the station breaks came at the fifteen-minute intervals. Forty-five minutes of Cherry Blossom music was broadcast tonight. Then it was over.

"Pretty gay crowd," said the announcer, and looked around the screen.

Tom looked too. The room was well filled, they were dancing, the management had provided favors.

"Swell music," Tom agreed, tapping his foot and shrugging a shoulder.

"Let's get going," suggested the announcer. "Hey, what's the big idea?" he asked, in amazement.

Tom had seen Lynn. At a corner table with Dwight. Her hand lay on the table. Dwight's covered it. He was leaning close, speaking to her, low, eagerly.

She was listening. Once she spoke. Once she nodded and smiled. Once she was very grave, shaking her dark head.

"My God!" said Tom aloud.

"Come on," urged the announcer impatiently. "Have you taken root?"

After a moment Tom stumbled after the other man, out into the wide sleeping gardens, where a light snow was falling, where the lanterns swayed in the wind, and those, whose little light had survived, bloomed like immense enchanted and very unseasonable flowers against the drifting flakes and the dark, unstarred sky.

Dwight had been saying, back there, in the noisy room, "But you must have known always that I loved you, Lynn. I've come to an agreement with — Mrs. Dwight. She will set me free. She's abroad now, we'll run it through, routine fashion, in Paris. And I'll come back for you? Or would you join me there — in the late spring? We could be married in England. You've never known an English spring, have you? It's very lovely."

She said slowly, "I don't love you."

"But you *like* me?"

This was where she nodded and smiled a little. She said, "I like you very much. But —"

"Darling, you'll love me. You must. I want you so much," he told her, "and I — need you."

She made a curious little gesture, with her free hand, bewildered. She shook her head.

"But why — *me?*" she wanted to know. "It seems — so strange. All the people you've known — the women —"

"I've never known any," he said, and believed it; "not since life began. There is only you. No one else has ever existed."

Tom had gone from her. Tom no longer cared or he would have returned to her before this. She did not know how near he was now, behind the screen, staring at her. She had no warning, no premonition. She felt tired, suddenly, of unhappiness and of struggle. But — David Dwight?

"Don't answer now," he said quickly,

very quickly. "I'll wait. You needn't say anything now. Look up, smile. I'll not speak of it again until you're ready. Shall we dance?" he asked.

Tom saw them rise, saw her go into his arms, before he left.

Tom's duties for the evening were over. He went straight to Lynn's apartment house and was announced to Sarah. She was home, as it happened, and alone. She opened the door to him herself. He came in, shaking the wet snow from his overcoat.

"Why, Tom!" she said, astonished.

It was late. She was ready, she had thought, to go to bed. To rest, not to sleep. She had not slept well recently.

"I had to see you. I've just come from a roadhouse, out Yonkers way. I saw Lynn there. With — Dwight. He was holding her hand across the table, looking as if he could eat her up — What does this mean, Sarah?" Tom demanded.

Sarah sat down in the nearest chair. She admitted after a moment, "I don't know —"

Tom said, standing over her, "She belongs to me. She knows it. What is she doing with — him?"

Sarah asked a question in her turn. "What has happened between you? Tell me, you *must* tell me, Tom, if I'm to help you."

He sat down, facing her, and told her briefly, in his boyish speech. When he had finished he repeated, through her long silence, "I didn't do it. She just jumped at the conclusion. Didn't give me a chance. I could produce Rawlson, of course."

"Rawlson knew?"

"Sure, he suggested it," Tom said, astonished, "in the first place."

Sarah was remembering. Dwight's question. Her answer, abstractedly given. She had seen Dwight and Bob Rawlson talking one day, on the main banking floor in a corner apart.

Dwight had done very well lately. She had heard he was going abroad, was, for a little space, retiring, on a long vacation. He had even said it to her carelessly, "I rate a vacation, do I not?"

But how on earth had Dwight first stumbled across Rawlson's path?

She asked Tom suddenly, "Do you know where Bob Rawlson lives — at home, I mean?"

"Why, yes," he answered, "it isn't far from here. Why?"

"Go there," ordered Sarah, "now, this instant! Never mind how late it is. Make him tell you to whom he has talked — recently. Force him to. You won't have to use much persuasion. After all, he approached you first. But find out."

"But — Lynn?" he asked. "Sarah, I'm nearly crazy. If you could have seen them — I — I damned near went in there and dragged her away from him. I — you know how I feel about her. I've been a fool, keeping away out of pride, stubbornness, call it anything you want. If only I'd come back, made her listen to me, brought Bob to see her, if necessary! But I couldn't understand — it seemed an awfully small thing to come between us. Even," he said defiantly, "even if I *had* done it."

"It wouldn't be small to Lynn. But you didn't do it. I'll talk to Lynn. Go now and see if you can find Rawlson, tonight. Leave it to me," said Sarah, and rose, tall, erect, a little white.

Somehow he knew he could trust her. He left and went out to find Bob Rawlson.

Sarah went downstairs and spoke to the superintendent, who knew her close intimacy with Lynn. She had, she told him, an urgent message to give the younger woman. She would rather not telephone it but would prefer to wait in Lynn's room until she came in. Incurious, the superintendent admitted her.

She waited there, through the longest

hours of her life. No, not the longest; she recalled those others; she had to.

Would Lynn come in alone?

As it happened, she did not. The car drew up at the door, shortly after one o'clock. The longest night had not been, after all, so long. They had dined late, lingered to dance — and talk. Tom had been in the inn from 8:30 until 9:15 and had come directly to Sarah's apartment.

"May I come in, just for a moment?" Dwight asked outside the door. "You know, I've never seen your place."

Lynn had her hand on the knob. "Why, it's open," she exclaimed in astonishment. "No, of course you can't come in," she answered.

"If it's open, I must," he answered. "Suppose the place has been broken into or something?"

"But that's nonsense! Still, I'm sure I shut the door."

Sarah listened, waiting.

Dwight turned the knob, the door swung. He stepped into the room, saying, over his shoulder, "Wait out there a moment, darling —"

Then — "Sarah!" he said, on the heels of that betraying endearment.

Chapter Twenty:

HIS ARMS, HIS KISS

"I was waiting for Lynn," Sarah told him. "I didn't expect you, too."

But, inevitably, she had.

Lynn, close on Dwight's heels, exclaimed, "Oh, it's you! When I found the door open I didn't know what to think — we were afraid someone had broken in."

She was flushed, but her eyes were tired. Sarah said evenly, "Shut the door, Lynn, and come inside. This is a curious hour for me to be calling." She tried to smile, failed, and went on, "But I had something to speak to you about, something important. McHiggin let me in —"

"I'll go," Dwight offered hastily, conscious of a growing discomfort. "I'll call you tomorrow, Lynn."

Easier to let him go; easier to say what she had to say, to Lynn's ears alone. But —

"I'd rather you stayed," she said steadily, "for it concerns you, David."

He raised his eyebrows. "My dear Sarah,

what can possibly concern me?"

"Sarah, dear, what is it?" she asked. For a moment her heart had missed a beat — *something important* — news from home? Bad news? But now she was at rest again, for if it had been news from home it could not have concerned Dwight.

She touched Sarah's cheek with her small, cool hand.

"Sarah — you look so tragic —" she began, ready to be frightened again.

Dwight stood leaning against the little bookcase. "May I smoke?" he asked, and without waiting for permission, lighted a cigarette. He speculated, his eyes expressionless.

It was to Dwight that Sarah addressed herself now.

"Do you remember our conversation this summer, at your house?" she asked directly.

Indiscretion seemed the better part of valor.

"Perfectly," he admitted coolly.

"Then you must recall that you gave me your word — which you have broken."

"Dear Sarah, you embarrass me! Lynn is looking wide-eyed from one to the other of us. It is past one in the morning. Cannot we postpone this interesting chat until another more seasonable — or reasonable — hour?" he inquired.

"No — Lynn," she said, turning her white face to the girl beside her, "last summer when we were at David's I went to him and asked him —"

"If my intentions toward you were honorable, darling," Dwight interrupted lightly.

Lynn colored. "Oh, Sarah —" she began, distressed.

Sarah ignored both interruptions.

"I asked him what he meant by his attitude toward you. I reminded him that you were engaged to Tom Shepard. He promised me that as long as you remained so he would —"

"Fade from the picture," Dwight explained. "And I did. But Lynn's no longer engaged to young Shepard," he reminded them both.

"How did you *know?*" Sarah asked him simply.

"She told me so," he answered, and smiled, a little.

"But you knew — before she told you. Or else you broke your promise first," Sarah persisted.

"Oh, I knew — or guessed."

"How — ?"

"One hears these things," he admitted vaguely.

"From — Robert Rawlson?"

"Rawlson?" he asked. "Rawlson?"

Blank amazement. Too well done. A picture flashed into Lynn's mind: Dwight's car at the curb, Bob Rawlson walking away from it, into the bank —

"It was from Bob Rawlson, was it not, that you also obtained information of the probable Seacoast merger with the First Citizens' organization?" asked Sarah.

"I don't know what you're talking about," he answered shortly.

Sarah said, quietly, "It doesn't matter, except to Lynn. Lynn quarreled with Tom because she thought that against her express wishes he had sold his confidential information to outsiders. That's neither here nor there. You know quite well what I'm talking about. Lynn confided in you last summer. You yourself told me so. It would have been singularly easy for you to find and approach the person who had made the original suggestion to Tom, and to learn from him the exact moment when it would be wise — and clever — to buy what stock you could through various investment houses and in small lots."

"Then Tom didn't —" began Lynn. Her face was colorless.

"No, Tom didn't. I'm certain of that," Sarah told her briefly, and turned to Dwight again. "You'll deny any complicity, of course. Although it was, I suppose, my fault. I haven't forgotten that you asked me with whom Tom was intimate in the bank; or that I told you, not thinking, young Rawlson."

"You're out of your mind," he said sharply. "I know Rawlson casually, as Norton's secretary. That is all."

"It doesn't matter," said Sarah again, "although I congratulate you upon your sagacity. It isn't everyone who does a little business on the side, while managing to separate two young people who care for each other, for his own purposes."

"Sarah," he asked, in magnificent bewilderment, "what on earth has come over you lately? It's not like you to take to melodrama."

She said shortly, "Never mind that. The fact remains that you're a married man. And that both you and Lynn should know better."

"I shan't," Dwight informed her, "be a married man very long. Or rather, not married to the present Mrs. Dwight." He

382

waited a moment, and then drove home. He wanted to hurt the woman sitting there, facing him, cool eyes and steady mouth and quiet hands, wanted to hurt her so that she would cry out. "Mrs. Dwight has done me the honor to consent to a divorce," he said with facetious formality, "and so I have asked Lynn to marry me when my freedom is obtained."

"Ah —" said Sarah, very low. She turned to Lynn, after a moment. "Is this true?" she asked.

Lynn spoke, for the first time in several minutes. "Yes, it's true, Sarah, he did ask me to marry him. But — I don't understand — about Bob Rawlson and Tom and —"

"That can wait. Do you love — him?" Sarah urged her, and indicated Dwight.

"Please, Sarah, this is excessively embarrassing and unnecessary," Dwight said. He was no longer smiling.

"No. He knows that. But — oh, Sarah!" Lynn bowed her dark head against the older woman's shoulder and wept, from bewilderment and fatigue. The broken words she uttered were not clear but one or two of them came, muffled, to Sarah's ears — "so lonely — so unhappy." Sarah put her arm around the girl.

"Because you thought Tom had failed you, you were going to marry David perhaps and be — more lonely, more unhappy?" she asked.

Lynn replied, "Yes," faintly. Then she drew away from Sarah and spoke, strongly, distinctly. "Oh," she said with violence, "I'm so ashamed. It's been my fault, Sarah, all my fault. You'll never trust me again. You see, that time in the country, I spoke — to — him" — she indicated Dwight — "about Tom, I told him the whole situation, asked him if — if what Tom was considering was unethical, dishonest. I felt that it was." She added, "I ought to lose my job for that, Sarah. I was out of my head, worried about Tom, about the whole business, and — a little drunk, too," she said defiantly, "not realizing what I was saying —"

Sarah took her eyes from Dwight's altered face. She asked, "Lynn, did you mention Bob Rawlson on that occasion?"

"No. Not by name. I said Tom had an acquaintance who'd advised him." Her little face was drawn, the black arrow on her forehead was clear against her pallor. For the first time in several crowded moments of realization she looked at Dwight, spoke directly to him, "Why did you do it?" she asked. "Why did you let me think, cause me to think, that Tom —"

He answered, smiling dimly, "My dear, when I advised you to forget the whole stupid matter didn't I tell you all's fair in love and business?"

She was silent, her lips shaking. Sarah answered for her.

"Perhaps. But it's hardly a basis for a happy marriage. You — have never had the ghost of a chance to make Lynn happy, David. You've much less now. Even if she had not learned what she's learning to-night, she would have married you with another man in her heart. You" — she spoke regretfully — "you couldn't make any woman happy, David, not any more. You've lost so much."

"What right have you to say that?" he asked violently. "I love Lynn. I *can* make her happy — I will make her happy. I have never," he said deliberately, not forgetting to stab, "cared for any woman as I do for her. She'll forget about this. I'll make her forget. I tell you I love her, I'd give her the world, if I could!"

Sarah said, " I suppose so. Yet you told me that once — I remember."

There was a deep silence. Lynn cried, raising her face from Sarah's shoulder —

"Sarah?" and Dwight repeated it. "Sarah!" he said, but on a note of warning.

Sarah said, "Not that that matters any more, either. Why you have mattered to me, David, for twenty years, is beyond my comprehension. But Lynn must know. It may explain things to her, when later she thinks it all over; may explain why I was so blind, so gullible —"

"You — and David?" asked Lynn. It was the first time she had spoken Dwight's Christian name. He heard it echoing sweetly, and was able to look toward her with a little, secret gratitude in his brief glance.

"Yes — I and David —"

"Twenty years ago," Dwight reminded Lynn smoothly.

"You were going to marry him?" asked Lynn of Sarah. "I — why didn't you tell me? I didn't know — or dream."

"No, there was no question of marriage between us. Dwight couldn't afford to marry — a nobody," Sarah told her evenly. "We were — lovers."

"An elastic term," Dwight remarked, hunting for his cigarette case. He was fighting, and he knew it, with his back to the wall.

"Not very. Not in this case. Shall I tell

her about Maryland, David, and the place called Heartsease? Shall I tell her about the apartment, here in New York —"

"No, no," cried Lynn suddenly. Childishly, her hands were at her ears. "No, don't tell me — anything more!"

"But I think I must," Sarah said.

"No, it — isn't necessary." Lynn found herself on her feet, standing and facing Dwight. "Why?" she asked, and again, "*Why?*"

He said soothingly, as one speaks to a child, "Darling, you would never have known, from me. What Sarah's motive is —" He shrugged. But he knew her motive. He said, "Don't look at me like that. It happened so long ago — it was over, so long ago. We were young and lonely and —"

"But — *Sarah?*" She couldn't understand it, couldn't reconcile it. Sarah, her mother's friend, Sarah who had taken her in, given her her chance, been kinder to her than Heaven. She said brokenly, "If it had been anyone but — Sarah — I wouldn't have cared, why should I? I'm not, after all, a child." Nor was she; at that moment she was entirely adult. "But to treat Sarah — like that!" She turned from him definitely, went down on her knees by the side of Sarah's chair and looked up into a face that was no longer calm, into eyes no longer steady. "It must have hurt you terribly to tell me. I — Oh, Sarah, how *could* he?"

Her head was on Sarah's knees. The older woman touched the satin-soft hair with her long capable hand. She said, shaken, "Don't cry for me, Lynn. As David says, it was over long ago. If you had cared for him I should have been silent, you would have never known. But you don't care for him, Lynn; you love Tom. I had to show you how little you care for — David. If you had cared you wouldn't have turned to me, thought first of me."

Dwight asked, after a moment, "Lynn, will you come here — to me?"

She rose unsteadily and walked a few steps toward him. His hands went out to her, pleading, eager, ardent. She shrank away perceptibly. These were the hands that had known Sarah, intimately and in love; the hands that had betrayed her. Sarah was her friend. She cried out, "Don't touch me — don't *dare* to touch me!"

Empty, defeated, his hands dropped to his sides again. He said sharply, "Lynn, you are being very foolish. Granted that I treated Sarah badly, many years ago; it has been, I thought, forgiven, has been, I hoped, forgotten. We have been good friends since." He appealed to the other woman, "Is that not so, Sarah?"

"I have been your friend," she answered evenly.

"She — she bears me no grudge. Look, Lynn, you know, you must have known that there have been other women in my life. You are modern enough, woman enough to understand that. I'm not a boy, to bring you first love, first passion." He stumbled over that a little, loathing, fearing that verity. "But I bring you something worth so much more. Last love, love that will endure. For the rest of my life." And, as she made no movement toward him, as her young, soft face hardened to a premature ageing and her eyes remained hostile, he cried out helplessly, "Oh, for God's sake, Lynn — this is beyond all reason! To — to repudiate me, for something which happened almost before you were born, for a moral scruple —"

He stopped, a little appalled. He had belonged so utterly to her generation a short time before. Not any longer. She said, "It's not a moral scruple. It's *Sarah*. Can't you see that makes all the difference? When I think, when I try to realize —" She fled back to the other woman, eyes warm for her, lips warm, arms about her. "Sarah, you've been so *unhappy!*"

"Not for a long time," Sarah told her. "And now perhaps you'd better go, David."

He looked at Lynn, but her eyes were averted from his own. He put his hand on the doorknob. He said, "I'll come back."

No one spoke. The door opened under the pressure of his fingers. Tom, racing past, down the hall, toward the elevators, stopped, wheeled, and flung himself into the room. He said, "Oh, no, you don't! You stay here!"

There was a moment of utmost confusion. Sarah stiffened a little in her chair and sighed as a man sighs who is in the last extremity of fatigue. Lynn cried, *"Tom!"*—incredulously. He looked like nothing on earth.

"We'll have this out!" he said.

"You'll excuse me," Dwight commented coolly, "if I say I don't care to stay — any longer."

"You'll stay," Tom contradicted. He was not quite himself, Lynn thought, her heart contracting. He's been drinking. He had not been, save of the heady wine of violence.

"Look here, you," said Tom, and addressed Dwight. "Somehow, you found out that there was something going on at the bank. I don't know how; it doesn't signify. So then you went to Rawlson, and got all the dope you needed. And you've made money on his tip. You'll make more, I guess. That doesn't concern me; I don't care how much jack you make or how you make it. What does concern me is — Lynn. Lynn thought I'd tipped someone off and was getting my whack. Well, I didn't. You did. I got it out of Rawlson." He looked with satisfaction at his knuckles. They, too, were bruised. "I'll say he worked for his money! He didn't tell me — until I made him. But before you go — you seem to be in a hurry — perhaps you'll be good enough to tell Lynn and Miss Dennet that I didn't have anything to do with this stock manipulation."

Dwight said clearly, "No, you didn't. You're too much of a fool. I'm not."

The door shut behind him.

"Well!" said Tom, and looked from Lynn to Sarah, who were staring at him in silence. "Well, that's that!" He felt idiotic. His fine high fervor had passed. He was let down. "I must look like the devil," he said, after a moment.

The spell that had been on Lynn's limbs

relaxed and released her and she flashed into life. She sprang to her feet and ran to him, putting up her arms. "Tom, are you *hurt?* Did he hurt you?"

"Who? Bob? Not as much as I hurt him," Tom told her grinning. "Hey, what are you crying for? I'm all right," he assured her.

"I'm not crying, I'm laughing. Yes, I am crying, but just because I'm happy." She was close in his arms now, she was saying, "Tom, please forgive me, *please* —"

Sarah got out of her chair and walked stiffly toward the door. She was terribly stooped. She said dimly, "Everything's all right now."

But they did not hear her; nor her going.

Tom put Lynn in a chair and managed to occupy the same chair himself. She said, "All these days and nights, I've been waiting; hoping — hoping you'd come back, Tom. I was ready to take you back, if only you'd come, even if you had done it. I'd gotten so I didn't care. But — but I would have believed you, if only you'd told me again."

"I was an ass," he agreed amiably, "flinging myself out like that. Of course everything looked pretty black, against me. Dwight? How the hell he caught on —"

She said, and it hurt her terribly to say it, "It was my fault. Down there in the country, I told him. I put it to him — as a case — a hypothetical case — to see what he'd think. But —" She stopped, remembering.

"Then how —" asked Tom, bewildered.

"He asked Sarah later, quite casually, if you had any close friends in the bank. He'd known I'd meant you, of course. I — admitted it. Sarah told him, yes, you went around with Bob Rawlson. The rest was easy."

"Too damned easy. He's cleaned up; there's no doubt of that. If it gets about it won't be healthy for him around here. I mean, people will sort of give him the Bronx cheer. And Rawlson will lose his job."

"He's going abroad — David Dwight, I mean."

"He'd better. And stay there too. The climate should agree with him." He shook her, a very little. "You — don't care, do you? About his going, I mean? You see, I saw you — at that Jap place tonight."

"Tom, you didn't! No, I don't care. I never want to see him again. Tom, were you really at the Cherry Blossom? You saw me?"

"With these old eyes. I was up there with Erickson, supervising the broadcast. I came back to town and went right to Sarah. I was — crazy, I tell you. I thought — all sorts of things. Sarah headed me off. She questioned me on the bank business, sent me to find Bob and get the truth out of him, told me, that is, to find out if he'd blabbed to anyone. So I did. I came back. I couldn't help it, no matter how late it was, to tell her. You could have knocked me over with a coupling pin when Bob did come across, spitting teeth and blood — Oh, sorry," he said hastily, as Lynn shivered. "I saw Dwight's car outside. Spoke to his man. Saw him coming out of here. Came in, and found you — and Sarah. Boy, she's a corker," said Tom sincerely, "If it hadn't been for Sarah —"

"Oh, poor Sarah!" said Lynn, remembering.

"Why — Here, not going to spill over again, are you?"

She would not tell him why. She never told him.

"Tom," she asked, "can you ever forgive me — for getting you into this mess? For telling David Dwight?" She said suddenly, in perfectly honest astonishment. "And I thought I was such a good business woman, so closemouthed, so loyal. But I was just a fool, because I thought him kind and wise, thought I could trust him."

"He was wise all right!" Tom grinned. It didn't matter. Nothing mattered. Lynn was — his own.

"But — how can you *trust* me?" she wailed. "Tom, I'll go to Mr. Norton, I'll explain, I'll tell him everything."

"Lord, don't! He might offer me my job back," said Tom, "and I'm nuts about my present one."

"But you do forgive me — for doubting you?"

"Sure, I do," he said uncomfortably. "Anyone would have doubted me. Talk about circumstantial evidence. And it was a lot my fault, not coming back and making you see reason. With a club if necessary. Treat 'em rough, that's my motto from now on. I'm good at that — and at making people see reason," he told her gaily and caressed gingerly his bruised knuckles.

Lynn said, "Mr. Norton should know. Rawlson's there — and —"

"Forget it," ordered Tom. "How much do you love me?"

"So much that I'll marry you, any time you want!" she told him.

She was not uncertain of retaining her position: she trusted Sarah to see her over that difficulty; and besides, the bank no longer talked of letting the married women employees go since business had grown better.

"There's room for us both here, till the lease runs out." She looked about the little room and tried unsuccessfully to fit Tom and his great height and breadth into it as a permanent picture. She laughed shakily. "You're so darned *big*," she complained, "but we'll manage. We'll go on working, both of us. And saving. And some day, we'll get a place of our own."

"You're darned right, we will. We'll get married tomorrow," he exulted, "and look here, Lynn, you needn't be worried about my job. I mean, I'm making good. I've been talking to 'em up there about some of my ideas. They're going to let me take a crack at the research laboratories. I've got a keen slant on things, I think — I've been working on an idea, it has to do with sending out more than one program over the same wire. It would save 'em money. They — they've been darned decent to me. The sky's the limit if I hit on anything that will make for progress. I'll work! And, gosh, Lynn, how I love it!"

"I know you do. Sometimes, I think, more than you do me."

"It's different," he said absently. Her heart contracted again. She would always share him with his work; he had, in a genuine sense, the creative mind, the mind that is curious and constructive and eager and visionary. She thought proudly, *I wouldn't have him any different.*

"We'll get married tomorrow! I have to wire home and see if they'll come on for it. I think they will. Mother and Father, I mean; I couldn't be married without them," she told him.

"Then we'll wait," he agreed, "but not long. Mother and Father — that sounds pretty darned good to me — They must be swell, Lynn, or they'd never had you — and Sarah — she's family, too. And Hank and Slim — we'll have a regular wedding party," he planned boyishly. He looked down at her and grinned, "Going to ask Dwight?" he wanted to know.

She shook her head.

"He wouldn't come," she said soberly, "even if I did; as if I'd ask him, after — everything."

"I suppose he wouldn't — 'Wedding bells are ringing for Lynnie but not for Lynnie and me,' " sang Tom, off-key. "See here, you — you didn't fall for him, just a little bit, did you?"

She said, "No," definitely. She added, "Although I did go out with him, Tom, quite a lot after — after we quarreled. I was — lonely."

"Sure, I understand. But he was crazy about you," said Tom. "You needn't deny it!"

She did not. She said nothing. She was to make no comment on the subject of David Dwight as long as she lived. Not even, when a year or more had passed and Tom, picking up a newspaper, chortled, "Well, here's a hell of a note — your old boy friend Dwight gets himself all married to an English show girl, aged nineteen. How's that? Feeling sort of low, Lynn?"

But that was still a year away.

"Tom, you must go," she said. "It's terribly late. What will people think?"

He rose, dumping her unceremoniously, picking her up again to kiss her, not for the first time that evening.

"I don't want to go. But I will. Now that I know I'm coming back," he said, "and pretty soon. To stay."

She said wistfully, "I wish Jennie could be with us — when we get married."

"Jennie?" He frowned. "Don't worry your head about her. Slim, poor devil, he's sunk, drinks too much. He told me you'd seen him."

"He didn't understand," she said, low. "She didn't want him to. I'll tell you some day. No," she said reconsidering, "I can't tell even you. But try to believe, Tom, that it wasn't all Jennie's fault."

"I'll believe anything you say," he told her, "but we'll have old Slim over a lot, won't we, and try to cheer him up and find some cute little trick to console him? Not as cute as you are," he added.

He kissed her again.

"Tom, you've got to go," she said, and then, "I'm so terribly happy. Sure, sure I'm forgiven?"

He was sure; he made her sure. Presently he was gone. Suddenly almost sick with fatigue, she undressed and went to bed. Lying there in the darkness she tried to think. But her thoughts were kaleidoscopic. Dwight, his hand on hers: "You must have known I loved you." Dwight, asking her to marry him — in the spring, in England. She thought, in utter astonishment, is it possible that — that I was even tempted? She thought wonderingly of Sarah — remembering how, the door opening, she had seen her there, waiting, her face a mask of tragedy.

Sarah —

She turned her tired mind from the scene which had followed — Then, Tom, the bruise on his cheek, his collar torn, his tie a string, awry —

Tom's arms, Tom's kiss, Tom's proved innocence; her own unconscious guilt, meaning, she discovered with a pang of astonishment and dismay, so much less than his embrace —

"Sarah, if I can make it up to you, show you how grateful I am for what you did for me —" she whispered in the darkness.

Chapter Twenty-One:

THEIR SKYSCRAPER

The next morning Tom called for her, his hours, as it happened, more or less coinciding with her own, or at least his early hours. They drove uptown in the "new car."

"It runs," said Lynn, "like a dream."

"We'll go honeymooning in it."

"Tom, I can't get away."

"Neither can I," he admitted cheerfully, "but there'll be next summer — and vacations. Man," said Tom, addressing the blue back of a traffic policeman, "man, ain't Nature grand!"

He parked in a great garage not far from the Seacoast Building. They walked — to breakfast and to work, together. Perched on the high stools — "Do you remember?" they asked each other simultaneously, and their coffee cooled while the white jacket attending their needs asked, "What, so early in the morning?" but grinned in sympathy nevertheless.

The great building hummed all around

them. "Jennie's gone," said Lynn, sitting there on the stool, "and Mara."

"They made a mess of things," Tom said bluntly. "We won't."

"Not," agreed Lynn, "as long as we love each other. And that will be always."

The cafeteria was filled with clatter and bustle, plates rattled, containers steamed, people tramped in and out. "Golly," said Lynn, gasping. "I'm late!"

She fled to work. Miss Marple, plucking a pencil from behind a newly exposed ear, asked sourly, "Why the bright and cheerful morning face? Someone left you a million?"

"Two," Lynn told her solemnly.

Sarah. It would be hard to face Sarah, she thought. Yet somehow it was not. Later, forced to go to her desk on business, she reached it almost with reluctance. Sarah looked up. Lynn stared at her. Sarah, in black, white collar, white cuffs, her eyes preoccupied, her face serene —

"About this report of Mr. Johnson's," Sarah asked.

Listening, Lynn's eyes were pulled, against her will, to the open door of Norton's office. Norton's small, dark typist sat there, busy. She saw no one else.

Sarah smiled faintly. "I understand Mr. Rawlson is — ill," she said.

Lynn laughed outright. "And how!" she agreed.

"I've been talking," said Sarah, "to Mr. Norton. You — needn't look so worried, Lynn. It's all right. He understands everything. And Rawlson will send in his resignation."

A moment later she watched Lynn leave the room, walking with her easy, light step between the big desks, the pillars. Sarah's eyes were heavy. She thought, *It hasn't made any difference to her, as far as I'm concerned. She won't speak of it again.*

Yet she did so, on her wedding day, her hand fast in Sarah's —

Dr. Harding was talking to Tom in the living-room of Sarah's apartment. Mrs. Harding, an older Lynn, was talking to the minister, wiping her pretty eyes, trying to smile — "It seems so strange to have her married — and away from home," she was saying, "but he seems a fine boy."

"If I knew how to thank you," Lynn murmured, "If I knew how to tell you how grateful I am, Sarah —"

Sarah stooped and kissed her. "You can tell me," Sarah answered, "by being happy, always, Lynn."

It was dusk. A little later Tom and Lynn would go away for their brief honeymoon week-end together.

Alone, after the Hardings had gone to their hotel, Sarah looked from her windows into the darkness of the night. She thought, *Queer, he should sail, tonight* —

She thought of the thing she had done, the loyalty she had shattered forever, for another loyalty. She thought of the look she had seen in David Dwight's eyes, a look of utter astonishment, astonishment too great for reproach. She had realized then that somehow she was an unacknowledged part of him; that without ever giving it consideration he had nevertheless counted upon her as the one stable thing in his shifting world. She had failed him for Lynn. She was not sorry. Yet now she bowed her head and wept, slow, difficult tears. They fell on her clasped hands and she regarded them amazedly — as if she had looked to see blood and saw instead something colorless, and evanescent.

She thought, *I'll never see him again.*

She loved him — without tenderness, without compassion, without ardor, without honor, or honoring. And she had been his enemy. Yet he was a scar that she must carry to her grave. She thought, *There's my work, I've that much left.*

Strange, to feel so empty and forlorn, as

if something had gone from her when for so many years she had had nothing, nothing but work, and memories and the hope that some day she might see recognition in eyes grown too accustomed to her as she now was. She had seen it, last summer. *"Sarah — Sarita —"* for a blinding moment.

She turned from the window.

Standing on the deck of the biggest of ocean liners, David Dwight sailed for France at midnight. He stood there, coat collar upturned, alone, watching the skyline. In the skyscrapers some of the windows were still lighted, pale gold against black. People moved about in there, did their work, toiled through the night. Scrubwomen had their obscure, ambiguous being. Night and day, there were human beings, active as ants, going about their varied concerns in these aspiring, terrifying masses of stone and steel.

"Good to be getting away," commented a pallid man, moving to the rail beside him, "from the incessant fever and fret of commerce and commercial people; good to be going to lands that are still able to dream."

He was a poet; and traveling first class

because he had inherited money. A price-less combination. Dwight turned; the light fell upon his worn face and brilliant eyes. Even poets read newspapers.

"I — I do beg your pardon, you're Dwight, aren't you, David Dwight?"

Stupid, absurd, but a vague comfort. His cold heart warmed, a little. He answered, smiling, "Yes, I'm Dwight — and yes, it is good to be getting away."

"That's the Seacoast Building, isn't it?" asked the poet. "It's lovely, I think, at night, with those few windows lighted below, and the tower glowing. It looks like a concrete embodiment of man's most magnificent dream. Seeing it from here, one forgets the taint, the imprisoned lies, the scramble for existence."

It was the Seacoast Building. From those tall towers nets were woven, nets of speech, of music, and flung all the wide world over. Dwight turned away.

"I've something in my cabin. Care to join me?"

"On Monday," said the poet, "the Sea-coast Building will be — just another sky-scraper, just another monument to man's insatiable greed."

And on Monday Lynn said, sleepily, hav-ing arrived in town very late on Sunday night, "Tom — for goodness' sake, wake up. We'll be late!"

On Monday, they made a sketchy breakfast in the little kitchenette and set off together for work. On Monday they stopped in the street and looked up, as if somewhere beyond their craning necks there was a message for them. Lynn said, a little awed, "It makes me feel dizzy, somehow: as dizzy as if I were looking *down*. Isn't it beautiful, Tom?"

"It's swell," said Tom, contentedly.

"I like," she told him, "being a part of it. I love it, and especially your working 'way up there in the tower, and me working down below. Under the same roof."

"There's a lot of us under it, and darned lucky to be there," Tom said sincerely.

The street was black with hurrying people. The winter sky was clear and cold and blue, the sun pale golden yellow. A plane passed overhead, its engine singing, its wings spread, casting its strange small shadow on the cool sides of the great building.

"Here, get going," said Tom.

He smiled down into her eyes. "It's great," he said, "being alive — having our jobs — being together —"

They vanished, with the hundreds of

others into the spaces allotted them beyond the great bronze doors.

Skyscraper. Roots embedded in earth, towers reaching to the far and azure empyrean. Symbol of man's need for stability, for endurance, for progress, for aspiration. *Skyscraper.* . . .